Sylvia stopped dead in her tracks and spun around, not realizing he was following so close behind. Her body barreled into his and she let out a soft *oof*.

Hugh gripped her arms, holding her tight so she didn't topple, his hands cool against her skin. Sylvia made the mistake of looking up, her eyes meeting his, and for a moment, she was lost in deep blue eyes.

"Sylvia…" Hugh said, his voice like honey. This was how he had spoken to her on those long, warm evenings in the Caribbean. She had fallen under his spell then, but she wouldn't fall again.

"No." She swallowed the sob that swelled in her throat, pushed herself away from him and took off at a run, not caring which path she took, turning left and right until she exploded out of the maze in relief. There were no footsteps behind her, no repentant viscount dropping to his knees and telling her what a fool he had been.

Author Note

Ever since I was ten years old and picked the battered copy of *Treasure Island* from the school library for my book of the week, there has been a special place in my literary heart for desert islands, exotic sunsets and even a little pirate treasure. The first book I wrote for Harlequin, *The Pirate Hunter*, brought all of that together and I think to this day, that was my favorite to write of all my books. That was why, when I first had the idea that turned into the story for *Her Secret Past with the Viscount*, I knew it would be another book I would find great pleasure in writing.

I loved the clash of the rigid Regency rules of society with the idea of being helplessly marooned on a desert island, and all thoughts of propriety and respectability immediately having to be abandoned. Even more fun, and where *Her Secret Past with the Viscount* takes up the story, is the aftermath of such a stay, and how two people who lived in such close proximity, who shared such intimacy, would struggle when returned to the real world.

I hope you enjoy Sylvia and Hugh's reunion in the rolling hills of Kent, and savor the memories of the Caribbean they bring to the story.

LAURA MARTIN

—

Her Secret Past with the Viscount

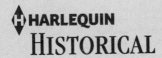

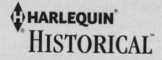

Recycling programs
for this product may
not exist in your area.

ISBN-13: 978-1-335-59571-3

Her Secret Past with the Viscount

For questions and comments about the quality of this book,
please contact us at CustomerService@Harlequin.com.

Harlequin Enterprises ULC
22 Adelaide St. West, 41st Floor
Toronto, Ontario M5H 4E3, Canada
www.Harlequin.com

Printed in U.S.A.

Laura Martin writes historical romances with an adventurous undercurrent. When not writing she spends her time working as a doctor in Cambridgeshire, where she lives with her husband. In her spare moments, Laura loves to lose herself in a book, and has been known to read from cover to cover in a single day when the story is particularly gripping. She also loves to travel—especially to visit historical sites and far-flung shores.

Books by Laura Martin

Harlequin Historical

The Brooding Earl's Proposition
Her Best Friend, the Duke
One Snowy Night with Lord Hauxton
The Captain's Impossible Match

Matchmade Marriages

The Marquess Meets His Match
A Pretend Match for the Viscount
A Match to Fool Society

The Ashburton Reunion

Flirting with His Forbidden Lady
Falling for His Practical Wife

Scandalous Australian Bachelors

Courting the Forbidden Debutante
Reunited with His Long-Lost Cinderella
Her Rags-to-Riches Christmas

Visit the Author Profile page
at Harlequin.com for more titles.

To Luke, in memory of our Caribbean sunburn
and lobsters on the beach.

Chapter One

It was beautiful sunny day when the ship set sail from Southampton, and for most of the voyage we were blessed with calm seas and blue skies. It lulled all the passengers into a false sense of safety, and soon I forgot my concerns about storms and shipwrecks.

Sylvia pressed her body against the hedge, wishing for a moment she could melt into the greenery and disappear. The party was much larger than she had been led to expect, and a hushed, reverent murmur had run through the crowd at a rumour the Queen might even make an appearance. This was not where Sylvia felt comfortable. These were not her people. As the daughter of a solicitor, she had been born firmly into the middle classes, and before the loss of her parents and brother her social calendar had been filled with dances at the Assembly Rooms rather than grand balls and garden parties.

Reminding herself this was necessary, vital for her

survival, she plastered a smile on her face and forced her feet to move away from the hedge. She had been invited as a curiosity, as someone to be paraded about and tell her story, and it was important she took advantage of the opportunity to make connections with some influential people. Even if all she really wanted was to be curled up in her favourite chair with a book in her hand.

As she stepped into the gathering, their hostess, Lady Montague, saw her and bustled over, calling to one of her friends on the way.

'Lady French, have you met Miss Thompson?'

'No, although I have heard a lot about you, Miss Thompson. You were quite the talk of the *ton* after your miraculous rescue.'

'It is lovely to meet you, Lady French,' Sylvia said, smiling as genuinely as she could.

'Tell me, Miss Thompson, what was it like being shipwrecked with the most eligible bachelor in England?' It was the question everyone asked, and Sylvia knew she should be used to it by now. She had a whole arsenal of answers, tailored for whatever audience she was faced with. For Lady French, she adopted a dreamy, faraway expression.

'Lord Wilder was the perfect gentleman,' Sylvia said with a delicate little sigh. 'He ensured my companion and I were safe and comfortable without ever once intruding on our privacy.'

Lady French nodded as if she had expected nothing less.

'You didn't become close whilst you were shipwrecked?' Lady Montague said.

'Lord Wilder is a dear friend,' Sylvia lied. In truth, she hadn't seen him for a whole year. An entire year of yearning and discontent and desperately trying to forget how his lips felt on her skin, how his eyes sparkled when he laughed. She knew the value of selling the fantasy. In her book, Lord Wilder was the hero of the tale, gallantly rushing to her rescue. People might be mildly interested in how she had learned to spear-fish with tools she had fashioned herself, but they mostly wanted to fall in love with a man who was a quintessential hero.

With her eyes flitting over the crowd, Sylvia stiffened. She had been assured he would not be in attendance. She'd checked three times with the hostess that Lord Hugh Wilder's name was not on the guest list for this weekend party at Somersham Hall, Lady Montague's country estate. He was meant to be in Southampton, preparing for his upcoming nuptials.

For a moment, she was overwhelmed by memories, the good mixed in with the bad. In the distance, she could make out his hearty laugh, and the sound shot straight to her core, making her yearn for a man who had broken her heart a year earlier, a break she was still struggling to piece back together.

'Please excuse me, Lady French,' Sylvia said, suddenly overcome by the urge to disappear. She didn't want to see Hugh, especially not here, where she was to be trapped for the entire weekend.

Taking her leave of the countess, she slunk away, hunching her shoulders and hoping no one would pay her any attention. It was difficult, as she had spent the last of her money on a brightly coloured dress, wanting to seem confident and exotic in the blue silk. It had been second- or third-hand, rescued and restored lovingly, but expensive for Sylvia all the same.

Desperately she glanced around her, dismayed to find she could not retreat to the house for a few minutes, for Hugh was positioned between her and the open doors of the summer room. Her options were limited to the gardens, but much was laid out in a formal parterre, and the low flower beds would do little to hide her if Hugh happened to glance over.

Instead she opted for the hedge maze. There was a narrow opening to one side, and once behind the first hedge she was all but invisible. Deciding she would simply follow the path for a couple of twists and turns and find somewhere to collect herself, she slipped in, feeling her body relax as soon as she was away from everyone's gaze.

Sylvia hurried along, going left at the first turn and then right at the second. Although it did not cover a huge area, she had heard the hostess boast the maze had a quarter of a mile of pathways and was easy to get lost in. Determined she would not spend the whole afternoon wandering the maze, she paused, thinking she would take a couple of minutes to herself and then head back to the garden party with a smile fixed firmly in place. Even if she had to face Hugh.

She thought of the last kiss they had shared, a passion-filled embrace full of relief and disappointment as the ship turned towards their little patch of paradise. They had been saved, but right then, Sylvia knew she was going to lose the only man she had ever loved. Part of her wanted to pull Hugh into the trees, to pretend they were not there, and continue with their marooned life on the small island.

Reminiscing was not helping, and Sylvia firmly pushed all thoughts of Hugh out of her mind, instead trying to focus her mind on charming the ladies and gentlemen at the weekend-long series of events.

She was almost ready to return when she heard the soft crunch of footsteps over the leaves and sticks on the path. She stiffened, not wanting to be caught in the maze, trapped by a couple who had thought to sneak off for an illicit liaison. Or even worse, by a lone man who had seen her slip in between the hedges and thought her solitary dash was an invitation for a persistent suitor to press his attentions.

She contemplated her options. It was only thirty or forty feet to the entrance. She could easily put her head down and run past whoever it was coming in, saving herself from any potential embarrassment. Or she could retreat further into the maze.

Cautiously she peeked around the corner and felt her heart thud into her stomach as she caught a glimpse of Hugh. He was moving slowly, deciding which turn to take, and he was alone. She let out a little involuntary gasp, and as his head shot up, she quickly retreated round the corner. Sylvia didn't stop. She didn't want to see Hugh, and she most certainly didn't want to see him alone in the middle of a hedge maze. Picking up her skirts, she began to run, twisting this way and that, in her hurry not taking any notice of which way she was going.

After a minute, she slowed, realising she was totally

and utterly lost, but still relieved that she must have also shaken off Hugh. Hopefully he had decided to turn back rather than conquer the maze. For a moment, she wondered if he had come in here searching for her, but quickly dismissed the idea. He was likely as disappointed as she was to be sharing the same weekend accommodations. Perhaps he was simply coming to inform her he would be leaving. She scoffed at the idea. The Viscount would be more likely to tell *her* to move on than leave himself.

'You always were so damn stubborn,' she heard him mutter from the other side of a hedge. Sylvia held her breath, hating the vibrant colour of her dress as she saw him bend down and peer into the foliage. 'I can see you,' he said, straightening. 'Wait there.'

After a moment of hesitation Sylvia ran, not stopping until she came out into the very middle of the maze. Silently she cursed. Far from being delighted that she had found the middle, she realised she had backed herself into a corner with no other exit other than the way she had come. *And* she was furthest from the exit.

Ten seconds later, Hugh appeared, blocking her only way out and looking furious.

'Why did you run?'

'You were chasing me.'

He looked at her as though she had grown another head, not speaking for a long moment.

'You always did make things impossible,' he murmured.

'*I* made things impossible?'

'Well, I certainly didn't.'

She closed her eyes, forcing herself to exhale deeply before she spoke again.

'Delightful as it is to see you again, Lord Wilder, is there something I can help you with?'

Hugh took a step towards her, and another, and Sylvia hated that she held her breath as he came closer. Some rebellious part of her was hoping he would sweep her into his arms and tell her he had made a grievous mistake, that she was the only woman for him and they were destined to be together.

'I came to tell you not to be such a blind, pigheaded fool.'

Not quite the declaration her heart secretly yearned for.

'I've missed you too, Lord Wilder,' she murmured, shaking her head. It was better this way, cleaner. She'd known at some point she would have to see Hugh again. At least he was consistent in his desire to push her away. This way she could banish whatever little feeling she had left for him, once and for all.

'This book, it will ruin you.'

Sylvia looked at him with a raised eyebrow. 'Come, tell the truth, Lord Wilder. It is not *my* reputation you fear for.'

'Of course it is. You are going to admit to the world we were alone on that island for three months. You will be shunned from polite society, and your life will be ruined.'

'Do you think me a fool, Lord Wilder?' Her voice was clipped and curt, and she felt her entire body bristling with suppressed anger.

He regarded her without answering.

'Do you credit me with so little thought, so little brain, that you think I would publish the truth of what occurred on that island?' She had written it down, exactly as it had happened, but that copy was just for her. It was locked in a box inside a chest with a huge padlock, and Sylvia was sure no one could get their hands on it. The manuscript she had delivered to her publisher contained a vastly different series of events. A more palatable version that preserved her reputation. 'Do not fear. You are soon going to become the darling of the *ton*. I have not told the truth. I have written you as a perfect gentleman, attentive to preserving my dignity at all times.'

Still he did not speak, and Sylvia took a step forwards, forcing herself to ignore the part of her that wanted to throw herself into his arms and press her lips against his one last time.

'I have written nothing that will make your fiancée think twice about marrying you.'

'This is not about Miss Willis.'

Sylvia shrugged and brushed past him, her heart thumping in her chest. She was almost at the path that led back into the maze when he reached out and gripped her wrist, holding it gently but firmly until she turned to face him.

'However clever you think you have been, it will not be enough. Abandon this idea, tell your publisher you have changed your mind, and forget about your ruse this weekend. Tell Lady Montague your family have sent for you, and get far away from the sharks here, or they will eat you alive.'

Sylvia felt the tears well up in her eyes and bit down firmly on her lip to try to control them. 'I have no family,' she said, pulling away.

'Your brother…?'

'He died. Eight months ago.'

'Sylvia…'

'Miss Thompson,' she corrected him.

He didn't say anything, his eyes searching hers, and she got the impression he was holding something back.

Sylvia took a juddering breath before speaking. It took every ounce of her self-composure not to launch into a tirade of how he had hurt her, of every wrong he had committed against her. 'I give you my word, your position will not be compromised. Your fiancée will have nothing to reproach you about, and you will only grow in esteem in the eyes of society,' Sylvia said, wrenching her arm away. She hated how much it hurt to be arguing like this. Once she had fooled herself that the only person he would be fiercely protective of was her. Straightening her back, she blinked quickly in the hope the tears would not fall onto her cheeks, and marched out of the centre of the maze.

She had taken only a few steps when Hugh's voice rang out behind her.

'You're going the wrong way.'

'How on earth could you know that?'

He shrugged. 'Innate sense of direction.'

'You cannot have an innate sense of direction in a maze. It twists this way and that.' Trying to prove her point, she carried on down her selected route, only to be met with a dead end.

Hugh was waiting for her back where she had started and pointed at the other path.

'Lucky guess,' she muttered and stalked past him.

'Shall I take the lead?'

'No,' she shot back over her shoulder. 'Stay here. We cannot be seen alone together.'

'If I wait for you to find your way out of the maze, I'll die of dehydration.'

'You always did have a penchant for exaggeration.'

'And you got lost on the trail from the forest to the beach more times than I care to remember.'

Sylvia stopped dead in her tracks and spun around, not realising he was following so close behind. Her body barrelled into his, and she let out a soft *oof*.

Hugh gripped her arms, holding her tight so she didn't topple, his hands cool against her skin. Sylvia made the mistake of looking up, her eyes meeting his, and for a moment she was lost in the deep blue eyes.

'Sylvia…' Hugh said, his voice like honey. This was how he had spoken to her on those long, warm evenings in the Caribbean. She had fallen under his spell then, but she wouldn't fall again.

'No,' she said, pushing him away a little more violently than she meant to. He stumbled, bouncing off the robust hedge, and collided with her again. This time he didn't reach out to catch her, and Sylvia fell forwards, her palms meeting the soft earth as she wondered how everything they'd shared had been reduced to this.

She swallowed the sob that swelled in her throat, pushed herself up from the dirt, and took off at a run, not caring which path she took, turning left and right until she exploded out of the maze in relief. There were no footsteps behind her. There was no repentant viscount dropping to his knees and telling her what a fool he had been.

A few people turned to look, and Sylvia quickly brushed the dirt from her hands and straightened her skirts. She tucked the stray strands of hair behind her ears and then walked with as much composure as she could muster towards the house. Lady Montague was hosting events all weekend long at her country residence. It wouldn't matter if Sylvia bowed out early this one time.

Chapter Two

That fateful night, all the passengers went to bed with no premonition of what was to come, although some of the seasoned sailors looked at the horizon with trepidation. A storm was brewing, and they hoped for a mere swell, but the Caribbean winds were unforgiving, and they were blowing trouble our way.

Hugh stood completely rigid, hating the way his collar rubbed against his neck and wishing he could tear his cravat from his shirt. He was the firstborn son of a line of firstborn sons that stretched back generations, to a time when the Norman kings had conquered Britain. The expectations of his role had been set out from the moment he could talk, and his father would have him parrot the roles and responsibilities of the Viscount.

One of the expectations was to be a model of dignity and respectability. No scandal should touch the viscountcy. To a lesser degree, it meant being perfectly turned out at all times. It might be acceptable for country squires and members of the gentry to sit around in their shirt-sleeves, but the Viscount Wilder should never show such a human side as giving even a hint he wanted to relax.

For a moment, his thoughts flashed back to the time on the Isla Ana. There he had worn only his shirt open at the front and his ragged trousers, and it had been heavenly.

Now was not the time to fall into the melancholy that accompanied his memories. This evening he had a job to do, and he would not be distracted from it.

He was certain Sylvia had not entered the grand ballroom. From his position opposite the double set of doors, he could see everyone who came and went, and he knew he wouldn't miss the arrival of the woman who still haunted his dreams.

Thinking about their encounter in the maze, he had to admit it could have gone better, but it was not only his lack of finesse that had been the problem. Sylvia was stubborn and found it difficult to admit when she was wrong, and this time she was very wrong.

'Lord Wilder, I am thrilled you accepted my invitation. Is your lovely fiancée not joining us?' Lady Montague said, beaming as she approached him.

'Unfortunately not, Lady Montague. Her father's health is declining, and she is devoted to looking after him.' It was a bald-faced lie. Honoria's father, Captain William Willis, was a weather-beaten scoundrel who drank too much and ate all the wrong things, but Hugh had a suspicion he would outlive everyone that surrounded him. He was far too stubborn to die.

'Oh, that is a shame. Do you know, I do not think I have met Miss Willis yet. Isn't that strange? All these events we attend together, and not once have I seen your fiancée.'

'Perhaps she is a ruse,' Hugh said, leaning in with a grin. For years he had watched his father charm the ladies of the *ton*. He might not have approved of the old man's affairs and mistresses, but he had picked up a few tips on how to best deflect questions you did not want to answer.

'Oh, Lord Wilder,' Lady Montague said, letting out a titter of laughter, 'you are too naughty. Do not tease me so.'

Hugh smiled and bent over his hostess's hand. 'It would be a perfect ruse, would it not?' he continued quietly. 'Invent a fiancée that no one has ever met. Declare yourself madly in love, and then keep supplying the excuses as to why she couldn't attend all the social events on the calendar.'

'I do not believe you, Lord Wilder.'

'It would keep all the ambitious débutantes at bay, and allow me to enjoy the season without worrying about fending off the unwanted attention of this year's batch of young women.'

'Now I am determined to meet Miss Willis,' Lady Montague said.

'To see what sort of young lady would be fool enough to put up with me?'

'Quite.'

Hugh bowed and moved away, pleased when Lady Montague stopped regarding him with her sharp eyes and focussed on her next guest. His glib comments and self-deprecating jokes could keep the gossips at bay for only so long. One day he really would have to introduce Miss Willis to his world—that or definitively find a way out of the tangle of lies and promises he was caught up in with the Willis family.

With a sigh, he rubbed his temples, feeling the tension beginning to build as he always did when he thought of the mess he had got himself into with Captain Willis and his daughter. Miss Willis was inoffensive in herself, a pleasant young lady who was interesting enough to talk to, but he felt nothing for her. In itself, a lack of affection was not an issue, not where marriages within the *ton* were concerned. Most were arranged for monetary reasons, or the joining of two great families. It was considered a bonus if you actually liked your wife. Hugh had even been prepared to settle for such an arrangement himself, until he had taken that fateful voyage and his life had been turned upside down.

As he tried to banish thoughts of the tangle his affairs were in, he glanced up and felt his heart squeeze in his chest. He wondered if Sylvia would always cause that reaction in him, whether one day, when they were both grey and old, he might catch a glimpse of her across a crowded room and his heart would skip a beat.

'Stop being so fanciful,' he muttered to himself. He was here for one reason and one reason only. Once he had persuaded Sylvia not to publish that damn book of hers and ruin the carefully curated charade he had sacrificed so much to build, he would leave and return to missing her from afar.

She entered the ballroom alone, head held high and chin raised as if she had been born for this life. Only someone who knew her well would notice the subtle signs of her nervousness. There was the way her fingers worried at the skin on her thumb, never resting, never still, and the almost compulsive way she would touch the front of her hair every minute or two, to check that the wispy, soft strands she disliked so much just on her hairline were staying in place.

Sylvia might look as if she belonged here, but he could tell she didn't feel it.

He suppressed the urge to go to her straightaway. Part of him wanted to take her by the shoulders and shake her, to make her realise what she was doing was beyond foolish, but he held himself back. People would expect them to interact, to talk, to dance even. He would have plenty of opportunity to make her see the error in her judgement.

To his surprise, Sylvia turned towards him, and her eyes came up to meet his. He thought she would look away, but she didn't, instead smiling broadly and moving in his direction.

'Lord Wilder,' she exclaimed loudly, leaning in and taking his hand. Immediately he could see she was playing a role, the part expected of her as a curiosity brought in to entertain. He wanted to refuse to be part of this, to pull away and glower at her, but he knew if he wanted to speak to her privately, he would need to play along.

'It is so good to see you again, Miss Thompson,' he said, raising her hand to his lips. He was satisfied to see the mask fall from her face for just an instant as his lips met her skin, but she quickly rallied.

'It has been too long,' she agreed, smiling but not able to meet his eye. Instead she looked at the assembled guests, some of whom were watching the exchange with interest. 'Ask me to dance,' she murmured so only he could hear.

'Miss Thompson, would you honour me with your next dance?'

'Of course, Lord Wilder, I would be delighted.' Their conversation was stilted, and Hugh wondered if this was all there was left between them. Theatrics and awkwardness.

As if in response to his invitation, the musicians finished the gentle swell of the piece they had been playing to welcome people in to the ball and struck up the first notes of a waltz.

Wordlessly Hugh led Sylvia to the area that had been cleared for the dance floor, thankful to see there were other couples taking their places to divert some of the attention away from them.

The waltz was Hugh's favourite dance. His father had hired a dance tutor to visit Elmwood Hall when Hugh was age twelve and home from school during the holidays. Demanding perfection in all things, his father wanted Hugh to be master of all he tried his hand at. A viscount was expected to host and attend multiple balls during the season, and Hugh's father would not accept anything but excellence when it came to dancing. Of all the things his father had pushed upon him, Hugh had not minded the dancing. At the time, it had sometimes seemed tedious, but now he could lead a young lady in a quadrille or waltz without even needing to think. It was hardly the most challenging skill he had learned, but it was useful on occasion.

'Do you remember the first time we danced a waltz?' Sylvia said quietly as he took her hand in his.

For a moment he was frozen, unable to move a single muscle. It was a memory he had desperately tried to suppress, the memory of their first dance. Of course, there hadn't been any music, just the sound of the gentle waves lapping on the shore. They had danced barefoot, silent at first and then giggling with laughter as Hugh had swept Sylvia across the sand. It had been one of those crucial moments in life where the whole future hinges on one decision.

'I am not here to reminisce about the past,' he said gruffly.

'Unfortunately, that is exactly what I am here to do.'

'Why do you want to rake over it all? Surely it is not a time you want to relive?'

He watched as she swallowed and looked away.

'I need three things from you this weekend,' she said, not answering him. Her voice was sharp, and he could see she was struggling to keep her emotions contained. 'One, I need you to pretend we're friends. An unusual friendship, admittedly, one that was born of extreme circumstance, but friends all the same. Two, I need you to be vague when you answer any questions about our time on the Isla Ana. I have changed some of the details in my book, and I do not want you to directly contradict anything I have said.' She paused, taking a deep breath.

'And three?'

'Three, I need you to come out and openly endorse my book.' Her eyes flickered to his for an instant, and he could see she knew he would never comply.

'No,' he said simply.

'No?'

'I will pretend we are friends, and I will be vague about our time on the island,' he said slowly. 'The first is a lie, but I am happy to go along with it. The second is something I always do anyway. I will do these things for you, but I will never say I endorse your book.'

'You should read it. You may be pleasantly surprised.'

He looked down at her, adopting his best haughty expression. In truth, he was trying to mask the anger he felt. He had sacrificed everything to shield Sylvia from the cruelty of the *ton* to maintain her reputation and ensure she came through this terrible ordeal as unscathed as possible. When they had been rescued, he was ready to abandon his principles for her, to abandon the sense of duty that had been drummed into him as a young boy, but she had pushed him away. So he had done the next best thing, arranging everything so she would be protected from the world, and now she was trying to dash that against the rocks too.

'I do not want to read it,' he said, his voice dangerously low. 'I do not want anyone to read it. Ever.'

'I have an early copy from my publisher. Perhaps I can lend it to you.'

'Listen to me, Sylvia,' he said, aware of the eyes on them, desperately trying to maintain a calm façade when in truth he wanted to grip her by the arms and shake her until she understood. 'This book will bring nothing but trouble.'

'I have had nothing but trouble this last year,' she said, and then cut herself off and looked away.

'Nonsense. It may have felt like a hard year, but believe me, when you publish all the sordid little details of our time on the Isla Ana, you will be hounded from society.'

'There are no sordid little details. I am not a fool, Lord Wilder.'

He leaned in, ensuring his lips were close to her ear so no one else had a chance of overhearing him. 'You may not have written about the time we made love up against that coconut tree, but you do not have to. Society finds the most ridiculous things scandalous, things you will not have even thought of. Stripping off your clothes to bathe naked in the natural pools, fashioning rudimentary garments from scraps of sail—all of these things may sell your book, but you will be shunned, whispered about.'

Sylvia pulled away and shook her head. 'You have no idea what it is like for anyone who is not born into your world, do you? *All* I need is to sell my book, to sell enough copies that I can eke out a small yearly income if I live modestly. This is it, the sum of my life. I have no living family, no money, no prospects. Either this gamble works for me, or I will have to seek employment. If I am fortunate, perhaps I will find a position in a respectable shop, but I am not trained for anything. I have no particular skill.'

They twirled, their eyes locked. Sylvia was tense in

his arms, her every muscle held rigid, defiance governing her expressions. The music swelled one final time and then faded away, and as the other couples made to move away from the dance floor, they lingered, neither wanting to be the first to break eye contact.

Chapter Three

I woke in the early hours of the morning, thrown from my bed by a dreadful swell. On deck there was shouting, muffled by the wind, and there was panic like nothing I have ever seen before on the sailors' faces. I dressed as best I could with the ship rolling this way and that and tried to control my nerves for the climb up to the deck to see if I could make myself useful.

As Sylvia closed her bedroom door behind her, she let the smile slip from her face. It was exhausting pretending to be something she wasn't. All evening she had smiled and talked, entertaining people with stories of the shipwreck and her time on the Isla Ana. Hardly any of them had been true, but all the same, she had felt Hugh's eyes on her. It was as though he was listening intently, waiting for her to slip up.

'A pox on Hugh Wilder,' she muttered as she set the candle down on the sturdy dressing table.

'*Pox on Hugh Wilder,*' a high-pitched voice mimicked.

There was a flutter of wings as Rosa came to sit on her shoulder, sharp claws digging in as she found a comfortable position.

'You understand, don't you, my darling?' Sylvia said, leaning her head towards the bird and feeling a wonderful warmth spread through her as the parrot nuzzled her back. Rosa was an accidental pet, one that Sylvia had never expected to follow her home, although now she couldn't imagine her life without the bird. She knew parrots were thought only to mimic the sounds they heard rather than engage in any meaningful conversation, but she did wonder sometimes if Rosa understood more than was generally thought. The words she decided to mimic were important and allowed a certain level of conversation.

'It was horrific tonight,' Sylvia said.

'*Horrific.*'

'Everyone was looking at me with that morbid curiosity. I felt like a bearded lady in the circus.'

'*Bearded lady. Horrific. Pox on Hugh Wilder.*'

'Yes, Hugh was there. Trying to stop me from publishing this book. A whole year and I have heard nothing from him, and now he pops up.' Sylvia shook her head and then began to unpin her hair, knowing she was being a little unfair but unable to react with anything but a burning anger. She had told him in no uncertain terms not to contact her before they had stepped off the ship onto the dock a year earlier. Her emotions had been high and no doubt her barely suppressed fury apparent, but she hadn't expected him to comply with her request so easily, so readily. He had become a ghost in her life, disappeared completely. Sometimes she felt as though he were close by, almost within reach, but never had she actually seen him, and long ago she'd had to accept the sense of him being close was nothing more than wishful thinking. 'He says he is worried about my reputation.' She snorted, and then laughed as Rosa tried to copy the sound. 'I expect he is worried his fiancée will find out what really went on whilst we were on the Isla Ana.'

Rosa flapped her wings and fluttered off Sylvia's shoulder, settling on one of the wooden bedposts and surveying the room.

'If he would stop being so pig headed and just listen to me, he would see he has nothing to worry about.'

'Pigheaded. Pox on Hugh Wilder.'

Sylvia flopped down on the bed and then stiffened. Twice she had offered him a copy of her book to show him there was nothing inflammatory or unsavoury in it. So far he had refused, but if she forced it on him, he would see for himself. Then he could leave her alone and retreat back to Honoria Willis and their fairy tale.

She stood and crossed to the small battered trunk. As she dropped to her knees in front of it, she paused, touching the leather. It had been her brother's and was well-travelled, the scratches and small rips holding secrets that now no one would ever divulge. Her own trunk, similar in looks but less well-travelled, rested at the bottom of the Caribbean Sea, lost forever to the waves.

Carefully she lifted the lid and took the beautifully bound book out, running her fingers over the spine with the gold writing. *The Rescue by Sylvia Thompson.*

Richard Townley was her publisher, a portly man with a
perpetual smile and jolly mannerisms who assured her
the first print run would soon sell out. He had printed
five hundred one copies of the book. Five hundred were
waiting to be delivered to the best booksellers in London, ready to be sold when the *ton* started to return
from their country estates after the summer heat. This
one copy was special. It was printed first and given to
her by Mr Townley, who made her promise to cherish
it as a great achievement.

'I will be back in a minute or two, Rosa,' Sylvia said.
'Back in a minute.'

With her hair loose about her shoulders, Sylvia
slipped from her room. She had been given a tour of
the house earlier that day, and she knew the guest bedrooms were all on this floor. When her bags had been
delivered upstairs, two maids had been giggling as they
made up one of the finer bedrooms, and they had mentioned 'the Viscount,' so she thought she knew what
room he was staying in. All it would take was a little
luck, and she could be there and back to her room without anyone seeing her.

She padded along the corridor in her satin shoes,
pausing at the top of the stairs to count the doors before
continuing on in the darkness. She had been one of the
last to bid their hostess good-night, with most people
having retired for the evening if they were staying, or
returned to their carriages if they were not. Downstairs
there was still a soft clatter as the maids cleared the mess,
but Sylvia doubted anyone would be about on this level.

Pausing before the heavy wooden door, she hesitated, checking each direction before she brought her hand up to knock gently.

The door opened quickly as if Hugh had been close by, and for a moment, they both stood in the darkness, just staring at one another.

Hugh had evidently been starting to get undressed, with his cravat abandoned over the back of a chair and his shirt open at the neck. Sylvia felt her body react to the sight of him and took an involuntary step forward, only stopping herself at the last moment from reaching out.

'You can't be here,' he said, leaning out past her and looking up and down the corridor.

'I merely came to give you something.'

He looked at her as though she had gone mad for a long few seconds, only startled into movement when there was the pad of footsteps on the stairs further down the hall.

Sylvia had to muffle a cry of surprise as he gripped her firmly by the arm and pulled her into his room, pressing her against the wall before closing the door with a muted click.

'What are you doing?'

'Are you truly that naive?'

Sylvia bristled. She may not be part of this world of balls and garden parties, but the same rules applied to women of her class as to his.

'Do not call me naive,' she said, shocked when he brought his hand up and pressed it against her lips. Admittedly she had been talking a little too loud if someone was now coming in their direction down the corridor, but there was no need to overreact in this way.

'Take your hand away,' she said, her voice distorted.

'Do you promise to be quiet?'

She nodded, drawing herself up to her full height as he removed his hand.

'You can rant and rave at me in a minute when whoever that was has settled in their room,' he murmured. 'Just be quiet for now.'

'I do not rant and rave,' Sylvia whispered. '*You* are the one overreacting here. I merely came to drop off my book. It could have been a simple exchange. You could have said, "Good evening, Miss Thompson, is there something I can do for you?" And I would have handed over the book and told you to read it before making any assumptions about it.'

He looked at her without answering, then simply pressed a finger to his lips. Sylvia felt her anger swell and pulse inside her. He had been like this the first few days after the shipwreck too. He'd assumed superiority, refused to let her take charge of anything meaningful, even dismissed her well-reasoned opinions.

At the time, she had wondered if Hugh would survive the shipwreck only to be murdered by her a few days later. Of course he had mellowed. He had seen what she was capable of, and over time they had grown to appreciate one another's talents. He had conceded she was a better spear-fisher, and she had admitted all shelter building should be left to him. Their partnership had blossomed. Right now it was as if he had forgotten other people had skills and opinions to offer as well.

After another minute, he nodded as if satisfied the risk had passed.

'Instead you dragged me in here, compromising me, when the exchange could have been short and pleasant, and I could be tucked up in my own bed now.'

'You came to give me your book?'

Sylvia looked down to the book clasped against her chest and nodded, thrusting it out towards him.

'I don't want to read it.'

She rolled her eyes, trying to pretend that didn't sting a little.

'I am not suggesting you read it for your own enjoyment.' She snorted. 'No doubt you have returned to the real world and forgotten how to enjoy anything, now your sense of duty has been sparked. I am suggesting you read it to see there is nothing ruinous about it.'

He sighed, running a hand through his blond hair. Sylvia saw a flash of the old Hugh, the one she had loved. Quickly she pushed that thought away. Too much had passed between them for any thoughts of love.

'I will repeat what I said earlier. It does not matter that you have left out the most scandalous parts of our time on the island, or that you have perpetuated this idea of a chaperon. You invite too close scrutiny to our time there. If people were allowed to forget about it, they would not question it. They would not wonder if the chaperon was real. They would not think how convenient it was for us to have another female companion who survived the whole time we were on the island and then died on the ship on the way home. Every time someone picks up that book, it threatens to ruin you.'

'Is it Honoria you worry about?' Sylvia said quietly.

She knew the pleasant daughter of the merchant and could not see her making a fuss over this.

'No,' he exploded, far too loudly. Hugh turned away, pacing the room. Then, with a flash of emotion, he strode over to her and grasped her by the arms. 'It is you. It has always been you. Everything I have done. Everything I have agreed to…' He trailed off, shaking his head, his eyes searching hers.

Sylvia frowned, then shook her head in disdain. How could he claim he had even spared a single thought for her this past year? After making his intention to marry Miss Willis clear, he had acted as though everything they had once shared was meaningless.

'What do you mean?'

The veil seemed to descend again over his eyes, and she saw him collect himself.

'Nothing. Forget I said anything. I will read your book, and then I will show you what will damage you. Perhaps then you will understand what a foolish idea it is to make yourself the centre of all this attention again.'

He was still holding her arms, his body just a fraction too close to hers. She could feel the heat of him, the tightly wound coil of energy as if he were ready to spring at a moment's notice. There was an intensity in his eyes that made it look as though they might burst into flames. She saw a longing in them, although what, for she couldn't be sure. With a soft shake of his head he dropped his hands from her arms, severing their connection.

For one insane moment, Sylvia wanted to reach out, to stroke his cheek and coax him back to her. She yearned to remind him of the man he had been, of the time they had spent together. Every night when she was dropping off to sleep, her thoughts flew to the Isla Ana. For a few wonderful moments, she could fool herself that nothing had changed, that she was drifting off to sleep on the sand in the arms of the man she loved.

She lifted her hand, but he saw the movement and caught it, his eyes searching hers before he turned away with a grunt of frustration.

'Go,' he said gruffly. 'Leave the book. We will talk tomorrow.'

It was a definite dismissal, one that she could not ignore despite the roiling fire he had ignited deep inside her. She hated that he could still affect her like this, hated the attraction she still felt to him despite how terribly he had treated her. Part of her wished she could forget Hugh Wilder existed. She wanted to wipe him from her memory entirely. Her life hadn't been easy these last couple of years with the death of her father and the shipwreck and then the devastating loss of her brother, but Hugh's betrayal had hit her the hardest. Her grief and loss she was slowly learning to deal with, but the way Hugh had completely abandoned her would scar her trust for the rest of her life.

It was humiliating to see he held her in such contempt, so without another word, she opened the door a fraction and peeked out before slipping into the corridor.

It was only when she reached her room, locking the door behind her, that she allowed the tears to fall onto her cheeks as she threw herself face down onto the bed.

Chapter Four

Lord Wilder was already on deck, working in his shirtsleeves to try to save the ship alongside the sailors. As soon as I stepped onto the slippery deck and saw the height of the swell around us, I knew there was no way a ship could survive, and mere seconds later, a giant wave swept across the boat and carried me from the ship. As I plunged into the icy waters, consumed by the darkness, I truly thought my time on earth was over.

Hugh nudged his horse with one knee, changing direction slightly as they plodded across the fields on the return journey to Somersham Hall. He hadn't slept and this morning he'd lay waiting for the dawn, restless and on edge, after a while deciding to take an early morning ride through the countryside near Lady Montague's country estate. After Sylvia had left his room the night before, he had tried to rest, but his whole body had been on edge, and it had been impossible to close his eyes without visions of her filling them. Instead he had lit his candle and read the book she had brought him.

Grudgingly he had to admit it was good, better than good. It was compelling, engaging and exciting. When he had read about the shipwreck itself, Hugh could imagine himself back there, being tossed in the salty water in the darkness, battered by the waves until it felt as though his whole body was bruised and broken. For months after he had often awakened in a cold sweat, reliving the moments of terror in his dreams.

The part on the island was also well-written, although she had not been lying when she had said it was completely made-up. On the surface, it was a tame read. There was no hint of the passion they had shared, of the longing they felt for one another and the intense desire that had exploded when they had finally given in to it. Instead she had written about the practicalities of building a shelter, of finding food, of making a life for themselves when they were not sure whether they would ever be rescued. She had mentioned the fictitious Mrs White multiple times, the older woman they had invented as a handy chaperon for their time spent on the island.

Still, his worries persisted. She had written it well, but that did not mean it was perfect.

Pressing his heels against Caesar's flanks, he increased his pace, feeling the liberation he always did when he was out on horseback. He loved riding, loved the sense of freedom it gave him when the rest of his life was spent in stuffy offices and studies, overseeing the vast administration that came with the viscountcy he was entrusted with.

He had risen with the dawn, knowing he would not sleep despite his night spent reading rather than resting. The house had been silent—even the servants had not begun to stir for the day's work ahead when he had slipped out. Even so, now he could see a solitary figure walking through the gardens. He was still a fair distance from the house, but he knew instinctively it was Sylvia. It was as though he were drawn to her, though he knew the best thing for everyone was for him to keep his distance.

Before he got to the gardens, he dismounted, leading Caesar by the reins so he did not inadvertently trample any of the carefully planted flowers.

Sylvia hadn't seen him. She looked lost in her own world, wandering amongst the flowers. Her hair was pinned into a loose bun at the nape of her neck, long chestnut strands already falling loose, and her dress this morning was nothing like the striking blue silk she had been in the day before. This morning she looked more natural, and he could imagine her as a water nymph as described in ancient Greek myths. Her dress was of white cotton, a woollen shawl about her shoulders, but despite her simple attire, Hugh found her irresistible.

Chiding himself for a lack of resolve, he hardened his mind and then coughed as he approached so as not to startle her too much.

'Good morning, Sylvia.' She did not correct him today, and he relished the sound of her name on his lips.

Once he had dreamed he would utter it every morning as they woke, her body warm against his.

'Good morning, Hugh.' She looked melancholy, and her voice was subdued. He wanted to go to her, to pull her to him, but that was no longer his role. He realised he preferred it when they were sparring like the previous night. At least then he didn't get the urge to comfort her.

'Couldn't you sleep?' he asked.

She shrugged, taking a seat on the low wall around an ornamental fountain. He was about to sit down next to her when there was a flutter of wings, and Hugh was surprised by the brightly coloured bird that came and settled on the wall next to her.

'Is that Rosa?'

'Rosa,' the bird said. *'Pox on Hugh Wilder.'*

'I can see you have taught her a few more choice phrases since I last saw you.'

Sylvia stroked the bird's head affectionately, and he marvelled at how tame the animal was.

'I have absolutely no influence over what Rosa decides to say,' Sylvia said, but he could tell she was trying to suppress a smile.

'I read your book.'

She looked up sharply, and he saw a hint of panic in her eyes.

'What do you think?' she said when he did not continue.

'You've been careful,' he said eventually, choosing his words with precision. 'I cannot deny that. There is nothing that would explicitly ruin your reputation, but I still think it is a bad idea to invite scrutiny to our time on the island.'

'We renewed our acquaintance less than twenty-four hours ago, and you have said the same thing over and over until it has made me want to scream. I *know* we are not friends, but would it kill you to politely enquire as to my health, perhaps ask what my plans are for after publication of the book? You are single-minded, Lord Wilder, and it is becoming tiresome.'

'How is your health?'

'Fine. I am as strong as an ox.'

'What are your plans after your book has been published?'

'I will look for a small cottage somewhere inexpensive.'

'Good. Now that's over, can we return to the matter at hand?'

Sylvia stood and let out a world-weary sigh. 'Let me make this easy for you,' she said, turning to him. 'Whatever you say, whatever you do, I am not going to tell my publisher to stop the launch of my book. What's more, even if for some mad reason I wanted to, I couldn't now. The books are printed, money has been invested, and there is no turning back. There is *nothing* you could say or do to change my mind.'

Hugh saw the sincerity in her eyes and felt his world contract as a flare of anger welled up inside him. He had sacrificed so much for this woman, agreed to so much to protect her reputation, yet she was intent on doing everything she could to destroy it.

'You do not know what you do.'

'I know exactly what I am doing,' she said, taking a step towards him. 'I am providing for my future. I have no hefty inheritance, no grand estate to seek refuge in. My father left nothing but debts, and my brother was not in this world long enough to make his mark. I have no family, no one to turn to, so I am doing the only thing that is left. I am looking out for myself.' She advanced further, the brightly coloured parrot flapping its wings and coming to rest on her shoulder. Together they made a formidable sight. 'So I am truly sorry that it does not fit with the image you want to put out into the world, and I really do not wish any strife between you and your future wife over this, but you ceased to deserve an opinion on what *I* do with *my* life the day you walked away from me at the docks.'

Hugh scoffed and then saw she was deadly serious.

'Think what you will of me, Miss Thompson, but do not fool yourself *into* thinking that I walked away from you.'

'My memory is as clear as day, my lord. We disembarked, and then you took your future wife by the arm and walked away without even deigning to say goodbye.'

'You had made it perfectly clear by then you wished to have nothing further to do with me,' Hugh said, trying to push down the memory of the devastation he had felt when he had first overheard her saying that they had no future together in the real world. For once in his life he had been ready to give up his every principle, every rule his father had drummed into him. He had been ready to present Sylvia to the world as his future wife. 'All I did was refuse to draw out the final goodbye. You had already pushed me away. That happened almost as soon as we boarded the *Chameleon*.' He shook his head, remembering the pain he'd felt when she had told him never to come near her again. 'You told me you never wanted to see me again. You warned me to stay away.'

'I did not push you away as soon as we boarded the *Chameleon*,' Sylvia said, her voice incredulous as if unable to believe what she was hearing.

'Clearly we were not on the same ship,' Hugh said. He shook his head in disbelief, torn between walking away and laying out the truth once and for all. He glanced up at the house, ensuring there were no twitching curtains to bear witness to their confrontation.

'You were the one who told Captain Willis there was no future for us, that we would never be married, not in the real world. It was one of the first things you said to him. The island was still in sight.'

'You heard that?'

'Every word.'

Sylvia took a shuddering breath before speaking. 'It was the truth, though, wasn't it? Despite what we shared on the Isla Ana. You began pulling away from me as soon as we saw the ship turning towards the island. You became distant, and I knew even before we started talking of England that you were imagining a future without me.'

'That is ridiculous,' Hugh said, but he had to turn his face away. On the day they were rescued, he had been consumed by thoughts of home, of what his life would be after he returned from the dead. Perhaps he had been a little distant with Sylvia, but it was only to be expected. The life they had built the previous three months had been ripped from them, and he had panicked as to how to bring together the two worlds that would have to collide.

'I said there was no future for us because I could see in your eyes you were already thinking of home, of a place where I did not belong. I refused to pine away for you whilst you wished yourself free of the burden of promises made when we thought we would never be rescued.' Sylvia's eyes flashed as she spoke. Somewhere inside, Hugh realised what a difficult decision this must have been for her, but right now he felt livid. Her fears had led to one of the most weighty decisions of his life, the decision to ask Honoria Willis to be his wife. 'And I was not wrong, was I? A few days later, you were engaged. To Miss Willis.' She almost spat out the name, and he inadvertently took a step back.

'You object to Miss Willis?'

'I have nothing against the girl,' she said, turning her face away and then snapping back round to face him as if unable to contain her fury. 'What I did object to was how quickly you made her your fiancée. You pulled away from *me* because I was not suitable to be your viscountess, yet Miss Willis was.' He had thought he would never tell her the truth, he would never admit the sacrifice he had made for her, but now he found it bubbling up to the surface, and he was unable to keep it in.

'I did that for you,' he said quietly. 'I proposed to Miss Willis for you.'

She scoffed, and he felt the sound as if it were a dagger in his heart.

'You proposed to your fiancée for me?' she asked, clearly incredulous.

'When it was clear you were scornful of the protection my name could bring you, I saw no other choice. Captain Willis is hardly the sort of man to keep your secrets without a significant bribe.'

Hugh watched as Sylvia puzzled through what he had just told her. She began shaking her head.

'No,' she said, the colour draining from her cheeks. 'It's not true.'

'Believe what you want,' Hugh said. 'It doesn't change anything. Our futures were set the day we were rescued from that island.'

For a moment, he wanted to open the whole terrible truth up for her to see. He wanted her to have to listen to the details of how Captain Willis had threatened to expose the intimacy Hugh and Sylvia had clearly shared and how when Sylvia had openly said she didn't see a future for them, the captain had offered his own solution. His daughter would become a viscountess, be mistress in a grand house, and in return, Captain Willis would perpetuate the lie that there was a third person rescued with them, a respectable lady who died on the voyage back to England. The marriage was the price of that lie.

'I never asked you to sacrifice your future for me,' Sylvia said quietly, and he could see the tears welling in her eyes. 'I never asked anything from you.'

'It doesn't matter now,' Hugh said abruptly. 'I know the value of a promise.' He just hated that his promise went against everything he had been raised to hold as important. Once he could have stomached marrying someone society would cruelly shun if he cared for her, but the daughter of a merchant sailor, no matter how wealthy, would never be accepted in the eyes of the *ton*, and he had failed at the first role of the Viscount: to provide an heir with an impeccable bloodline.

'I don't...' Sylvia began to say, but Hugh held up a hand to silence her. He wished he hadn't begun this conversation, and now all he really wanted was for it to be over. There was no going back, no point in arguing over who said what or felt most wronged. Every day of his life, he would wake up with regrets, and he didn't doubt Sylvia would too, but there was no easy way out of this predicament. The past year he had been consumed by his quest to find a route out of the marriage to Miss Willis, some way that would preserve Sylvia's reputation. When he was feeling optimistic, sometimes he imagined them coming together again, with all the animosity lost and the affection found, but he knew that was a lot to wish for. Initially he would settle for *not* having to marry Miss Willis. It was not straightforward, though, as his travails this past year would attest, and he could not simply bow out, saying he had changed his mind. He believed in owning one's decisions, no matter how bad. This was his burden to bear.

Bowing abruptly, he turned and led his horse away, pretending he didn't hear when Sylvia called after him.

Chapter Five

Fate smiled upon me that dreadful night, for I should have been lost at the bottom of the ocean with all the other poor souls from the Lady Catherine. Instead I was tossed around until, exhausted, I managed to grab onto a shattered piece of wood from the sinking ship. For hours I clung on until the storm peaked and then abated, leaving a scene of devastation behind it.

'Miss Thompson, you were not at breakfast. I do hope nothing is amiss. My guests are looking forward to your book reading later this morning.'

Sylvia summoned a smile she didn't feel and turned to the hostess.

'Nothing amiss, Lady Montague. I often enjoy an early morning stroll around the garden, and yours is so beautiful, I quite lost track of time.'

'Lost track of time,' Rosa squawked from Sylvia's shoulder.

'What a beautiful creature,' Lady Montague said,

taking a step closer. 'You will bring her to the reading later this morning?'

'Of course, Rosa will be there in all her glory.'

Lady Montague smiled and turned away, taking a couple of steps before speaking over her shoulder. 'Persuade Lord Wilder to attend too. It will make more of an atmosphere.'

Sylvia nodded, smiling until the older lady had slipped back into the dining room before letting out a groan of despair. A small reading to an interested group of ladies, that was how Lady Montague had phrased it when she had first invited Sylvia to be part of her weekend house party. That hadn't sounded too terrible—perhaps even with the right select audience it would be enjoyable—but Sylvia could see exactly how this was going to go. She would read one or two select passages whilst the ladies all sighed and fluttered their eyelashes at Hugh, not really listening to anything she said. They would huddle round him, asking how he had found the strength to be so brave, to survive when no one else had, forgetting all the time Sylvia was sitting right there. It wasn't that she liked to be the centre of attention, far from it, but sometimes she wished for the freedom to express herself and be seen, as she would have been if she had written the book as it had actually happened.

Worse, Sylvia was supposed to produce Hugh as if he were a willing participant.

It had been three hours since she had encountered him in the gardens early that morning, three hours during which all she had managed to do was brood over his words. The hours and days after their rescue was hazy in her mind. So much had happened in such a short time, but she could see by the look in Hugh's eyes he spoke the truth. He had overheard her tell Captain Willis she and Hugh did not have a future, and when the scoundrel sea captain threatened to make trouble for her, Hugh had agreed to marry the sailor's daughter.

No wonder he looked at her with such fire in his eyes. He blamed her for getting himself trapped into an engagement he didn't want. His honour stopped him from breaking things off with Honoria Willis, yet from the long talks they'd had whilst trapped together on the Isla Ana, she knew Miss Willis was not the sort of wife he had been raised to marry.

Sylvia closed her eyes and shook her head. They hadn't spoken much about their futures whilst trapped on the island, talking in more abstract terms of what had been their hopes and dreams. It had seemed too dangerous to plan anything when they both had believed they may never be rescued. Still, she knew Hugh had been expected to marry someone of an impeccable bloodline with a fortune to match. It was why she had thought he had begun to pull away from her when it was clear they would be rescued, and why things had hurt even more when he announced he was marrying Honoria Willis, the daughter of a rogue merchant trader, so far removed from the life she had stepped aside to allow him to go back to.

Looking at the stairs with trepidation, Sylvia knew what she had to do. Nothing had changed, not really. She still needed her book to be a success, and for that to happen, she needed the influential ladies of Lady

Montague's social circle to talk about it, to spread the word until there was such a fuss around it that a second print run was needed almost immediately. That meant she needed Hugh. At the very least, she needed to try to persuade him to accompany her.

The walk up the sweeping staircase seemed to stretch on forever, and Sylvia had a sinking feeling in her stomach as if walking to her doom. Her feet felt as if they had great weights tied to them as she advanced along the corridor, and when she eventually got to Hugh's door, she could not bring herself to knock.

Before she had summoned the courage to rap on the wood, the door was thrown open and Hugh stepped out, almost barrelling into her but pulling himself up short.

'What are you doing standing there?' His words were abrupt, and he didn't look pleased to see her.

Sylvia cleared her throat, feeling herself bristle at his tone. The first few days they had spent together on the Isla Ana had given her a similar feeling. Hugh was assertive and didn't hold back from telling people if he thought they were doing something wrong, and in those early days, they had clashed incessantly.

'I was about to knock on your door.'

'Whatever for?'

Tamping down the curt response she wanted to give, Sylvia forced herself to breathe deeply and smile.

'Lady Montague has arranged for a few of her guests to attend a reading I am giving from my book. These are influential women, the sort of women that others emulate. If I can get them interested it would be ideal.'

'What has that got to do with me? Go do your reading. I am not stopping you.'

Sylvia knew he was going to say no before she even asked the question, but she pushed on anyway.

'Lady Montague suggested it may be more entertaining, more of an event, if you are in attendance too,' Sylvia said through gritted teeth.

'You do not need me to read a chapter or two from your book.'

'No,' she started slowly, not wanting to admit most of her audience would be more interested in Hugh than in what she had to say. 'I don't *need* you, but I suppose it would make it more exciting I can read a little, and then the ladies will be able to ask any questions of both of us.'

'In the year I have been back, do you know how many times I've been asked all the inane questions people come up with? *How did you survive? What did you do for shelter? Did you have to eat insects?*'

'At least yours are about your experience,' Sylvia muttered. 'All of the questions I am asked are about you.'

He looked at her with genuine curiosity then, and for a moment, she thought he might relent and agree.

'I do not want to add to this spectacle. You know my views on raking this all up. It is a bad idea, and as such, I won't add to the interest around it by fanning the flames of the fire.'

Sylvia bit her lip, wondering how she could persuade him but realising she barely knew the man. The Hugh of a year ago, the man she had fallen in love with, belonged to another world. That man she would wrap her arms around and tease with kisses until he relented, grumbling about whatever it was she had asked him to do, but secretly happy to do whatever she asked of him, whatever made her content.

Trying to suppress the tears she could feel forming in her eyes, the memory of their first few weeks on the island came to her. Initially Hugh had been aloof and distant, but with time, she had cracked through that hard, brittle shell and slowly revealed the man underneath. Then they'd talked for hours, whether they were standing in the shallows spear-fishing or climbing trees to collect the highest hanging fruit. Sylvia had been reluctant to admit to herself the infatuation she had felt for Hugh until the night he had asked her to dance with him on the beach. Then, as she had looked into his eyes, she had seen the same desire she felt reflected in his. For the first time in weeks, she felt that flicker of hope and happiness despite the uncertainty of their circumstances.

'Please excuse me,' he said, inclining his head stiffly and retreating back into his room, starting to close the door.

'Hugh, I need the book at the very least,' she said, throwing out a hand to stop the door closing in her face. He grunted and disappeared into the room, returning a moment later with her book in his hand. With one final shake of his head he handed it over and then pushed the door closed behind him, leaving Sylvia rejected in the hall.

Sylvia stood for a long time, unmoving. Unsure what to do next, but with a sinking heart, she realised there was nothing she could do. She and Hugh shared nothing any more, nothing but memories, and it seemed he was keen to forget those as quickly as possible too.

'This is the last place I would expect to find you.' A familiar voice invaded the silence of the library. 'Hiding away at Lady Montague's country estate. Don't you have a wedding to plan?'

Hugh turned in his chair and grinned, then stood quickly and pulled the other man into an embrace.

'Turner, now, this is a pleasant surprise. What are you doing here?'

'My wife is Lady Montague's third cousin or great niece or some other distant relative. We're here for the weekend, but our carriage lost a wheel, so we were a bit late arriving.' Sir Percy Turner collapsed into the chair opposite Hugh, leaning back and relaxing completely. Even though it was only half past ten in the morning, already he looked a mess, with his clothes dishevelled and his hair flopping about in an unruly fashion. Hugh had known Sir Percy for nearly twenty years, with both of them starting at Harrow together one blustery autumn morning, and never had he seen him perfectly turned out. 'More to the point, what are you doing here?'

'You're not wrong,' Hugh murmured.

'I understand from my wife your Miss Thompson is doing a reading from her new book.'

'Yes, more fool her.'

'You came here to try to stop her?'

'I came here to try to persuade her to give up on the

whole idea of inviting scrutiny to our time on the Isla Ana, but the stubborn dolt will not listen to me.'

'I am curious to meet this young lady,' Sir Percy said, the corners of his mouth tugging upwards despite his best efforts. 'I don't think I've ever known anyone able to vex you as much as she does.'

Sir Percy knew most of the truth when it came to the salacious events of a year ago. Hugh hadn't meant to tell him despite their years of friendship, but one evening when mourning everything he had lost, Hugh had become rip-roaringly drunk and spilled his secrets to his friend. Sir Percy was supportive in a gently teasing way, although the normally mild-mannered man didn't hold back when he told Hugh he was a stubborn fool for not telling Sylvia how he felt. Hugh had mumbled that his feelings were far too complex to put into words whilst wishing they weren't further complicated by the fiancée he had secreted away in Southampton.

'She is vexatious,' Hugh said. 'She will not listen to sound advice and insists on doing everything her own way.'

'Just like someone else I know.'

'I listen to advice.'

Sir Percy scoffed. 'If you were fixing a chair and a carpenter came along and told you to do it another way, you would double down on your own method and struggle on, regardless of what the expert said.' He paused, looking at Hugh keenly. 'Isn't Lady Montague gathering her ladies now for a reading?'

Hugh grunted.

'Shouldn't you be there?'

'Sir Percy, I have been looking for you everywhere,' Lady Turner said as she hurried into the room. 'Miss Thompson is going to start her reading in a moment, and I do not want to miss it. Will you accompany me?'

She drew up short as she saw Hugh and then broke out into a beatific smile. Many people did not know why the diamond of the 1808 season had chosen the amiable but absent-minded Sir Percy as her husband out of the many suitors eager to make her their wife. There had been men with greater fortunes and men with more impressive titles all vying for her hand, but the diamond had chosen the underwhelming Sir Percy Turner. When asked, she gave an enigmatic smile and said she was drawn to her husband's kind eyes.

Hugh knew differently, although he didn't argue that his friend had kind eyes. He knew Lady Turner was one of the most astute people in society. She had seen the kindness in Percy, the devotion, and his solid, hard-working outlook on life.

'Lord Wilder, what a delight. Percy did not tell me you were going to be here.'

Hugh stood and took Lady Turner's hand.

'Am I to hope that you've come to your senses and realised your true feelings for Miss Thompson should be shouted from the rooftops and have decided to use this weekend's party to express them to her?'

'Hardly a suitable venue,' he said softly.

'I see I am hoping in vain,' Lady Turner said. 'Shall I leave you. Percy?'

'No,' Sir Percy said, taking his wife's arm. 'Let us

see what Miss Thompson has to say. I am intrigued to hear the other side of this story.'

Hugh watched as they walked away and then sighed. He knew he would follow them. Sylvia's book might not be contentious, but at any moment the truth could slip from her lips, and the ladies in her audience might realise how scandalous a time their three months on the Isla Ana had been.

He followed the Turners into the hall, pausing outside the drawing room before entering. Sylvia was at the front, arranging her space with her back towards him. The parrot that had taken a shine to her on their third day of being marooned was perched on the back of her chair, no doubt ready to perform. The bird had never particularly liked him, favouring Sylvia as she gradually worked on gaining its trust.

'Lord Wilder, what a wonderful treat,' Lady Montague said as she spotted him. Quickly she motioned to a footman to bring over another chair and placed it directly next to Sylvia's. Sylvia turned, and her eyes locked on to his. As often happened, he felt a spark of attraction flare between them. He might have resigned himself to a different life, but he could not deny the relentless force that pulled him towards Sylvia.

'Lord Wilder,' she said, her voice low, but she couldn't disguise the slight tremor. 'You came.'

'I came, Miss Thompson.'

She nodded in acknowledgement and then turned away. It was only when she sat in the chair and looked out at the assembled audience that he could see how nervous she was.

Hugh knew she struggled when all eyes were on her, especially when it was the eyes of ladies of a different social class. There was something so judgemental about the ladies of the *ton*. At the moment, they looked engaged, excited even, but Hugh was aware that one wrong comment, one snub to the wrong person, and Sylvia would be excluded entirely. She was a momentary fascination, that was all. In a few months, the interest of society would have moved on to other things, and Sylvia knew it.

'Ladies and gentlemen,' Lady Montague said, clapping her hands together as if controlling a naughty group of school children. 'It is my pleasure to introduce to you today a young lady who has been championed by the Queen herself. Miss Sylvia Thompson was caught up in a tragic shipwreck that saw many of her companions die and then was trapped for months on a desert island. She is here for your entertainment.'

'Thank you, Lady Montague,' Sylvia said, standing up and smiling at the assembled group. Hugh looked out at the crowd. It was mainly made up of ladies, with a few gentlemen scattered here and there. For now they looked engaged and interested, and as he watched, Sylvia seemed to bloom under their attention. He knew she was a naturally reserved person, but although she called herself shy, he didn't quite believe it. She had a quiet authority, not pushing herself forwards like many did even when they had nothing to say, Sylvia preferred to wait until she was sure of her facts or opinion, then give it in a measured way.

'Good morning, ladies and gentlemen. Thank you

for coming to listen today. As Lady Montague said, I am Miss Sylvia Thompson, and a year ago, my life was turned upside down by the sinking of the *Lady Catherine*. There are many things I am thankful for every single day, but foremost for being alive.' She turned to Lord Wilder and smiled. 'I doubt I would be standing here today without the bravery and sacrifice of Lord Wilder, the true hero of my story.'

There was a hearty applause, and Hugh stood for a moment, acknowledging it. This was going to be an uncomfortable half an hour.

Chapter Six

I drifted for hours, barely conscious. My lips were cracked, my skin burning and my head pounding. When I was lucid I mourned the loss of all the poor souls from the Lady Catherine, but most of that day I floated in and out of a delirium. The island, when I first spotted it, seemed fanciful, as if merely a figment of my imagination.

The first time Sylvia looked up from the book, she almost stumbled over her words. Her audience was sitting enraptured, actually listening. She had spent half the night worrying that no one would turn up to her reading, and the other half worrying they would sit sniggering if they did attend. Instead everyone actually seemed to be enjoying her account. She was reading an extract from about a quarter of the way through, detailing how they tried to build a shelter to shield them from the thunder and rain of an approaching storm. It hadn't gone well, but the story was a good one and raised some laughter from the crowd.

Sylvia knew not to press her luck and also was keen to leave her potential readers wanting more, so after fifteen minutes, she gently closed the book and looked up with a smile.

There was a gentle round of applause, and Lady Montague stood.

'How fascinating, Miss Thompson, I do not know how I would have survived in your position. How fortuitous Lord Wilder was marooned with you.'

'Fortuitous indeed.'

'The Queen was most curious about your story, was she not, Miss Thompson?' Lady Montague asked.

'She was. I was overcome by her grace and generosity when she bade me attend her to tell her my story.'

'You actually met the Queen?' one eager young lady said, her eyes wide.

'Yes. She invited me to take tea with her.' It had been a strange few weeks after she had arrived back in England on the *Chameleon*, and at first she had felt lost, as if set adrift. Then a childhood acquaintance had reached out, having heard of Sylvia's plight, and invited her to a dinner party. The woman had started life as a clerk's daughter, but she had married well and cultivated her social relationships. That one dinner party had led to a flurry of invitations for Sylvia, each a little grander than the last, until she was socialising with the titled and wealthy. Sylvia had forgotten to breathe for half a minute when one of these ladies, the Countess of Somerset, announced the Queen had expressed a desire to meet her. Never in her entire life had she expected to be invited to take tea with royalty.

'An honour indeed,' Lady Montague said, and Sylvia realised how wily the older woman really was. Sylvia might be using this gathering for her own ends, but they were at least transparent. Lady Montague was gaining something out of the arrangement too. She was aligning herself with the Queen of England, showing interest and favour to the same person the Queen had blessed with her attention. It would elevate Lady Montague in the eyes of society and might even win her favour with the court.

Thinking how exhausting it must be to play these games all the time, Sylvia looked out to the crowd for the next question, but Lady Montague was not yet finished.

'Tell us, my dear, what you and the Queen talked about.'

'She wanted to hear my story, in as much detail as possible, and she was fascinated by my bird.' As if on cue, Rosa fluttered down from the back of the chair where she had been perching, looking like a statue she was so still, and paraded on the carpet in front of the guests. 'Whilst we were there, a feather from Rosa's tail came loose, and the Queen ordered it to be made into a brooch.'

'The bird is your pet?'

Sylvia smiled softly, inclining her head. 'I would not presume ownership over Rosa. She is a highly intelligent creature. I would never try to keep her captive.'

'She is free to fly away?'

'If she wishes. And sometimes she does, but she always finds her way back home.'

'Is she dangerous?'

'No, not at all. Her diet is made up of fruits and seeds, and although her beak does look ferocious, she mainly uses it for cracking the shells of nuts.'

'She does peck, though,' Hugh said from his seat next to her. Rosa turned and regarded him with a haughty expression, and Sylvia had to suppress a giggle.

'Unfortunately, Lord Wilder and Rosa's acquaintance was cursed from the very first,' Sylvia said. 'Rosa has not once pecked me.'

'What happened, my lord?' One young lady asked.

Hugh motioned for Sylvia to tell the story, and she felt a swell of gratitude. Hugh might be gruff, but he was not the sort to intentionally steal her moment.

'We were celebrating,' Sylvia said, unable to stop the smile from spreading across her face at the memory. 'We had successfully caught a fish for our dinner, and it was the first time we had eaten anything but fruit in a long while. We managed to start a fire and cook the fish, and as we sat down to eat it, Rosa swooped in. Lord Wilder, in his panic, thought Rosa meant to steal our hard-earned dinner and tried to shoo her away. Of course she was merely curious and took offence at Lord Wilder's attempts, and when he extended a hand, she pecked him on the finger.'

The parrot spread her wings and fluttered, rising a few feet off the ground before coming to rest on Sylvia's shoulder.

'The bird hasn't warmed to me since,' Lord Wilder murmured. 'But she followed Miss Thompson everywhere.'

'There is a simmering animosity between you,' Sylvia said, directing her words to Lord Wilder.

'I am willing to call a truce if the bird will too.'

'What do you say, Rosa? Will you take Lord Wilder's hand of friendship.'

'Pox on Hugh Wilder,' Rosa squawked, drawing a swell of laughter from the crowd.

'Thank you, Miss Thompson and Lord Wilder, for your wonderful insights,' Lady Montague said, taking her place at the front of the room. 'In honour of your trials on the Isla Ana, I thought I would arrange a little challenge for any guests that wanted to play.'

When she had first returned to England, Sylvia had been swept up in a whirl of dinner parties and balls. It had been her first peek into the world of the *ton*, so she knew from those experiences that often games and activities were arranged at these house parties in a bid to get the ladies and gentlemen mixing and having fun. It had seemed frivolous at first, but everyone seemed to enjoy them.

'I hope you will indulge us, Lord Wilder,' Lady Montague said with a sweet smile.

Sylvia could see the moment of hesitation, but good manners won out, and Hugh inclined his head.

'In the garden, I have gathered some materials you might use to make a shelter. I want you to imagine you are marooned on a desert island, with no hope of rescue. A storm is approaching, and you need to build a shelter. I suggest, ladies, you find a gentleman to assist you, and shall we say you have an hour to perfect your creation.

I will be the judge, and you are competing against Miss Thompson and Lord Wilder.'

A swell of conversation filled the room as the ladies rose, some of them selecting their gentlemen from the guests in the room whilst others went off in search of someone to do the heavy lifting.

Lady Montague approached Sylvia, clapping her hands. 'You did wonderfully my dear. Everyone loved you.'

'Thank you for the opportunity,' Sylvia said.

'And Lord Wilder, you looked perfectly brooding sitting in that chair. Did it take you back to your time on the island?'

'It did, Lady Montague.'

Lady Montague beamed and then began to usher them out of the room.

'I like to fill the day with something practical. Otherwise, all these house parties begin to feel the same,' Lady Montague said as she showed them to the lawn beyond the parterre. 'In a few months' time, people will still be talking about this, whereas can I remember anything about Lady Mottisham's garden party last year?' She shook her head. 'Not a thing. You have to be different, memorable.' Lady Montague looked at Sylvia and nodded in approval. 'I think we see eye to eye there.'

Already some couples were choosing their materials from a large pile laid out on the lawn. There were sticks from the nearby wood, reams of old material cut to various sizes, ropes and twine and a few less useful objects.

'Make me proud, Miss Thompson. Show everyone what a real shelter should look like.'

Their hostess walked away, leaving them standing in front of the pile of sticks.

'I feel like I am in a bad dream,' Hugh muttered.

Sylvia bent down, not wanting to agree with him but finding it hard to see a positive in the situation.

'She must be mad,' Hugh continued, looking after their hostess. 'What sane person makes two shipwreck survivors relive a part of their horrifying ordeal?'

'I don't think that was her intention.'

'She may as well throw us in the lake and see if we sink or swim.'

'She is merely trying to make this weekend memorable. I doubt she has considered the experience was traumatic.'

'And therein lies the problem. Perhaps she could consider it.'

'I suppose people *will* remember this more than if I had just done the reading.'

'We should refuse.'

Sylvia felt a flicker of panic and reached out to lay a hand on Hugh's arm. She had no right to ask anything of him, she knew that, but in her desperation she must try.

'I need Lady Montague's favour,' she said quietly. 'Please, Hugh, do not spoil this for me. You do not have to participate—I will build this on my own—but I beg you do not say anything to Lady Montague.'

For a long moment, he considered her request, and she found herself holding her breath.

'Fine,' he growled eventually. 'Let's get this over with.'

As he selected a sturdy stick, his hand brushed against Sylvia's, and a crackle passed between them. The reading had been relatively painless. Sylvia had chosen an innocuous passage that contained the right balance of humour and peril. Her description had taken him back to that evening on the island as they struggled with the paltry materials they had, barely able to communicate as their voices were whipped away by the wind.

The shelter they had ended up with had lasted one night, surviving the storm only to tumble around them in the morning when his foot had caught one of the stabilising poles. It had been the first shelter of many, each a little better than the last, each lasting a few more days than its predecessor.

Of course, he hadn't built anything in a year. Manual labour was not part of the role of the Viscount, but as he gripped the stick in his hand, he realised there was a certain satisfaction to be had from building something tangible from a collection of materials.

They worked in unison, selecting their materials quickly and retreating to a quieter part of the garden, although he was sure never to be out of sight of the house and the other guests. He hadn't sacrificed so much to protect Sylvia's reputation only to ruin her now.

'Here?' she suggested, picking a level patch of grass.

'To the left a little.'

She frowned but moved without a word.

'No, to the right,' he corrected her as she stepped too far.

Sighing, she stepped back.

'How is this, master builder?'

'You know the rules.'

He thought he saw her roll her eyes, but she parroted them back to him.

'Check the terrain is level and solid. Make a stable frame. Overlap everything.'

The task was irritating and a waste of his time, but he did feel a small swell of pleasure to be working alongside Sylvia again. As soon as he had the thought, he banished it. The last thing that should be on his mind was pleasure. The whole point of him being here was to persuade Sylvia not to publish her book and ruin herself. Once that single task was completed, he could return to the much more arduous task of extricating himself from his engagement to Miss Willis. Only then could he even begin to think of enjoying himself, of perhaps even enjoying Sylvia's company again.

'Hold these together,' he said, selecting a piece of rope to wind around three sticks leaning against one another. Expertly he looped the rope round and tied off the end, making the first support secure. As he finished his knot, his hand brushed against Sylvia's again, and they both drew back quickly. He made the mistake of looking up into her brown eyes, and for a moment, he was lost. It was as if time had slowed and everything else but Sylvia faded away.

Her appearance had changed. Her hair was neatly styled now instead of hanging long and loose down her back, and her skin didn't have the deep tan she had developed whilst on the Isla Ana. She was very slightly plumper too, with a healthy layer of fat to cover the bones that had protruded by the end of their stay on the island.

Despite everything, Hugh felt an irresistible attraction to Sylvia. Once they had shared everything, been as intimate as the most devoted of husbands and wives. He knew every inch of her skin, had kissed her all over from her toes to the top of her head. When he had first lost her, it felt like a part of his body had been ripped away and he had been left half-formed, bloodied and incomplete.

It was agony now seeing her again, being so close yet knowing they would never again share what they had on the Isla Ana. Part of him yearned for that physical connection, wanted to sweep her into his arms and forget about all the heartache and anguish, but he knew that could not be, not now. Their history was too complex to even imagine a short but passionate fling, and he had promised himself he would find a resolution to the unwanted engagement to Miss Willis before he even allowed himself to consider what the future held for him and Sylvia.

'Do you think that is tied too tight?' Sylvia asked, looking at the rope that held together the second set of sticks.

He tugged on the sticks, satisfied with his handiwork. 'No.'

'Look, it is affecting the angle the sticks are standing up at, making it lean.'

Hugh took a deep breath. 'You do realise it wouldn't matter if we piled up the sticks, threw a sheet over the top and had done with it. This is a game, a piece of meaningless frivolity, nothing more.'

Sylvia shifted from one foot to the other. 'It is a game,'

she said quietly, 'and I agree the shelter hardly needs to withstand a storm, but I do believe if you are going to do something, you should do it well.' She looked at him, eyes ablaze, but her tone was still measured. 'There was a time when you thought so too.'

'You are mistaken,' he said, hearing the coolness in his voice. 'I believe in spending time and effort on things that matter and eschewing those that do not.'

'You decide what matters, I suppose.'

'Yes.'

Sylvia nodded her head silently, and he could see she was holding back. Restraint was something she had mastered this past year. He'd seen her spitting fire when they were alone, but out here, in the open, she was wary of what other people might see or overhear. He should applaud her for it. Restraint was one of his father's golden rules. A viscount should be poised and in control at all times. He should be in charge of whatever situation he found himself in.

There was something unsettling about the way she swallowed the words that were vying to slip out, though. The Sylvia of old would have told him exactly what she thought, but now she was too aware of someone overhearing.

'Thank you for your help, my lord,' she said after a moment. 'I am sure I can finish things from here. There must be more pressing calls upon your time.'

He ignored her thanks and continued to press the collection of carefully tied sticks into the ground and then loop a rope over the top to string between the two strengthened poles.

'I said you can go,' Sylvia repeated, louder this time, an unmistakable edge to her voice.

'I can, but I will stay until the shelter is finished.'

'I don't need you, Lord Wilder. I can cope on my own.'

'You have made that abundantly clear,' he murmured, keeping his face impassive.

Sylvia blanched, and he saw her slowly start to lose her tight grip on her composure.

'I have had no choice this last year,' she said, her voice quiet but her eyes filled with fire. 'I have had no choice but to cope on my own.'

'It was the life you chose,' he said, knowing the words would hurt her but unable to stop himself from saying them.

'*This* was never the life I chose. I had no options. I got off that ship at the docks in London all alone with no money and no living family in this country to find out my brother was gravely ill and probably wouldn't survive the voyage home. I didn't choose to be alone.'

Hugh was aware of the terrible loss she had suffered, she had told him of the death of her brother so soon after they had returned from the Caribbean. The cruelty of the situation did not escape him. Captain Willis had insisted they return to England rather than making the short journey to Port Royal once he had rescued him, and that action would have meant Sylvia did not see her brother again before his death.

'I do not mean your family,' Hugh said quietly.

She looked at him as if unable to believe he thought this whole mess between them was her fault. He saw a swell of anger and sadness in her eyes.

* * *

Sylvia forced herself to breathe deeply, reminding herself how much damage she would cause if she told Hugh exactly what she thought of him out here in the open.

Looking over her shoulder, she satisfied herself that no one was watching them, and then she took a step closer, raising her hand and poking a finger in his chest.

'You became distant and cool towards me. What was I supposed to think? I was devastated, but you had told me of the expectations everyone held for you in the real world. I could only assume you meant to fulfil those rather than any promises you made to me in the heat of the moment.'

'So this disastrous situation we find ourselves in is anchored on an assumption you made.'

'Do not lay this at my door. If you had spoken to me about any of it then, perhaps things would have been different, but that ship appeared and you changed into someone I didn't know.'

'This is the man I am, Sylvia. The one you thought you knew from the Isla Ana was not real.'

Sylvia wanted to scream and shout, to rail against this statement, but she could see the resignation in his eyes. He did seem like a different man now. Perhaps that realisation was the push she needed to move on. This past year, she hadn't been able to sleep without dreaming of Hugh. She'd imagined him everywhere, willed him to spring to her rescue with a declaration of undying love on countless occasions, but he hadn't. She needed to stop thinking about him, stop ruminating on what they could have had. Their worlds were different, and she would never fit into his.

'At least we agree it was for the best,' Sylvia said, desperately trying to blink away the tears. All her anger had dissipated now, draining away and leaving her feeling empty and sad.

'For the best,' Rosa echoed from her perch on a low branch nearby.

None of it felt for the best. Again Sylvia felt as though her heart had been squeezed until there was nothing left but dust.

Silently Hugh finished building the shelter, his face a blank mask. He had this uncanny ability to hide what he was feeling, to completely shut off his emotions from the outside world. She knew in his childhood his father had expected perfection in all things, but alongside that, she wondered if he had advocated for never letting one's true feelings be known.

'There,' Hugh said once he laid the material over the top. It was a solid shelter for one built so quickly. Although it would never survive the violent storms of the Caribbean, it was sturdy enough for the purposes of this competition. 'Finished. Please excuse me, Miss Thompson. I think it is probably best if I take my leave now.'

Sylvia nodded, knowing she should thank him but her mind still playing over his words again and again.

'Finished so soon, Lord Wilder?' Lady Montague said as she approached. 'Well, that is an impressive structure.'

Hugh gave a little bow and then took another step, but Lady Montague caught him by the arm.

'You must stay and help me judge the other entries. I insist.'

'I am sure you are very capable of doing that yourself, Lady Montague.'

'I am capable, but you add a little something to the proceedings, do you not think?'

Sylvia watched as Hugh smiled briefly at their hostess before removing her hand from his arm.

'I will unfortunately have to decline this morning,' he said, sounding genuinely regretful. 'I think I may have to leave the party early. I have some unmovable commitments, unfortunately.'

Sylvia felt her heart sink a little. As much as it was stressful having Hugh here, she wasn't ready for him to walk out of her life for good. After this weekend, she knew there would be no reason to ever see him again. Their lives barely overlapped. They did not share the same friends or acquaintances, didn't move in the same circles. When she said goodbye to him as they left Lady Montague's country estate, there would be no plans for any future meeting.

Still, her pride stopped her from stepping forwards and asking him to stay.

'Stay, my lord,' Lady Montague said with a winning smile. 'I promised my guests both Miss Thompson *and* you for the weekend. I do not like to disappoint them.'

Sylvia raised her eyebrows. She had explicitly asked their hostess if Hugh was invited to the house party this weekend, and Lady Montague had told her he was not. She wondered if the older lady suspected the animosity between them. That thought sent a shiver down

Sylvia's spine. If Lady Montague did, then others must think the same.

'I am afraid you will have to on this occasion,' Hugh said, his tone curt.

'You are making a mistake. I am a very useful friend to have. It hasn't escaped society's notice that your future wife is from a different social class. Marrying you will only get her so far, but if you ensure she is surrounded by influential friends…'

Sylvia saw Hugh hesitate as he contemplated Lady Montague's proposal and then nod his head sharply. 'Fine. I will stay.'

'Wonderful,' their hostess said, clapping her hands. 'Meet me in front of the house in five minutes. You two can judge the competition.'

They both stood in silence as Lady Montague left, quiet long after she had disappeared from view, checking on some of her other guests.

Chapter Seven

My legs were like those of a newborn calf when I first tried to stand after so long at sea. Dry land was a blessing, and for a long while I sat and sobbed, mourning all those that had been lost. It was only after I had been on the beach for twenty minutes I realised I was not alone. Further along, lying washed up on the sand, was the body of a man.

Hugh stood rigid, not wanting to move unless he lost his carefully curated control.

Somewhere behind him, Sylvia shifted, and after another few seconds, he felt her hand on his arm. Her touch was gentle but not tentative, and slowly she increased the pressure to bring him round to face her.

'Hugh,' she said quietly. He loved it when she used his given name, even though it went against every rule of propriety. It made something inside him swell, and quickly he tamped the sensation down. He needed his wits about him now, not to be overcome by his emotions.

Silently he shook his head, but she had a determined look on her face that made him pause.

'Hugh,' she repeated. 'Look at me.'

His eyes came up to meet hers momentarily, and he felt the old pulse of understanding pass between them. He and Sylvia were from different worlds, raised in different ways, destined for different futures, but there was a connection between them such as he had never had with anyone else. She could tell how he was feeling merely by looking at him, as he could with her.

'I'm sorry,' she said quietly, her eyes brimming with tears.

It could have been an apology for a thousand things, but instinctively he knew she was apologising for putting him in this situation. It didn't mean she would change her mind about pressing ahead with her book, but she did care that he was involuntarily caught up in the fanfare and fuss that surrounded it.

'She shouldn't use Miss Willis like that,' Sylvia said. 'It isn't fair.'

'I find most things these people do are not fair.' Hugh took a deep breath and shook his head. '*This* is not your fault.'

'I know you don't want to be involved in any of this.'

'I do not, but I chose to come here. There are many things I could blame you for, Sylvia, but Lady Montague's holding me hostage is not one of them.'

'Is Miss Willis concerned about taking a step into society?'

Hugh shrugged. He didn't know. He'd hardly spoken to the woman. 'I expect so.'

'Is it something you've discussed?'

'Why this sudden curiosity about Miss Willis?'

'It is not sudden,' Sylvia said, and he could see she was working hard to keep her voice measured and calm. 'I know nearly nothing about the young woman, but she is part of our story whether I like it or not.'

'You don't like it?' he said, the question slipping out before he'd had chance to think.

There was a slight pause, and he saw the colour flood to her cheeks. 'I have nothing against Miss Willis,' Sylvia said eventually. 'But I am struggling to forgive her father for the bargain he pressed you into.'

'The captain never pretended he was anything but a rogue. At least he was honest in that.'

Sylvia snorted and then covered her mouth quickly with her hand. '*Rogue* is too gentle a word for him.'

For a moment Hugh thought back to the moment when Captain Willis had sat him down and poured them both a large tot of rum, before proceeding to blackmail him into proposing to Honoria.

'Perhaps you're right.'

'You don't have to go through with it for me,' Sylvia said, her eyes searching his. She continued quickly. 'Perhaps you have grown to care for Honoria, and if that is the case, then I will keep my words to myself, but I do not want you to marry her solely to protect me.'

'It is not something that can be undone easily.' He was putting it mildly. This past year, after a month or so of inaction caused by the shock of returning to the real world, he had tried multiple approaches to extricate himself from the engagement to Miss Willis. Initially he had tried reasoning with Captain Willis, then offering him obscene sums of money to buy his way out of the engagement. He had phrased it as a contribution to Honoria's dowry, but the captain was rich enough to provide a king's ransom of a dowry for his only daughter all by himself and had laughed Hugh out of his house. Hugh had even tried to find some titled but penniless gentleman who would be all too pleased to be paid to marry Honoria, feeling guilty as he did so at playing with the young woman's future. That had not gone well. The young gentleman in question had spent fifteen minutes with Captain Willis and his daughter before fleeing the house and declaring no amount of money would compensate for having that man as his father-in-law. Hugh was inclined to agree.

Now he was running out of time. Until recently, Honoria had seemed in no rush to hurry their union along, with Captain Willis handling most of the communication between them, but a few weeks earlier, he had received a letter from Honoria asking him to visit her so they could discuss their future and confirm their plans. He had delayed, but the clock was ticking, and soon he would have to decide if he would break his promise and subject himself and Sylvia to the vilest of gossip or marry a woman he barely knew and didn't care for.

'Surely there is a way, if you wanted to get out of it.'

'My word is my bond. I proposed to Honoria. I made the decision, knowing the consequences. I will not go back on my word.' Instead he would continue to try to find another way, but Sylvia did not need to know about the struggles he faced.

He watched as Sylvia bit her lip and knew he shouldn't have given her this burden to carry. If he had kept his counsel, she would never have known the lengths to which he had gone to ensure her reputation was safe. Shaking his head, he knew there was no way back now. He couldn't claw the words from her mind, so she would have to live with it as he did.

'Lady Montague is not wrong,' he said, his eyes flitting over the group of guests beginning to assemble in front of the house. 'Miss Willis will find the ladies unwelcoming, unforgiving even, of her social climbing. They will not be kind. She will need any support she can get.' Whatever he decided, he had no desire to hurt Miss Willis. She was innocent in this, a mere pawn in her father's game. If the worst happened and they were forced to marry, he didn't want her life made any more miserable.

'I suppose two more days of your time is a small price to pay to guarantee Lady Montague will advocate for her once you are married.'

'A small price,' Hugh murmured, wondering if it were true. Two more days in Sylvia's company, two more days of this turmoil. She was still there, the woman that he had loved. Sometimes he found himself looking at her and dreaming as if the past year had not happened, as if they still had the chance to start their lives together. It was a cruel trick of his mind, and if he stayed here much longer, he thought it might drive him mad.

'If you are staying, perhaps I can make things a little easier for you,' Sylvia said, her brow furrowed. 'I propose a truce. I know your feelings on me publishing my book, and you know there is nothing I can do to stop it now it is printed and on its way to the bookshops. I will try to keep out of your way as much as possible, and we put on an amiable front when we are with other people.'

It all sounded very reasonable. Hugh didn't feel reasonable right now. He felt backed into a corner. First Sylvia was pushing him to accept there was no action he could take to stop her from ruining her reputation with this book of hers, and now Lady Montague wanted him to play a role in the story she was trying to present to her guests. He felt pushed and pulled in every direction except the one he wanted to go in.

For a long moment he did not speak, and then finally nodded his head. Later he would work out if there was a way for him to escape the commitment he had made to Lady Montague, and then he planned to get as far away from Somersham Hall as possible, but that would be easier to do if he wasn't bickering with Sylvia the whole time.

'A truce,' he said, turning back to face her and offering her his hand.

Tentatively she took it, her palm warm against his.

'Shall we go and judge the shelters?' Sylvia said quietly.

'I cannot think of anything I want to do much less.' Hugh said.

'There are hundreds of things. I am sure you would rather pass judgement than be bitten by a hungry shark. Or chased by a swarm of angry bees. Or disturb a hibernating bear.'

Hugh smiled grimly. 'All of those sound positively

delightful compared to pretending to care about the frankly terrible shelters the ladies and gentlemen have erected here.'

'Do not let Miss Hague hear you say that. She's looking very proud of the...*structure*...she has built.'

'It is a pile of sticks with a piece of Lady Montague's old sheet thrown over the top.' He groaned, shaking his head. 'What have I done to deserve this?'

'I thought this was what passed for fun in your circle,' Sylvia said as she fell into step beside him.

'I have never understood the need for a hostess to shepherd her guests into ridiculous pastimes.'

'Your family never hosted an event like this?'

'My father enjoyed society,' Hugh said slowly, thinking back to the balls that had been hosted at Elmwood Hall, Hugh as a young boy peering through the banisters as the guests had arrived. 'My mother not so much, but she knew her duty. They were balls though, with dancing and music, nothing as ridiculous as this. I can remember a few garden parties when I was young, but they were hosted for the locals. At most there was pallmall and hoops for the children.'

They reached the main lawn in front of the house, and Hugh was glad Lady Montague waved them over. He wanted this part of the morning to be over so he could retreat to the privacy of his room and not have to put on the polite façade that was expected of him.

'Time is up, everyone,' Lady Montague said, a look of glee on her face. She waited until everyone gathered on the main lawn, their shelters dotted around the edges. 'Lord Wilder and Miss Thompson will now make a round of your shelters and award a prize for the best, but first let us see what the experts have produced.'

Twelve guests had taken part in the challenge, split into six pairs, and it was a comical sight to see the normally pristine gardens littered with makeshift shelters. No doubt a bevy of servants would soon be summoned, ready to restore the garden to its previous glory.

Lady Montague ushered the guests first to Hugh and Sylvia's shelter, leading the way as if she were a general leading her troops into battle.

'What a marvellous shelter, Lord Wilder,' a young woman said as she fell into step beside him. 'So sturdy.'

'Thank you,' he murmured, trying not to engage her in conversation, but she either didn't notice or ignored his mild brusqueness.

'Tell me, did you make separate shelters for you and the ladies whilst you were on the island?'

He thought of the tiny wooden structure they had first erected. It had been barely big enough for one, but they had lain with their bodies pressed together as the storm raged overhead.

'Of course,' he lied. 'One for myself and then a little distance away, one for the ladies.'

'Miss Thompson made no mention of a second shelter in the reading she did this morning,' the young woman said keenly. Hugh flashed Sylvia a look. *This* was exactly what he had been worried about. Some minor detail that a perceptive reader would pick up on and puzzle over. It took nothing for a reputation to be ruined. He knew that first-hand.

Hugh shrugged, trying to look as nonchalant as possible. 'Perhaps she mentions it later in the book. There were two shelters, a small one for myself and a slightly larger one for Miss Thompson and Mrs White.'

Mrs White had been one of the passengers on the *Lady Catherine*, but she had perished with all the others during the storm. She was a widow with no living family, going to take up a position with a family in Port Royal as their governess. Her lack of family had been the reason they had chosen her There was no one to hurt by the false tale they wove, no one to curse that she had survived the storm and the time on the island only to die after being rescued.

'It must have been difficult work building the shelters. It isn't like everything would be laid out for you as it was for us here,' the young woman said.

'It took time to gather the right materials,' Hugh said, trying to keep his answers short and his manner polite but with an edge of curtness. Unlike Sylvia, he did not enjoy talking about his time on the island. He tried not to think of it at all. Every time the memories crept in, he was almost overwhelmed by a sense that he had lost something wonderful that he would never get back. Hugh knew people would view him as mad if he ever expressed such a view—no sane man *wanted* to be marooned on a desert island—but the feeling was there all the same. Whilst on the Isla Ana, he had experienced a freedom like he had never known before. A freedom from his responsibilities, a freedom from the expectations of the world, even a freedom from his own expectations. There had been nothing to think of except how to survive. Of course, at first that had been a concern, but once they had found a natural spring that had provided them with fresh water and worked out how to gather the abundant fruit of the island and even catch a fish or two, it became obvious they *could* survive.

'It was very lucky the ladies had you to provide for them.'

Hugh didn't answer, thankful to be spared any more questions by their arrival at the shelter they had built.

'What an incredible example,' Lady Montague gushed. 'So stable, I feel this could survive anything a tropical storm threw at it.'

Hugh glanced at Sylvia and saw the smile tugging up the corners of her lips. He knew she was remembering the time about halfway through their stay on the island when a storm had ripped their entire shelter and whisked it up into the air. They had been naked at the time, making love whilst the rain pattered overhead, and as they scrabbled apart, trying to keep everything dry, Sylvia had been unable to stop laughing. It was one of his favourite memories, and often in the early hours before dawn when he lay awake in bed, it was that image that came into his mind.

'We did not have rope on the island,' Sylvia said as she stepped forwards, 'but we were able to fashion something much like it from some thick vines that grew around the trees. The sheet here is much like the ripped sails we used that washed up on the beach after the shipwreck.'

'Fascinating,' Lady Montague murmured. 'Now, shall we move on to the next shelter? Mr Priest and Miss Kimble, I think that is yours just over there, is it not?'

The couple in question nodded, leading the way over to a mess of sticks that looked like it would fall over in the slightest breeze.

'Do not crush them,' Sylvia murmured as they paused in front of it.

'A good effort,' Hugh managed to say as he walked around the shelter, inspecting it. 'Although I am a little confused as to how you get into it.'

'Ah, yes, we did forget about a door,' Mr Priest said, his cheeks turning red as he stumbled over the words.

'Shall we move on to the next one?' Lady Montague said.

They continued around the garden, moving in a loop from one patch to the next, each shelter as bad as the last, but Hugh did his best to make a positive comment about each. He felt Lady Montague's eyes on him and knew what was expected of him for his half of their bargain.

'Do you have a winner, Lord Wilder?' Lady Montague enquired at the end.

He cast his eye back over the garden and chose one shelter that had been marginally more stable than the rest.

'Lady French, I think your shelter was my favourite. You clearly thought about the best way to make it sturdy and built from there.'

There was a smattering of applause, and Lady Montague nodded in approval.

'Excellent choice, my lord. Lady French and Mr Willard, you are our winners. Although I am sure everyone would agree that if they were in the wilderness with no shelter, it would be Lord Wilder they hoped would happen by.'

Hugh even managed to summon a smile, thankful this farce was almost over, at least for a while.

'Refreshments will be served on the east lawn in fifteen minutes,' Lady Montague announced as people began drifting away, some back to the house and others to stroll around the gardens in the sunshine.

As Sylvia took a step towards the house, he caught her arm, the touch making her stiffen.

'Walk with me,' he murmured, indicating a path that headed in the opposite direction to the east lawn.

Sylvia frowned but fell into step beside him.

'Did you hear what that young woman said to me?'

'What young woman?'

'I don't know her name. Some young woman, small, blonde, white dress.'

'You could be describing half a dozen guests here.'

'It does not matter who it was. It matters what she said.'

'I thought people of your class prided themselves on knowing everyone. Don't you sit around with miniatures learning who people are and what noble line they have descended from?'

He blinked rapidly a few times.

'Where have you got that idea from?'

'Lady French said something about learning her miniatures when she was a young lady.'

'I have no idea what constitutes an education for a young lady, but it is hardly important right now. Will you focus?'

'Fine. What did this mystery young woman say?'

'She asked if we built one shelter or two on the island.'

Sylvia nodded, waiting for him to say more.

With an exasperated sigh, he continued. '*This* is exactly what I am worried about. Exactly the reason you need to tell your publisher you have changed your mind. In the reading, you mention building a shelter, singular, which is obviously what we did, because it was bloody hard work, and we did not have endless materials available to us. That young lady wanted to know if in fact we shared a shelter or if we built two.'

'What did you say?'

'That we built two, of course.'

Sylvia nodded, and he couldn't understand why she wasn't more disturbed by this. She seemed calm, nonchalant even, whereas he felt a roll of panic inside.

'Good.' She paused, looking at him, and then seeming to realise he needed more of a response than that. 'Now she knows.'

'Do you honestly not see the problem?'

'People are always going to question things, Hugh,' Sylvia said quietly, stopping and turning to face him. 'Half the population has probably already decided we succumbed to our baser instincts whilst trapped together, and the other half think we would never do anything as scandalous. I expect they come to their conclusions based on their own moral sense and an assumption that most people think and act in the same way as they would themselves.'

He was stunned into silence by her words.

'No one can prove anything, just like we can do nothing about any speculation. People will talk, and they will have their own opinions on whether we broke the rules of propriety, but as long as there is no confession that we were intimate, then it is only assumptions and theories.'

'You truly cannot be that naive.'

'I thought we agreed we would stop talking about this.'

'How can we? At the moment, you enjoy a position of privilege, of being feted and celebrated. If there is even a whiff of scandal, a rumour that takes hold, then you will be cast out to live on the edges of society. Believe me, it is not a happy place to be.'

Sylvia scoffed. 'How would you know? You are beloved by the *ton*. I honestly believe that you could confess to multiple murders, and the ladies and gentlemen would pat you on the back and tell each other that boys will be boys.'

'I have seen it,' he said stiffly, not wanting to dredge up old memories. 'I have seen how a scandal can destroy a person.'

This made Sylvia stop, her eyes coming up to meet his. For a long moment, she didn't speak, and then she stepped forward so she was closer to him. He had this urge to wrap his arms around her, to draw her closer and protect her from the world, but he knew that was not his role right now. Perhaps one day he might work a way through this mess, and then his thoughts would be free to turn to Sylvia. Right now, the best way he could protect her was to ensure she didn't irretrievably ruin her reputation. That was why he had to keep pushing even if it made her hate him.

'Who was it?' she asked, her voice quiet and her eyes focussed on his.

'It doesn't matter.'

'Of course it matters.'

'My mother.' He took a step back, knowing if he kept standing so close, he would do something they both would regret. He had this urge for comfort, for a human touch, but Sylvia could not be the one to give it to him now.

'What happened with your mother?'

It wasn't something he liked to talk about. When the scandal had occurred, he had been young, still at school, and his peers had taunted him mercilessly. He had been astute enough even at the age of fourteen to know not to react poorly, taking the teasing and hoping some other matter would soon arise to divert attention away from himself. Then the tragedy had occurred, and after his mother's death, there had been no more outright cruelty, just whispers that followed him round corners and haunted his every step.

'She did something foolish, and the gossip and scandal that followed destroyed her,' he said shortly, looking off over Sylvia's shoulder, not able to meet her eye.

'You never told me about this, about your mother.'

'You didn't need to know.'

She took a step back as if he had slapped her and gave a short nod, but there was a wounded look in her eyes that he couldn't ignore.

'It was a different world. On the island, for once my mother's scandal and the tragedy of her death did not follow me. I could live free of that burden and just remember her how I wished to, the kind, affectionate woman who was determined to stand up to my father so I would have at least a little normal childhood in between his lessons and rules.'

'You cannot do that here?'

'No. I cannot mention her name without people's faces clouding over. They do not remember the charities she supported or the way she advocated for the poor and needy. They don't even remember how her face lit up with laughter or how she could always find the positives in everything. *All* they remember is she dared to have an affair and was stupid enough to be found out.' He took a deep, shuddering breath. 'I do not want that for you, Sylvia.'

Her eyes were locked on his as if searching for something deep inside.

'I understand,' she said so quietly he wondered if he had imagined it.

Reaching out, she placed a hand on his arm and squeezed. It was a gesture of affection, one that seemed to convey a thousand words, and for a long moment, Hugh couldn't move.

'I'm sorry about your mother,' Sylvia said eventually. 'She sounds like she was a wonderful woman.'

'She was.'

He felt the familiar lump in his throat that appeared whenever he thought of his mother and suddenly had the urge to get far away. He wanted to be on horseback, charging through the countryside, but it would take too long to saddle Caesar. Instead he bade Sylvia a quick goodbye and strode off through the gardens, searching for some solitude.

Chapter Eight

*At first we dared not leave the beach lest a rescue
boat come searching for us and we missed it, but
as the day wore on, our thirst got the better of us,
and we decided we had to stave off dehydration as
a main priority. Our first steps into the interior of
the island were daunting. A thick forest came down
to the edge of the beach, and under the canopy,
you could imagine all sorts of exotic and dangerous creatures living.*

'I thought I might find you in here,' an unfamiliar voice
said as the door to the library opened and shut again.

Sylvia lowered her book to see a beautiful young
woman beaming at her.

'Lady Turner, but you must call me Mary. I know we
are going to be great friends, you and I.'

Sylvia felt her mouth open in astonishment at the
whirlwind that had entered the room. Normally the ladies and gentlemen of society were fastidious about
their etiquette, and in the early days, she had struggled

with how to address people so as not to cause offence. Once she had called the Duke of Hampshire *my lord* instead of *your grace*, and there had been a titter amongst the assembled group. Never had any of the people she had met during her brief foray into society invited her to call them by their given name.

'Have we met?' Sylvia said, rising from her perch on the window seat.

'No. Although I feel like we have. I am Sir Percy's wife, although I hate to be defined that way. It is always how I am introduced, Lady Turner, wife of Sir Percy, as if my greatest achievement was to marry.' She shrugged, her head tilted to one side as if she considered what she said. 'Perhaps it was. I'm hardly going to discover a new continent or put my name to the next innovation of industry.' She beamed at Sylvia. 'Sit down Miss Thompson, do make yourself comfortable. Lady Montague has arranged a game of pall-mall on the lawn, so most of the guests are out there flirting with one another. I doubt we will be disturbed.'

Sylvia nodded, not knowing what else to do, wondering what this effusive woman wanted with her.

'How are you coping with all this dreadful attention?'

'Lady Montague has been very kind,' Sylvia said carefully.

Lady Turner snorted. 'All that woman thinks about is social advancement. She wants to hold the grandest balls, be the first to take an interest in the latest trend. It must be exhausting.' She looked carefully at Sylvia, taking a seat opposite her. 'Doesn't do to speak badly of your hostess, though, does it? He said you were intelligent.'

'Who said?'

'Ah, yes, you don't know who I am. Past my name and that of my husband, my finest achievement.' Her eyes sparkled, and Sylvia felt herself warm to the young woman. You had to have your wits about you to keep up with her, but she seemed genuine and kind. 'Sir Percy is good friends with Lord Wilder, the best of friends. They have known one another since Harrow, and you understand what sort of bonds are forged at school. I think Lord Wilder helped my dear Percy survive, and Percy showed Lord Wilder not everything is bleak in the world.'

'Lord Wilder told me about Sir Percy,' Sylvia said, remembering how he always spoke of his friend with a smile.

'I have been begging Lord Wilder to introduce us to you this past year, but you know how stubborn he is. He refused. So I thought I would come and introduce myself. I do hope you don't mind.'

'It is a pleasure, Lady Turner.'

The young woman turned and checked the door to the library was closed, then focussed again on Sylvia.

'My husband sometimes tells me I am too forward, but I think if something is worth saying then you should not waste time on subtlety, so I do hope you will forgive me for being blunt. Lord Wilder is a mess, and that man hates anything that isn't properly ordered. At first we thought it was the stress of the shipwreck and being marooned for so long, but slowly he has recovered physically and I think emotionally from those, yet still he is far from the man who left England a year and a half ago.'

'I am sorry to hear that,' Sylvia murmured.

'Yes, I expect you are,' Lady Turner said. 'Now, Lord Wilder is a very discreet man, and he can handle his drink very well, but when he does allow himself to become inebriated, that stony exterior cracks and all these secrets just spill out.'

Sylvia shifted in her seat, trying to keep her composure. There was a chance Lady Turner was testing her, trying to trick her into revealing more than she meant to. The young woman seemed genial, but Sylvia did not know her or her motivations.

'You do not need to worry, Miss Thompson. Neither I nor my husband would do or say anything to harm Lord Wilder, but we are concerned about his happiness.'

'His happiness?' Sylvia echoed.

'Yes, as I am sure you are aware, having been so close to Lord Wilder, currently he is *not* happy.'

'No,' she murmured. 'He isn't happy.'

'And—if I may be blunt—the reason he isn't happy is you.'

Sylvia blanched, desperately trying to stop herself from reacting too violently. She held in a gasp and instead managed a noncommittal *mmm* sound.

'But he hasn't seen me for a year.'

'Therein lies the problem, or so I assume. He has missed you terribly.'

At this Sylvia had to stifle a surprised laugh.

'I hardly think so.'

'I would wager he has thought of little else but you this last year,' Lady Turner said quietly.

'He is engaged.'

'Yes, but I am sure you know the truth of the matter.'

Sylvia nodded. 'I do now. I understand he proposed to Miss Willis as part of a bargain with her father to preserve my reputation. I have told him I do not want him to sacrifice himself like that.'

'Good, although I am sure it did little to change his course. *Stubborn*, as I said. He has a misguided belief that duty and honour should come above all else, and now he has proposed to the Willis girl, he will not be able to back out.'

'I never asked him to do that for me,' she said quietly, 'but I know that is the kind of man Lord Wilder is.'

'You know about his mother?'

Sylvia looked up at her companion, studying her. 'A little. He told me this morning his mother was affected by a scandal, an affair. Past that I do not know the details.'

'It was an affair with a family friend. Lord Wilder's father was a beast by all accounts. Charming in society but a brute a home, you know the type. He believed that his wife was his property rather than his partner, and she had to obey all his rules. The old Lord Wilder had numerous affairs, and not discreetly. For years Hugh's mother did what she was told, but then one day, she fell in love. She succumbed briefly, then broke it off, but already news of the scandal had got out, and there was so much gossip and cruelty.' Lady Turner shook her head in disgust. 'It drove the poor woman to suicide.'

Sylvia covered her mouth with her hand, the thoughts whirring in her head.

'This is why Lord Wilder is so intent on protecting everyone from scandal.'

Lady Turner nodded grimly. 'He has seen first-hand the devastation gossip can cause. I expect the idea of losing someone else he loves to scandal is more than he can bear.'

'He doesn't love me.'

'Let us agree to disagree for now. Whatever he feels for you, he puts protecting your reputation above anything else.'

'That is why he has been so against my book being published.'

'I do not wish to gossip about Lord Wilder's past, but I thought it important you know.'

Sylvia played the dozens of conversations they'd had about inviting scandal and protecting herself from gossip these last couple of days over in her mind. It made sense now, his desperate need to try to protect her against a hazy, unsubstantiated threat. It also explained a little why he was so quick to agree to marry Miss Willis.

'I have misjudged him,' Sylvia said quietly. 'And perhaps been a little harsh in my words.'

'There is still time to right things.'

Silently Sylvia nodded. Her heart burned for Hugh and for all he had suffered. She herself had lost her mother when she was young. In itself it was a tragedy that changed a child's life, but that had been unavoidable. Hugh's loss was even more tragic because if people had been less judgemental, more understanding, his mother might still be here today.

'Do you love him?' Lady Turner said, her eyes shining brightly.

Sylvia opened her mouth to answer and realised she didn't know. She had loved him, throughout their time on the island. She'd loved him then with a great intensity like she had never known before or since. Perhaps too much had passed between them now for that same love to thrive. She knew she wasn't part of his world, part of the future that had been planned out for him for years. Neither was Miss Willis, but now she understood his motivations for pushing on with that engagement, it hurt a little less.

When they had sighted the ship off the east coast of the Isla Ana, Sylvia had not felt the happiness and relief she had expected. They had overcome many of the initial hardships of life on the island and enjoyed a peaceful harmony. She had been right to worry. As soon as it was clear they were going to be rescued, Hugh retreated into himself. It was as though something had flipped inside him, and gone was the carefree man she knew and loved, replaced with the serious Viscount whose first and only thought was for his duty. *That* was the man who had returned on the *Chameleon*. And that was the man who was here now.

She didn't know if she could love that man.

'I did love him,' she murmured, and then shook her head. 'It doesn't matter. It is too late. His life is on a different path, and so is mine.'

'It doesn't have to be,' Lady Turner said.

'It does. What you are hinting at is impossible, but I can offer him my friendship. I think I have been too defensive and not understanding enough of what he has suffered.'

'I suppose it is a start,' Lady Turner said, slumping back in her chair. 'If only the fool could see what would be good for him.'

The door to the library opened, and a short and un-kempt man with an amiable face came into the room. Lady Turner stood up and held out her hand.

'Percy darling, meet the lovely Miss Thompson. Miss Thompson, this is my husband, Sir Percy.'

'Delighted to meet you, Miss Thompson,' Sir Percy said, beaming at her. 'Can I assume my wife has already shared her views on our mutual friend?'

Sylvia inclined her head, and Sir Percy chortled and looked lovingly at his wife.

'You cannot change fate, my dear. If they are meant to be, they are meant to be.'

'Nonsense,' Lady Turner said, straightening up as if preparing for battle. 'I do not believe that for one second.'

'My wife, the challenger of destiny.'

'I have imposed myself on Miss Thompson long enough, Percy. Will you accompany me on a stroll through the gardens?'

Sylvia watched as the couple bade her goodbye and left the room arm-in-arm. Slowly she sank back down into her chair. She felt as though the whole world had shifted under her feet. So much more made sense now. Closing her eyes, she knew she had to talk to Hugh, to show him she appreciated what he had done for her and understood why he became so concerned about scandal, but she didn't know how to broach the subject.

With a sigh, she stood, knowing she would only ruminate on the matter if she didn't go and do something about it straightaway. With butterflies in her belly, she set off to find Hugh.

Chapter Nine

Nothing in the world tastes as good as fresh, pure water when you are dehydrated. I wanted to dive into the bubbling little pool, but ever the protector, Lord Wilder warned me to slow down. For the first time since the storm, I felt a glimmer of hope. With fresh water on the island, perhaps we might just survive.

Sylvia paused for a moment, wishing she had brought her shawl out with her. There was the first chill of the evening in the air, and the sun was beginning to drop lower in the sky. She had been searching for Hugh for an hour and as yet hadn't found any trace of him. Soon she would have to admit defeat and return to Somersham Hall to ready herself for dinner. There was a musical recital afterward this evening, with a talented violinist coming to entertain the guests before Lady Montague invited the ladies and gentlemen to step up to the piano. Sylvia would content herself with listening. When she

was growing up, funds hadn't stretched to music lessons, and although she had learned a little from her
mother, she was not ready to play in public.

She had hoped to find Hugh out here in the wider
estate. One of the grooms had informed her he had sad-
dled his horse and ridden out in a hurry earlier this afternoon. There was the possibility he had left the estate,
but Sylvia had assumed not. He would want to make
an appearance at dinner later given his assurances to
Lady Montague.

Overhead the clouds had drawn in, the sky heavy
and threatening rain. The air had a heavy, oppressive
feel, and Sylvia wondered if there might be a storm to
break the string of hot sunny days there had been over
the last week. She glanced back over her shoulder at the
house, now only a small speck in the distance. It would
take at least fifteen minutes of hard riding to get back.

Debating for a moment, Sylvia turned away from the
house and looked at the hill in front of her. At the top
was a grand folly, a ruined castle that looked at least five
hundred years old but that had been built half tumbled
down only a few years earlier. Lady Montague liked to
talk of the beauty it brought to the estate.

There was a tower and wall, crumbled at one end.
Sylvia felt as though she had covered much of the rest
of the estate, or at least cast her eye over it from the
various hills and vantage points. If Hugh was still on
Montague land, then perhaps she would be able to see
him from the top of the tower.

'Five more minutes,' she murmured to herself, picking up her skirts and hurrying to the base of the hill.

Five more minutes then she would have to admit defeat, something she did not like to do.

The first drop of rain hit her face as she was halfway up the hill, and Sylvia cursed under her breath, knowing she had made the wrong choice. Unlike many of the ladies here at Lady Montague's gathering, she had a finite number of dresses. There was the beautiful blue silk one she had bought with the last of her money to make an impression, a practical brown dress she used for everyday wear, a pink dress lined with lace she wore to the evening gatherings, and this flimsy white cotton garment the modiste had assured her all the young ladies wore to garden parties.

The modiste hadn't been wrong. The young unmarried ladies were all dressed in similar white cotton gowns with tiny flowers embroidered on them or with a ribbon sash to bring some colour. They might be popular, but the dresses were highly impractical. Any activity more vigorous than sitting quietly and reading put you in danger of staining the pure white material, and the thin cotton was liable to tear. Right now her hem was dusty, but if the rain started in earnest, no doubt the whole skirt would be splattered with mud.

Sylvia shivered as she neared the top of the hill, glancing up at the sky and knowing there was going to be a downpour. By the time she made it back to the house, she would be soaked to the skin. Her hair would be a mess and her skin blotchy. She was hardly going to be the ideal dinner guest.

'What are you doing here?'

Sylvia was so caught up in her thoughts that she hadn't

noticed the reins to Hugh's fine horse looped over the low stone wall.

She picked her way over the rough ground, searching the wall to see where the voice had come from.

'Up here.'

Directing her gaze up, she finally saw him sitting halfway up the wall in a crumbled section that had left a little alcove. It was the perfect spot to shelter from the rain, if you could manage the climb.

'I was looking for you,' she said.

He raised an eyebrow. 'You found me.'

Sylvia hesitated, wondering if she should ask him to come down. It was raining in earnest now, and she could feel her hair flattening against her head.

'I needed to talk to you.'

He spread his arms, as if inviting her to speak.

For a moment, she eyed the wall and considered the climb.

'Don't think about it,' he said, a note of warning in his voice.

The command was enough to spur her on, and quickly Sylvia gathered her skirts in one hand and reached up for a handhold. The stones were slippery in the rain, and immediately she regretted her rash action, but now she had started, there was no way she could admit defeat.

Slowly, testing out each foothold, she climbed, ignoring Hugh's protests above her, until she pulled herself onto the ledge, spinning round to sit down before finally letting out the breath she had been holding. It reminded her of one of their pivotal moments on the Isla

Ana. About two weeks after the *Lady Catherine* had
sunk and they had washed up on the beach, Hugh had
still been dreadfully formal in how he addressed her
and interacted with her. They spoke to discuss how they
would split the tasks for the day, what he would take
care of and what he would entrust to her, but little more
than that. Frustrated that once again her companion
would not trust her with anything more complex than
collecting water from the spring, Sylvia had resolved to
show him exactly what she was capable of. There were
some banana trees close to the beach, with the fruit far
too high up for them to reach from the ground. Up until
now, they had eschewed the fruit in favour of food that
was easier to gather, but Sylvia wanted to try the mysterious yellow fruit and had resolved to climb a tree to
gather some. Hugh had returned from his mission to
collect wood for his fiftieth attempt to start a fire to find
her halfway up a banana tree. He had been furious, yet
helpless to do anything but watch as she gathered some
of the fruit and carefully wriggled her way back to the
ground. Quietly he had accepted a proffered banana,
and the next day her share of the jobs had been a little
more interesting than merely collecting water.

'That was foolish,' he said now. 'You're filthy.'

Sylvia looked down at her dress and had to suppress
a groan. The once pristine white cotton was streaked
with sandy-coloured dirt, and it was beginning to crease
from the rain.

'You could have come down.'

'I could.'

They sat there in silence for a minute. Now Sylvia was here, she didn't know what to say.

'I came looking for you,' she said eventually. 'I wanted to talk to you, to apologise.'

Hugh remained quiet, and Sylvia turned to level him with an assessing look.

'I am sorry for what happened in the garden. I know this is a less than ideal situation for you, and you are here primarily because of me.' She turned to look at him. 'Lady Turner told me about your mother. I am sorry, Hugh. Losing her that way must have been terrible.'

'She shouldn't have spoken about it. You didn't need to know.'

Sylvia was quiet for a while, fishing around for the right words so her next statement sounded as sincere as she wanted it to.

'I understand now so much more why you acted as you did, why you are so concerned about protecting me from a scandal.'

'It has nothing to do with my mother,' Hugh said, shifting his body slightly so he was angled away from her.

'I didn't come here to start a fight,' Sylvia said softly. His hand was lying in between them. She reached out and placed hers next to it so their little fingers were just touching. Quickly he glanced up at her before looking away again. 'I wanted to tell you I understood and that I appreciate everything you have done for me. I am sorry it has changed the course of your life so much.' She took a deep, juddering breath, realising this next part was important to her, more important than she had realised before today. 'I miss you, Hugh. I miss you terribly. I know nothing can ever be the same—everything has moved on, and we are different people—but perhaps we can move on as friends.'

He wasn't moving, his face impassive and his body slightly hunched in on itself.

Sylvia drew her knees up to her body, partly to shelter better from the now heavy rain outside and partly to hug her herself as a way of reassurance.

'You think we can be friends?' he asked eventually. 'After everything that has passed between us?'

'I think I would like to try. What is the alternative? Never seeing one another again? Crossing the street when we spot one another in London or making excuses to not attend an event because we live in fear of the other person being there?'

'Perhaps it would be easier that way,' he murmured.

For a long while, neither of them spoke, and Sylvia considered whether she really did want them to be friends. Of course it would be painful, seeing him move on with his life whilst she was left behind, but she *had* missed him these last twelve months. Everyone told her time was a great healer. Perhaps one day in ten years' time, they would be sitting together, surrounded by their families, able to view their time on the island with nostalgia without any regret left.

Hugh turned to her, and Sylvia saw some of the familiar fire in his eyes, fire she hadn't seen during this trip. It sent a shiver down her spine, and she knew it would threaten everything she had just proposed.

'You wish to share a friendly stroll? Sit and take tea

with one another? Perhaps even go to the theatre together?'

Sylvia swallowed. As he said the words, she could see it would be a bad idea.

'All the time knowing there was this unspoken feeling between us.' His voice was low and intense.

'What is the alternative?'

Slowly Hugh leaned forwards, twisting his body so he was facing her straight-on. She let out a little exhalation as he caught her by the waist, holding her firmly. She could have wriggled free if she had wanted, but right now, Sylvia could think of nothing but his hand separated from her skin by a few thin layers of cotton.

Her eyes flicked to his lips, and her mind was flooded with memories of how he had kissed her. He was a devil with his lips, trailing them over her skin, building up the pleasure until she shouted out, unable to bear the anticipation. Despite everything that had passed, Sylvia knew she would give anything for one more consequence-free kiss.

He was only inches from her now, his eyes locked on hers.

'You think no one would notice this heat between us?' he murmured.

Sylvia knew he wouldn't kiss her. Somewhere inside, his honour and sense of responsibility would hold him back, but it would take very little for her to move forwards and brush his lips with her own. She didn't have a fiancé waiting for her, but she couldn't pretend that would be the only consequence of a kiss.

Still she didn't move away. It was as though she were

hypnotised, bewitched by his eyes and the hint of a promise within them.

He raised a hand and ever so lightly trailed his fingers over her cheek. It was the gentlest of movements, but Sylvia felt a sob of sadness rise up inside her. The thought that she could have had this, she could have had him, if only she had been a little bolder, sprang to her mind. He had become distant when they were rescued, but she knew now he would have married her. It might have been out of duty at first, and she had told herself that she hadn't wanted to be that burden to him, but maybe that would have been better than this.

Rallying, she caught hold of the thought. She couldn't believe that. She would not be a burden, and she refused to settle for a marriage where she wasn't completely and utterly loved. Hugh would have done the right thing, but deep down, she thought he would have resented being pushed into taking the honourable path rather than fulfilling the duty that was expected of him.

Even with all of this raging in her mind, Sylvia couldn't bring herself to turn away. There was a desperation in Hugh's eyes now along with the desire, and she felt as though she were looking at a man drowning.

'Enough,' he murmured, holding her gaze for one more second and then slowly pulling away. She could see the tension in his body, the self-control, and although she knew it was necessary, she felt the gulf between them acutely.

Without another word, he stood on the ledge, having to bow his head a little so as not to scrape it on the stones above.

'The rain is easing,' he said as he offered her his hand.

Sylvia sat unmoving, trying desperately to work through what had just happened.

'Hugh…' she began but was cut off by a shake of his head.

'We can't do this, Sylvia. *I* can't do this.'

'All I suggested was friendship.'

'What you are suggesting is a lifetime of purgatory.'

'Being my friend would be purgatory?'

'I think you know exactly what I mean.'

She studied him for a long moment, and finally she nodded, realising she did know. Having him near would be a constant reminder of what had almost been, the lives that they could have led. Perhaps he was right. Perhaps it would be easier to keep their distance and pretend they were nothing more than two people who had once shared some time on an island together.

Slowly she reached up and placed her hand in his. As he pulled her up, her body brushed against his. It was the lightest of touches, but Sylvia felt as though a great pulse of energy sped through her, making every inch of her skin tingle.

Chapter Ten

As the sun dropped lower in the sky, we had to face a terrifying prospect, spending the first night in an unknown place with no light and no way of knowing what might be creeping up from the forest behind us. Even the crippling exhaustion I felt wasn't enough to allow me to close my eyes, until Lord Wilder came to my aid, promising to sit close by and stay awake whilst I rested.

Caesar was sheltering where he had been left, under an overhanging part of the wall, and so he was relatively dry as Hugh led him out into the open. The rain was still coming down, although not as heavy as a few minutes earlier, and they really could have done with sheltering for longer, but he couldn't risk being cooped up with Sylvia for another moment.

She stood, looking pensive pressed up against the stone wall, her dress dusty and streaked with dirt. Wisps of her brown hair were falling loose, and she looked dishevelled but beautiful.

Hugh had to turn away. What she was offering was far too dangerous to contemplate. Of course he dreamed of kissing Sylvia, of a life where they did everything side by side. The thoughts crept in whenever he lowered his guard, whenever he allowed himself to be distracted. Right now, though, he had to focus on persuading Miss Willis and her troublesome father to take something else he was offering instead of his freedom, and until that was accomplished, he shouldn't even be thinking about Sylvia other than how best to protect her.

Time spent with Sylvia could only be a distraction from that. Friendship was impossible. Every time he laid eyes on her, he was almost overcome by a roiling mass of emotions, positive as well as negative. He acknowledged he still felt resentment for her and irritation at her insistence she knew best, but he could not deny there was more there too. Attraction, affection, a desire to protect, all competing for dominance.

If he let her too close, if he conceded to this idea that they could be friends, he knew he would struggle with controlling the desire, just like he had a few minutes earlier.

'Come here,' he said, his voice gruff.

Sylvia walked over, slipping a little on the wet grass. He held his hands out to boost her up onto Caesar's back, and she stepped forwards with her eyes downcast. Only as she gathered up her skirts and put her foot in his hand did she look at him, and he saw the same turmoil he felt reflected in her eyes.

The words he wanted to utter stuck in his throat, so

instead he lifted her up, acutely aware of her body as it brushed past his.

'Sit forwards,' he instructed, and then he pulled himself up behind her, reaching for the reins around her waist.

Caesar was a big horse, tall and powerful and fast. He liked nothing more than for Hugh to lean low across his back, loosen the reins, and let him run free. He could easily carry two of them for a short distance, but it was not roomy up on the horse's back, and Sylvia's body was pressed against Hugh's. As the horse began to walk forwards, Sylvia adjusted her position a little, wriggling her bottom in a way that made Hugh suppress a low groan of pent-up desire.

'Hold on,' he said, nudging Caesar with his heels. The sooner they were back at Somersham Hall, the sooner he could get away from the woman inadvertently taunting him with her presence.

Caesar broke into a gentle trot, not bothered by the rain and not needing to be guided on direction, seeming to know they were heading back to the warmth of the stable.

Sylvia said something, her voice whipped away on the air, and Hugh had to lean forwards to try to hear her.

'What did you say?'

She turned, the movement making her body tilt into his. He cursed that she didn't seem to be aware of every movement, every time their bodies touched. It was unfair that he was the only one tormented by her presence.

'Do you think there will be a storm?' There was a hint of panic in her voice, and he was momentarily taken back to the first storm they had experienced together. Sylvia had shaken in terror as the thunder and lightning had raged overhead, and she had looked at him imploringly. It was the first time he had taken her in his arms, and from the moment her warm body sank into his, he knew he was lost.

'Not yet,' he said, eyeing the clouds. There was a bank of dark grey cloud rolling in from the east, still a fair distance away. The rain was even lighter now, and he thought there might be a respite before the main storm reached them. 'We will be back at the house long before any storm reaches us,' he said, trying to soften his voice. 'And there may not be one at all.'

The estate was not vast, and within a few minutes, the house was in sight. Hugh headed for the stables, thinking it best if he and Sylvia entered the house separately. She could claim to have got caught out in the rain, and he could take his time brushing down Caesar and ensuring he was comfortable for the night.

As they entered the stable-yard, the sound of Caesar's hooves on the cobbles must have alerted the grooms, for a young stable-boy rushed out to assist them. Hugh handed the boy the reins so he could hold Caesar steady whilst Hugh dismounted. Then he reached up to help Sylvia down.

She was shivering a little, her skin cold to the touch despite the mild temperatures. Her dress was plastered to her body in places and no doubt uncomfortable.

'Get inside, go to your room and dry off,' he instructed. 'Ring for a maid.'

Sylvia nodded and turned away almost immediately.

She took a few steps before turning back, her eyes coming up to meet his and hold his gaze.

'Thank you for the ride, Hugh.' Her voice was a little flat, emotionless, and he had the urge to go to her and gather her in his arms, but it was not what either of them needed.

She walked off, posture stiff, her head held high, looking as regal as someone could with a filthy dress and bedraggled hair.

When she had disappeared, Hugh slumped. Coming here had been a terrible idea, and the whole weekend so far had been nothing but a disaster. If he had any sense, he would take the reins from the stable-boy, vault onto Caesar's back again, and ride off before he could get himself into any more trouble. It was only Lady Montague's offer of support to Miss Willis that made him stay. He might not want to marry the girl, but there was no sense in making an enemy of Lady Montague if by cruel fate he and Miss Willis did end up as husband and wife.

With a curse, he motioned for the stable-boy to lead Caesar away, following behind to see to the horse once the stable-boy had removed the saddle.

Sylvia felt damp and uncomfortable as she crept through the open front door into the house. She was hoping she might be able to make it to her room without anyone seeing her, for she knew she looked a mess. Lifting her dress so it didn't leave a muddy trail on the marble floors, she was nearly at the staircase when Lady Montague stepped out into the hall.

'Miss Thompson…oh, dear, what on earth happened?'

Sylvia grimaced, taking a second to try to compose herself before she turned to face her hostess.

'I went for a walk about the estate, but alas, I got caught in the rain.'

'How unfortunate. Ring for a maid, and someone will bring you some hot water and take that dress away to see what can be done.'

'Thank you, Lady Montague.'

Sylvia was about to turn and continue upstairs, her cheeks flushed with embarrassment at having been caught in such a state, when she noticed a young woman with raven-black hair loitering in the doorway behind Lady Montague.

'You know Miss Willis, I think?'

Sylvia felt as though time stopped as the pretty young woman stepped forwards, flashing Sylvia a cautious smile. She was immaculately presented and wearing a fine dress, with not a single hair out of place.

'Miss Willis, yes, of course, I trust you are well?'

The young woman smiled beatifically as if she were a saint giving out alms to the poor, bestowing them the pleasure of her beauty as well as her charity.

'Very well, thank you, Miss Thompson. It is wonderful to see you again.'

'Is something amiss?' Sylvia asked, not knowing how to make the question seem less blunt.

'Amiss?' Miss Willis echoed.

'Lord Wilder did not mention you were coming.'

Sylvia wasn't sure if she imagined the young woman's

eyes narrowing ever so slightly. By the time she spoke again, her expression was neutral and unreadable.

'It would seem my message didn't arrive,' Miss Willis said, turning to their hostess. 'I do not wish to be an inconvenience, Lady Montague. Once my horses have rested, I can return home. My groom is seeing to the carriage.'

'Nonsense,' Lady Montague said, looking very pleased with the situation. 'I invited Miss Willis to the party a few weeks ago, but unfortunately she wrote saying she was unable to attend. When her circumstances changed, she sent me a note, but it never arrived.'

Sylvia looked at the two women in front of her, trying to work out where the conspiracy originated. Miss Willis looked the picture of innocence, smiling demurely. She may have been born to a man who was more at home amongst the sailors in the dockside taverns, but she had received an impeccable education, and on the surface she looked as though she belonged here. The young woman must have a reason for wanting to be here, and at the moment, Sylvia couldn't decide if Lady Montague was in on the secret or if she was just drawn by the potential drama of the situation.

'Now, with all my guests here, unfortunately all the bedrooms are occupied, but seeing as you and Miss Willis know one another well, I thought you would not mind sharing a room for a few days.'

It took some effort to force a smile onto her lips, and Sylvia opted to merely nod rather than try to force anything through her clenched teeth. She couldn't think of much worse than having to share a room with this young woman. Miss Willis had always seemed perfectly pleasant, but she was engaged to marry Hugh. It made everything far too complicated for a friendship between them, but she supposed she could be civil for a few days.

Sylvia didn't like sharing her space, not after a year of fiercely guarded independence. She lived modestly, aware of her rapidly dwindling funds, but however small her rooms, she always chose privacy over everything else.

'How wonderful, Miss Thompson,' Miss Willis said. 'We have so much to catch up on.'

'I will let Miss Thompson show you to the bedroom, and I will see you both for dinner at seven.'

Lady Montague left them, and for a long moment, Sylvia and Miss Willis stood without moving. Eventually Sylvia turned, aware of the little pool of water that had gathered near her feet as she had lingered in the hall, and started upstairs.

'It *is* lovely to see you again Miss Thompson,' Miss Willis said as she hurried to keep up.

'Have you been keeping well?' Sylvia was practiced at the art of making small talk. This past year she had managed to hold most people at arm's length by asking the mundane and being content with superficial platitudes for her answers.

'Quite well, thank you,' Miss Willis said, and then let out a little sigh. 'I lie. In truth, I am in turmoil, Miss Thompson. A turmoil I think only you can help me with.'

They were outside the bedroom door now, and Sylvia paused with her hand on the door handle. After a moment, she opened the door, knowing this would be better addressed in the privacy of the room.

Inside the room was warm and stuffy despite the air coming through the open window. Still Sylvia shivered, telling herself it was the damp dress and nothing more.

Miss Willis closed the door behind her and moved quietly over to the bed, perching on the edge. She made no move to avert her eyes whilst Sylvia got undressed, instead watching her every move.

Self-consciously, Sylvia wriggled from the wet fabric and draped the dress over the back of the upright chair. She was aware the rainwater had soaked through to her chemise and petticoat, rendering them almost transparent.

Miss Willis hopped up and crossed the room, coming up behind Sylvia and unlacing the ties of her stays as if they weren't about to have a very serious conversation. Sylvia remembered the young woman had gone to boarding school from the age of twelve. No doubt she was used to being surrounded by other girls, and privacy was a foreign concept.

As she turned to walk back to the bed, Rosa fluttered from her perch on top of the curtain pole, making Miss Willis let out a yelp of surprise.

'You still have that bird?'

'Rosa, yes.'

'She's beautiful,' Miss Willis said as she watched the parrot carefully. 'I remember how devoted she was to you in the ship. Everyone kept saying she would fly home, but she stayed with you, even as the winds grew colder and the sea rougher.'

'She's stayed with me ever since.'

'You let her have her freedom?'

'Completely. Sometimes she disappears for a day or two, but she always comes back to me.'

'That is devotion,' Miss Willis murmured. Then her sharp eyes came up to meet Sylvia's. 'Speaking of devotion, or more precisely a lack of it, I expect you know why I am here, Miss Thompson.'

Sylvia was saved from answering by a knock at the door followed by a maid slipping into the room carrying in basin of steaming water. It looked heavy, and the maid moved slowly as she carried it across the room and set it on the little table.

'Shall I take your dress, miss?'

'Yes, please, Agnes.'

'Is there anything else I can do for you, miss? I can come back and do your hair for dinner if you wish?'

'There is no need,' Miss Willis said with a smile at the maid. 'I will do Miss Thompson's hair.'

Agnes curtsied and hurried from the room, closing the door behind her with a soft click.

The warm water was glorious against her skin and Sylvia took her time dabbing away the dirt. It gave her something to occupy her hands whilst she tried not to look at Miss Willis. It was ridiculous, really. She had nothing to be ashamed of. Since Hugh and Miss Willis had become engaged, Sylvia had not done a single thing to jeopardise their engagement. She might have thought some distinctly scandalous thoughts, but thinking something was not the same as acting on it.

'I believe Lord Wilder is here,' Miss Willis said eventually.

'Yes, he is.'

'Good. Do you know the last time I saw him was three months ago?'

'That is some time.'

'It is, isn't it, Miss Thompson? This past year I have seen him a total of five times.'

It wasn't much, not when they were supposed to be planning their nuptials and their life together.

'My father is incandescent with rage. He thinks it a slight on our reputation.'

'Is your father well, Miss Willis?' Sylvia said, desperately reaching for a subject to distract her companion, but the young woman wasn't going to be led that easily.

'He is the picture of health, thank you. He drinks far too much, of course, and I do not think that will change, no matter what I say. He has been making threats.'

'Threats?'

'Against Lord Wilder. And you.'

Sylvia felt all the blood drain from her head, and she had to clutch the sides of the heavy bowl to steady herself.

Slowly she turned to face Miss Willis, finally admitting to herself that there was no way out of this conversation.

'He tells me nothing, of course, but when he has been drinking, he flies into these terrible rages, storming about and saying Lord Wilder needs to be careful or he will expose everything.' Miss Willis regarded her in silence for a few seconds before pushing on. 'It is interminable, this waiting, but I think I could bear it if I knew what was to come at the end.'

'Surely you will marry Lord Wilder?'

Miss Willis shrugged, looking down at the hand that was tracing patterns on the bedsheets.

'It has been a year, Miss Thompson. I begin to doubt the devotion of my fiancé.' She spoke with a hint of a wry smile on her face, and Sylvia realised Miss Willis had grown up a lot in the past year. She had been aboard the ship when they were rescued from the Isla Ana, and then she had seemed to be a young, impressionable girl. Now she had a new maturity about her, an understanding of how the world worked. 'Then I heard he was to spend the weekend here with you.'

For a long few seconds, the two women just looked at one another, and then Sylvia set down the washcloth she had been dabbing her neck with.

'You fear there is something between Lord Wilder and me?'

'I know there is *something* between you, Miss Thompson. I may have been naive when you were brought onto my father's ship, but I could see the way you two looked at one another. Perhaps it was a fleeting feeling of companionship, born of the months you spent together. Perhaps it was something more. That I do not know.'

Sylvia nodded, turning away, not knowing what to say to the young woman.

'I have not seen Lord Wilder for a year, not since he escorted you away from the docks when we disembarked your father's ship. I have had no correspondence with him in that time.'

Miss Willis's eyes narrowed, and she leaned forwards. 'I have not come here to make trouble for you, Miss Thompson, so I beg you to be honest with me. I am in some terrible purgatory. Betrothed to a man I am almost certain does not care for me, but that is not the worst of it. Many marriages start that way and are very successful. I am betrothed to a man who I think would drag his heels until both of us die of old age. And then there is…' She trailed off, shaking her head.

'Lord Wilder has never shirked his responsibilities.'

'Yet here I am,' Miss Willis said, spreading her arms out.

Sylvia nodded, unable to deny the truth of the young woman's words.

'That is why you decided to come here?'

'I knew Lord Wilder was here and would be for the next few days. He informed me so himself, although he appears to have forgotten to pass on my invitation from Lady Montague. It seems our fates are rushing towards some sort of conclusion, and I wanted to be here for the ending, whatever it will be.'

'You may not believe me, but I wish you luck with your endeavours,' Sylvia said quietly. Miss Willis was an innocent in all this, told by her father she would be marrying the dashing Lord Wilder and one day soon become a viscountess, a social climb she must once have only dreamed of. Then left not knowing the true feelings of her betrothed, not knowing if or when he would fulfil his promise to wed her.

'Thank you, Miss Thompson.'

'Lord Wilder does not know you were planning to attend?'

'No.' Miss Willis gave a quick smile. 'I cannot wait to see the look on his face when he sees me. I am hoping it will be restitution for all the months of waiting he has put me through, unsure when he might visit next.'

No doubt he would maintain his calm and dignified demeanour, but Sylvia knew underneath he would be shaken by his two worlds colliding so suddenly without any input from him.

'Come, let's get dressed for dinner,' Miss Willis said with a sudden change in her expression. 'I meant what I said to Agnes. I will do your hair. I used to practice on the girls I shared a room with at school. I'm quite good.'

Sylvia selected her dress for the evening, the blue silk she had worn the day before, and after changing her damp undergarments, she slipped into it, surprised when Miss Willis stepped behind her to help her secure it.

'Sit.' She was directed to the chair and sat, her stomach a writhing mass of nerves, but Miss Willis's hands were gentle, and soon Sylvia found herself relaxing. There was only a small mirror on the wall in the room, nothing at the height Sylvia could see whilst seated, so for ten minutes she had no idea what her companion was doing. She could be making her look like Medusa for all she knew.

The feel of someone else's fingers in her hair took her back to childhood, to the happy days when her mother had been alive. Her father had earned a decent income as a solicitor, but despite that, they had never enjoyed the trappings of wealth. A few poor investments, trusting the wrong people, had left them scraping together enough money each month for the rent on their house and other essential expenses. It meant Sylvia had never had a maid. When she was younger, her mother had helped her to dress and spent hours plaiting and pinning her hair. Once her mother had died, Sylvia had needed to learn how to do these things and much more, taking over the running of the household for her father. Often she had wished for a sister, someone to share the excitement of getting ready for the dances at the local Assembly Rooms with, someone to gush over dresses, even if they were second-hand and subtly mended. Her brother had not been interested, his focus on finding some way out of their small-town life.

'There,' Miss Willis said, stepping back and nodding as if pleased with her handiwork. 'Perfect, if I say so myself.'

Sylvia stood and crossed to the little mirror, exclaiming in surprise as she saw the intricate way Miss Willis had twisted her hair and pinned it. The style was beautiful, perfectly complementing Sylvia's face and softening the angles.

'That is lovely. Thank you.'

Miss Willis beamed. 'I always wished for a sister to practice on. I can do my own, of course, but it isn't quite the same.'

'You have a real talent, Miss Willis.'

They finished the routine of dressing and readying themselves for the evening ahead, and as they moved around the room together, Sylvia could see there was a new tension to her companion's shoulders. She knew

asking the question could open up subjects she would
rather avoid, but the young woman was alone here,
striking out into the world for the first time, and Sylvia was aware how desperately nerve-wracking that
could be.

'Are you worried about something more than seeing
Lord Wilder, Miss Willis?'

The young woman looked up at her sharply, eyes
wide, and then her shoulders sagged a little.

'This is not my world,' Miss Willis said quietly.
'However much my father wishes it to be. Do you know,
when I was young, my parents and I lived in a tiny room
above one of my father's warehouses. Everything we
had went back into his business. I would play with the
street children as my companions, and we would be
able to afford only one meal a day.'

Sylvia nodded her head in understanding. This was
not her world either, although she had never suffered
the hardships Miss Willis had. In life most people were
born into a certain social level and stayed there. Your
friends were from the same class as you, your husband,
everyone you came into contact with. The odd person
took a step up or a step down, through good luck or bad,
but most people stayed exactly where they were born.

'I felt the same way when I started coming to these
events,' Sylvia said softly. 'And although I cannot say
I enjoy them now, no one has ever been unkind or malicious. It was always a fear of mine, but I have not experienced it.'

'You hear of the ladies of the *ton* being cruel.'

Sylvia shrugged. 'They are like every other person

on this earth. Some are kind, some less so. Their social status means they do not have to worry about certain things the rest of us do, but it does not change the people they are at heart.'

Miss Willis nodded, raising her chin and dropping her shoulders as if to prepare herself to go into battle.

'Shall we make our way to the drawing room?' Sylvia offered the younger woman her arm, and after only a moment's hesitation Miss Willis took it.

Chapter Eleven

That first sunrise on the Isla Ana was a magical thing. As the darkness began to fade, the sky lit up with every shade of red and orange you could imagine, making it look as though the whole world was on fire. I had awakened to the dawn chorus of unfamiliar birdsong, and Lord Wilder and I sat watching the spectacle in silence, too in awe of this natural phenomenon to spoil it with words.

Hugh shifted uncomfortably, unable to stop himself from glancing at the door, although his companion must have noticed his attention was not completely focussed.

'It is the little things that make a great performer,' Mr Oliver Sacrist was saying, gesturing over his shoulder to the violin that had been laid carefully on a table, positioned so it looked like an object of worship placed at the altar.

'Mmm,' Hugh said, hoping the violinist would not see the lack of interest in his eyes. It wasn't that he disliked music or musical recitals, and he could certainly appreciate the talent and dedication it took to be a master of any instrument, but he had an active loathing for the violin. It stemmed from childhood when his father had declared a mastery the piano was not enough and told his son he would be required to learn a new instrument. A few days later, a shiny new violin had arrived, along with a music teacher. Every day Hugh would struggle to make more than the most cutting screeching sound, and every day he hated the instrument a little more.

His father had been incandescent, telling Hugh he wasn't practicing enough, even applying the rod to his hands to teach him to move them faster. Hugh had been six years old, and each night he had crawled into bed cursing the instrument and wishing all violins of the world would burst into flames.

Over the course of a few years, he became a decent violinist, thanks to the tireless teacher and the desire not to have his hands whipped. Never once did he enjoy playing the instrument, and as soon as he went away to school, away from his father's influence, he packed up the violin in its little case and took pleasure at seeing it gather dust in the corner of his room.

Now even hearing the string instrument catapulted him back to the terrible feelings of fear and disappointment.

'Most people that play practice, but every time I pick up my violin, it is to *perform*. Do you see the distinction? I always imagine I am on stage, faced with hundreds of people who appreciate my music, my talent. It makes every note I play count and demands perfection every time I draw the bow across the strings.'

Hugh nodded again, thankful when Lady French sailed into the room, spotted the violinist and weaved her way through the crowds to accost the man.

'Mr Sacrist, it has been too long since I last heard you play,' Lady French said in her overly loud voice.

Hugh inclined his head silently and took the opportunity to slip away, turning towards the doors that led into the drawing room from the grand hallway. It was no surprise Sylvia was one of the last to arrive. She had been soaked to the skin, her clothes a mess and her hair dripping from the rain. It would take longer than usual for her to ready herself for the evening, and he doubted she would be in a rush to arrive. Although she had chosen to attend this party, and no doubt others like it, he knew it was not where she naturally felt happy. Despite his words to her, he did understand why she was doing all this, why she had written the book and why she was now trying to ensure its success.

Hugh had never met any of Sylvia's family. Her mother had died when she was younger, her father a few months before she had boarded the ship to Port Royal. It was her brother she was going to join in the Caribbean, her last surviving close relative. Now she had revealed her brother had died soon after she had returned to England and left her on her own. He may have left her some money, some modest savings, but as a secretary to the governor, he was hardly likely to have a big income, and no doubt the money was now running out. That was why she was so desperate now to make a success of the book.

He could see in her mind at least this book could provide her with a little independence. Decent sales could mean enough money to rent a modest room somewhere, perhaps even a small cottage. It would stave off the need for her to find an unskilled job or marry.

Hugh frowned to himself, knowing he should wish her the happiness of a husband and a family, but unable to do so right now. He hated the idea of her in someone else's arms, even though everything he was doing was so she could have a chance at a normal life.

Pushing the thought from his mind, he glanced up, almost dropping the glass in his hand at the sight that met him. Walking through the door, arm-in-arm as if they were the closest of companions, were the two women in his life. Sylvia was dressed in blue, her skirts falling about her like the cascade of a waterfall. Her hair was pinned beautifully, and her cheeks had a healthy glow about them. He couldn't tear his eyes away from her, but he had to assume everyone else in the room stopped what they were doing and stared at her too.

Next to Sylvia was Miss Willis, her raven-black hair a contrast to Sylvia's brown. Her dress was pale pink and her eyes lowered demurely. She looked like a picture of the perfect débutante, and Hugh wondered if she had been reading some sort of guide as to how a young lady should act in company such as this.

For a long moment, he could not move. Ten seconds passed and then twenty. It was only when he realised all eyes were on him he managed to summon a smile and force his legs to stumble forward. Out of the corner of his eye, he saw Lady Montague smirking, and he wondered if she had arranged this as some sort of cruel form of entertainment. He wouldn't think her above such a scheme. She seemed to revel in the drama of others and enjoyed moving people as if they were pieces on her own personal giant chess board.

'Miss Willis,' he said, taking his fiancée's hand and bowing over it. It took all his effort to go to her first, to turn away from Sylvia, but he knew he had to keep up appearances of being the devoted fiancé. 'What a surprise. I did not know you were coming.'

'How could you, my lord, when you failed to pass on the invitation from Lady Montague?' Miss Willis said.

He looked at her sharply, and she raised an eyebrow in challenge.

'Thankfully Lady Montague wrote to me a week ago, checking I had received the invitation and letting me know I would be most welcome at her little gathering.'

'Did she indeed?' Hugh murmured.

'I shall leave you to catch up,' Sylvia said, her eyes fixed firmly on a spot over his shoulder.

'No,' Miss Willis said firmly, gripping hold of Sylvia's arm. For an instant he saw something like understanding pass between the two women, and he frowned in confusion. 'Stay.'

'Would you like a drink, Miss Willis? Miss Thompson?' Lady Montague said, gliding over, reminding Hugh of a snake even down to the rapid flick of her tongue over her lips before she spoke. 'Isn't this delightful, Lord Wilder? You, your future wife, and the woman you spent three months with in the Caribbean, all in one place.'

'Delightful indeed,' he murmured.

'Miss Willis, I am keen to introduce you to everyone. Take a turn about the room with me, and I will show you who is who.'

Hugh watched as Sylvia surreptitiously squeezed the young woman's arm. There it was again, the show of solidarity. They barely knew one another, and from what he could gather, they had not spoken since the return of the *Chameleon* to English shores when he and Miss Willis had stepped off the gangplank, leaving Sylvia behind. Yet they looked as though they were confidantes, sisters even, united together.

'Thank you, Lady Montague. That is most kind,' Miss Willis said as she allowed the older lady to guide her away.

'What is happening?' Hugh snapped at Sylvia. He knew he should modify his tone, knew the words were too harsh, but the whole situation felt overwhelming. She gave him a haughty look and spun away. Despite the eyes that were on them, he reached out and caught her arm. His touch was gentle, but he knew she would not shrug him off and make a scene.

Ever so slowly, Sylvia turned back to face him.

'Come and sit with me,' he said, motioning to an empty sofa tucked into one corner of the room. It allowed a modicum of privacy, and Hugh was relieved when Sylvia gave a short, sharp nod.

'What are you doing with Miss Willis, looking like you are the closest of friends?' Hugh asked as they sat.

'She is a nice girl, pleasant,' Sylvia said, giving Hugh a pointed look. 'You might know that if you spent some time with her.'

'*You* are advocating for my marriage to that girl?'

Sylvia sighed and closed her eyes for a long few seconds. He could see the strain on her face, the tension in her shoulders, and realised she was walking a tightrope, placing one foot after the other and trying not to fall, like the most seasoned acrobat.

'I want you to be happy, Hugh,' she said quietly. 'Good Lord, is that too much to ask? I want us all to be happy. Me, you, even poor Miss Willis, who never asked for any of this.'

'She never refused it either.'

'Said with the conviction of a man who has to answer to no one. I do not know everything about Miss Willis's circumstances, but I doubt she has had a say in any aspect of her future. I admire her for coming here, for taking hold of her own destiny and trying to work out what her life is going to look like.'

Hugh sank back in his seat, running a hand through his hair. He knew he was being so defensive because he had acted poorly towards Miss Willis. Of course Sylvia was right. The young woman had never pressured him to marry her. The arrangement had been made without her knowledge. Then he had spent the past year trying to extract himself from the marriage by negotiating with Captain Willis, rather than speaking to Honoria directly. Perhaps that was where he was going wrong. He eyed his fiancée and realised he knew scant little about her. She was young with a vibrant personality and pleasant manners. With a jolt of surprise, he realised he had never asked Miss Willis what she thought of the marriage. His main concern had been the vengeful Captain Willis.

'God's blood,' he cursed, muttering the words under his breath so only Sylvia would hear. 'It is all a disaster.'

'I think Lady Montague is to blame for this latest stirring of the pot, though,' Sylvia said, motioning over to where their hostess was introducing Miss Willis to a seated young couple. 'I think when she suggested to me I should do a reading here at her house party, she decided she would make it as memorable as possible for her guests. You, Miss Willis, and I are not guests. We are entertainment.'

'Entertainment,' Hugh muttered, knowing Sylvia was right. 'And if we leave, it stirs up more scandal and gossip than if we stay and pretend we are all great friends.'

Sylvia nodded morosely, her eyes still fixed on Miss Willis. 'She is doing well, especially given how nervous she was.'

'She told you she was nervous?' He hardly expected the two young women to be friends, and it made him a little uncomfortable to think they might discuss their hopes, their dreams…their disappointments.

'She didn't have to, not in so many words. You forget Miss Willis and I are in similar positions. Neither of us belongs here amongst these people. Until you agreed to marriage, she would have been looking for her future husband at local dances, not mingling with some of the most influential people of the realm.' Sylvia paused and motioned to the room in general. 'You may feel at ease here, but most in this world wouldn't. It is like asking you to attend a tavern in Whitechapel. You would feel wildly out of place. I know how Miss Willis feels.'

Sylvia looked pensive, and he wondered if she was remembering the first time she stepped into a ballroom as grand as this.

'She didn't have to come,' he said quietly, even though he knew why she had. A whole year they had been engaged, and the matter of their marriage was far from settled. It was not something he was proud of.

'You need to talk to her, not me,' Sylvia said, smoothing her skirt down over her knees.

He was saved from answering by the Montagues' butler entering the room and announcing dinner was ready.

At dinner he was seated as far away from Miss Willis and Sylvia as was possible. Even though he knew Lady Montague had conformed to the social expectation that the seating plan was structured by rank and importance, still he suspected malicious compliance from their hostess. Every so often he would catch Sylvia say something to Miss Willis over the table, and he strained to hear their words, but there was too much chatter closer to him to make anything out.

The meal passed in a blur. He couldn't have told anyone what he ate, for it was as if he were being driven by clockwork, his fork moving to his mouth without him seeing or tasting what was on the end of it. Thankfully, with Mr Sacrist present and eager to start his recital, the ladies and gentlemen all moved together from the dining room together. He had almost caught up with Sylvia when Lady Montague stepped in.

'I can see you're eager to be with your betrothed, Lord Wilder. Let me help you with arranging the seating.'

'That is kind, Lady Montague, but I am perfectly capable of choosing my own chair.'

'Nonsense. Sit here with Miss Willis next to you, and Miss Thompson can sit on her other side,' Lady Montague said, beaming. 'That way dear Miss Willis is completely surrounded by friends.'

It was hard to argue with the sweet tone in her voice—he would have looked unnecessarily churlish— so he satisfied himself with giving Lady Montague an admonishing frown, which she proceeded to ignore, and then sat down.

Part of Hugh was aware this mess was of his own making, yet as he sat next to Miss Willis, with Sylvia just out of reach, he felt the overwhelming urge to flee. It wouldn't fix anything. It would instead make everything a lot worse, but the urge was still there. He shifted in his seat, angling his legs one way and then the other, crossing his arms on his chest and then uncrossing them and laying his hands in his lap. Next to him, Miss Willis was looking straight ahead, pretending to be oblivious to the situation.

After a minute of his fidgeting, as the rest of the small audience took their seats, Sylvia leaned back, reached her arm behind Miss Willis and placed her fingers gently on his shoulder. It was a move meant to calm him, to settle him, and Hugh immediately felt some of the tension ebbing away. The touch was fleeting but enough to remind him why he was doing all of this.

The performance was masterful. Even Hugh could admit that. The violinist swept them through four pieces of music with different moods and tempos. At the end, the audience stood and clapped for Mr Sacrist, who took a series of deep bows, enjoying the adoration.

'Ladies and gentlemen, if you would like to move through to the drawing room, I am sure some of the ladies present will treat us to their own musical performances,' Lady Montague said.

'I think we need to talk, Miss Willis,' Hugh said, feeling a weight in his chest.

'We do, my lord, but not now. Everyone is watching us, our every move.'

Hugh glanced up and saw Miss Willis was right. Eyes were on them. Everyone was intrigued by the sudden appearance of his fiancée and wondering if their love story was real or a woven web of fiction. He nodded stiffly and offered her his arm.

Behind him he was painfully aware of Sylvia waiting for them to leave before she made her own way through to the drawing room.

Chapter Twelve

It took us two days to venture further afield than the sweet spring of fresh water. Our hopes of rescue were rapidly dwindling, and although we thought we had washed ashore on an island, we were not sure. Part of me hoped we would trek a short distance through the thick forest and be rewarded by some sight of civilisation, but after no more than fifteen minutes of walking, we emerged out onto another beach, confirming our fears that we were on a tiny speck of land in the middle of the ocean.

Sylvia sat rigid for the next half an hour, not hearing a single note of the piano pieces the various ladies and gentlemen played. Her eyes were fixed on a spot firmly in front of her, hands placed one on top of the other demurely in her lap. She hoped she looked serene, the picture of calm, but inside her thoughts were in turmoil.

'Miss Thompson,' Lady Montague said, jolting Sylvia out of her reverie. 'Why don't you play for us?'

Sylvia swallowed hard, trying to summon a smile for the older woman.

'There are much more accomplished players here today,' Sylvia said, not moving.

'We all have out different styles, Miss Thompson. It is not a competition. No one will be judging you.'

'I am sure another of the young ladies would like to take my place,' Sylvia said, looking round desperately.

No one moved. No one said a word. She felt the panic begin to rise inside her and knew her cheeks were flushed pink out of embarrassment.

'Let me accompany you, Miss Thompson.' Hugh's voice startled her. 'I know what a beautiful singing voice you have, and I have been eager to get my hands on the piano.' He stood, offering her his arm, which she took after only a moment's hesitation.

'What are you doing?' she murmured to him as they walked across the room, everyone's eyes on her.

'I don't like bullies,' Hugh said, looking down at her, a softness in his eyes that she hadn't seen for a long time. 'And Lady Montague is a bully. I will not let her humiliate you.'

'What will you play?'

'I thought I would play "Waves on the Sea".'

Sylvia pressed her lips together, hoping he wouldn't notice the tears forming in her eyes. 'Waves on the Sea' was the song her mother used to sing to her to help her fall asleep at night. It was haunting and beautiful, and on the long nights on the Isla Ana, Sylvia would often sing it to Hugh.

'I will play and you can sing.'

'I've never had a singing lesson.'

'You don't need any singing lessons.'

He took a seat at the piano, and Sylvia stood next to him, looking out at the room. All eyes were on them, everyone fascinated to see what this strange partnership would perform. Miss Willis sat alone, but as Sylvia looked at her, the young woman glanced up and gave Sylvia a reassuring smile.

Hugh played the first few notes, his fingers dancing across the keys, and then it was Sylvia's cue to start singing. It was far too intimidating to look at the faces in the room, so instead, she angled her body a little and looked at Hugh.

She sang from her heart, trying to forget the audience, trying to pretend it was just the two of them spread out on the sand, watching the stars in the cloudless sky as she sang of shipwrecks and storms and sailors who would never see their homes again.

There had been one evening, in the aftermath of a storm, the island strangely quiet and the sea calm as it lapped against the beach, when Sylvia had sat alone, humming this tune to herself. She hadn't realised Hugh was there until she felt his hand on her shoulder. Then his presence beside her, closer than he should sit. He'd turned to her with a flicker of desire in his eyes and asked her to sing for him.

After the last note rang out, there was a moment of silence. Sylvia risked a peek at the assembled guests, wondering if she had horrified them. Miss Willis was the first to move, clapping her hands together in applause, and that sound seemed to wake up the rest of the audience and prompt them into vigorous clapping.

'Where have you been hiding that voice, Miss Thompson?' Lady Montague asked, her face a picture of composure. 'And Lord Wilder, what a talent you are on the piano. You truly are the perfect duo,' she said, and Sylvia saw the older woman's eyes flick sideways to take in Miss Willis's reaction. Hugh was right. Lady Montague was a bully. All she had done this weekend was manipulate and set people against one another in the hope for a reaction, for an event to make her gathering memorable, even if it meant ruining lives along the way.

They returned to their seats, and Sylvia waited a few moments before quietly excusing herself. She needed some air. The room had grown unbearably stuffy with the number of guests seated in one place, and she felt as though the heat was pressing down on her chest. After slipping into the hallway, she made her way to the library and the glass doors that opened to the terrace beyond. Thankfully they had not been locked, and she was able to push down on the handle to open one and move out onto the paved terrace.

It was cooler outside, and there was a slight breeze. The ground was wet from a recent shower, but there was no rain falling at that moment. The clouds were still thick and dark overhead, blocking out the moon and the stars and threatening a storm, although it had looked that way most of the day, nothing yet had materialised. She shuddered at the thought and realised she was thankful Miss Willis would be sharing her bed tonight. At least if the storm did come, she would have someone there beside her when the lightning flashed in the sky and the thunder crashed, making her feel like the whole world was going to come crashing down around her.

'You should not linger out here alone.' Hugh's voice came from behind her.

Sylvia spun quickly, almost tripping over the skirts of her dress. Once she had righted herself, she frowned.

'You shouldn't be here. It is safer if we are not seen together.'

'Lady Montague is organising card games. She is currently occupied trying to find the best combination of people. We have a few minutes, I think, before we are missed.'

Sylvia nodded, suddenly tired of arguing with him.

'You sang beautifully in there.'

'Thank you,' she said quietly. 'Thank you for rescuing me from humiliation, too.'

'Of course. She shouldn't have pressed you.'

'We cannot all be as accomplished as the talented Lord Wilder,' Sylvia said with a small smile.

'Not many people in this world can,' he murmured.

They fell silent for a moment, both knowing they needed to talk about more than the superficial, but neither wanting to be the one to delve into the tangle of emotions and practicalities they faced.

'It's such a shambles Sylvia,' Hugh said quietly, his posture sagging. Normally he was perfectly presented. He walked tall, he was immaculately groomed, and never was there a single crease in any of his garments. It was part of this perfectionism that plagued him, Sylvia knew. For him to allow some of that façade to slip, he must be struggling

'I know,' she said quietly. There was no other way to describe the situation they were in.

'This past year...' he began, and then trailed off.

'Then do not do it. Do not go through with this bargain you have struck,' Sylvia said softly. The mask was slipping from Hugh, and she could see some of the vulnerability peeking through. It was a glimpse, nothing more, but it reminded her of the man she knew him to be.

'I have given my word.'

Sylvia closed her eyes, realising it hurt just as much now she knew the truth behind his motive for asking Miss Willis to marry him as it had when she thought he had merely wanted to distance himself from Sylvia. She hated that his principles meant he would not fight for her.

'Then marry her,' Sylvia said. 'If the strength of your promise is the most important thing to you, the most sacred vow not to be broken, then you have to accept it and all the consequences that will come, but dallying will not help the matter.'

Hugh turned to her, the turmoil visible on his face.

'If I marry her, there is no way out, no other option. That is it for the rest of our lives.'

Sylvia felt a stab of pain at his words but nodded solemnly.

'How can I do that, Sylvia? How can I marry her when I...' His eyes held hers, and he trailed off. She felt her heart surge in her chest and then shatter into a thousand pieces as he didn't finish the sentence. She knew what he was going to say. *How can I marry her when I love you?* He'd told her that he'd loved her on the Isla Ana, and perhaps he still thought he did now.

Sylvia took a deep breath, realising she was going to have to be the strong one, the one to break this entanglement once and for all. It would mean hurting him, pushing him away, but perhaps one day they would both find peace.

She stepped closer and placed a hand on his chest, feeling the thud of his heart through the material of his shirt and waistcoat. It was an intimate position, and she felt her body instinctively sway closer to him, but she resisted the urge to wrap her arms round his neck.

'I loved you,' she said quietly, trying to keep her voice low and steady. 'On the Isla Ana, I loved you with all my heart. Despite the terrible situation we were in, I felt happy, contented.' She paused, breaking off and taking a few steadying breaths before continuing. 'But you were a different man then. Free from the weight of responsibility, free from your duties and obligations. I can understand now what you did for me on that ship home, and I will be forever grateful for the deal you made with Captain Willis to save my reputation.' She didn't add the silent words her mind was screaming. She didn't tell him it was only his change in demeanour towards her, the sudden coldness when he realised he would have to bring Sylvia into his world, that had pushed her away in the first place.

'Sylvia…' Hugh said, but she shook her head, placing a finger on his lips.

'Listen to me, Hugh, really listen. If you had asked

me to marry you when we'd left the island, I would have said yes.' She paused as he closed his eyes and let his head drop back. Quickly she ploughed on 'I would have said yes, but it would have been the wrong decision. Our love was a fantasy, not made for the real world. We value different things. You value your traditions and the sanctity of the role of the Viscount, and I do not fit into that mould. We would have been miserable, pining for something that once was, never able to be as happy as we were on the island.'

'You do not know that.'

'You value protecting the viscountcy above everything else,' Sylvia said softly. 'And I was not the right choice to be your viscountess.'

'Miss Willis is?' he said, shaking his head.

'That is a separate matter between you and your conscience. You have made her a promise. It is up to you whether you break it, but it does not change the fact we are not destined to be together.'

'Even if we want each other.'

'Even if we want each other.'

They stood there, body to body, for a long moment, neither moving, neither speaking. Sylvia had so much more she wanted to say, so many thoughts and opinions on what had happened this past year, but she knew she had to keep them to herself. Now wasn't the time to start flinging accusations and recriminations around. They had both made mistakes. She should have pressed Hugh to talk to her when she had seen him withdrawing, listened to how he was feeling instead of thinking it was all about her. And he shouldn't have tried to anticipate how she would react to him from a few snippets of conversation taken out of context.

'We had our moment, Hugh, and it was a wonderful moment, but it has passed now. We both need to move on from the Isla Ana and stop living in the past.'

Out of the corner of her eye, she saw him raise a hand, and then she felt his fingertips against her cheek. It was almost enough to make her try to claw back the words she had just uttered, almost enough to make her bundle him into a carriage, race to the nearest port and find a berth on any ship heading for the Caribbean to try to relive their time there.

'You're right,' he said, his lips barely moving, his fingers still on her cheek. 'I need to stop living in the past.'

For ten more seconds they stood there, face to face, resisting the urge to do something foolish, and then Hugh gave a resolute nod.

'You always were wise, Sylvia.'

She snorted. 'You have never admitted that before.'

'Then perhaps it is I who am the fool.'

Sylvia steeled herself for the flood of emotions she knew she would feel when she stepped away and then turned quickly, not wanting Hugh to see her expression. Part of her believed everything she had just said. Certainly she felt as if they were perfect for one another in a very specific set of circumstances, but not in the lives they currently occupied. She would not live up to his high expectations of what a viscountess should be, and he would focus too much of his time and energy on things other than her. Still, a small part of her had wanted him to fight for her, to care enough that he said to hell with convention and honour and duty, and swept her off into the sunset.

'It is done,' she murmured to herself, too softly for Hugh to hear. Now she had to reconcile herself with drawing a line underneath her time with Hugh on the Isla Ana. There could be no more fantasising, no more wishing things could have been different. She would plough all her energy into making a success of her book and trying to decide what more she wanted from life. The idea of ever falling in love with someone else seemed preposterous right now, but Sylvia was self-aware enough to know everything was horribly raw in this moment. Perhaps one day she would open her heart again, and this time she might find a man who was willing to fight for her no matter what the circumstances.

From somewhere behind her, she heard the faint click of the door to the library, and she knew she now stood alone on the terrace. The loneliness threatened to overwhelm her, and she gripped hold of the stone balustrade to steady herself. This was what it had felt like when she had first returned to England, when she had first watched Hugh walk away from her. Quietly she resolved that she wouldn't let him hurt her this way again. From this moment, she would work on letting go of the memory of the man she had spent three months loving. That man was as good as dead. Now she needed to look to building her own happiness.

Chapter Thirteen

Those first few days, my mood fluctuated between a deep melancholy at the thought of never seeing home again and a mania of the like I've never experienced before. For long hours, I would do nothing but sit on the beach, staring at the horizon. Then it was as though something flipped inside me, and I would be driven to jump up and race about the island, gathering food and scouting out the best spots for a shelter.

Sylvia woke surprisingly refreshed as the light filtered through the curtains. After the talk she'd had with Hugh the evening before on the terrace, her thoughts had been in turmoil. She had fled to her bedroom, hoping for some peace before Miss Willis came to join her. Sylvia had expected to lie awake all night, mulling over her words, dwelling on the past and trying to push away maudlin thoughts about the future. Instead she had dropped into a deep, dreamless sleep, undisturbed by Miss Willis when she had returned some time later that evening.

This morning she felt a flicker of hope inside her, This past year, she had fooled herself into thinking she had moved on, but in reality, she had been waiting for this moment. Part of her had yearned for Hugh and what they once had, and without the conversation they'd shared last night, she probably would have gone on dreaming about him forever.

'Today is a new day, a fresh start,' she murmured to herself.

Beside her, Miss Willis shifted in bed, her dark hair fanned out across the pillow. Sylvia rose silently, pleased to see the white dress that had been so crumpled and stained the day before draped over the back of a chair in perfect condition, the only sign it had been laundered a slightly damp hem.

She dressed quickly and fixed her hair in a simple style. Then she slipped from the room, leaving Miss Willis to sleep.

Downstairs the servants were beginning to set the table for breakfast, but it looked to be another twenty minutes until they would be ready to bring the food up from the kitchens.

Opting for a little fresh air, Sylvia stepped outside, her feet crunching on the stony path. The sky was clear and blue, and it promised to be another glorious day after the rain of the night before, but the grass was wet, and there was still a chill bite in the air. Sylvia strolled slowly, enjoying the beautiful blooms in the flowerbeds and the sound of birdsong in the air. The house was still quiet, but she could hear a distant clink of metal on metal. At first she assumed it was coming from the stables, but as she turned her head to listen, she realised it was somewhere out in the gardens, beyond the maze.

Curious as to what could be making the noise, she followed the sound, pausing every now and then as the clinks ceased and then resumed. After a couple of minutes, she rounded a hedge and stopped in surprise.

Foils drawn, Hugh and Sir Percy were fencing, attacking and defending robustly. Lady Turner sat on a stone bench, shouting encouragement every now and then, her face turned up to the sun.

'Jab him, Percy. Don't hold back.'

Lady Turner spotted Sylvia and waved her over to the bench.

'Come, my dear, join me. The sun is glorious. I'm a vain creature, but I love the feel of the sun on my face. I couldn't stand to have freckles, of course, so these early morning spells in the sun are all I allow myself.'

Sylvia perched down beside Lady Turner, her eyes fixed on the two men in front of them. Lord Wilder was clearly the better swordsman. He moved with grace and ease, transferring his balance from foot to foot as he parried and blocked. Sir Percy was less graceful, his steps heavier and his movements with his sword hand slower, but he went at it with great enthusiasm.

'My husband taught me to fence when we first were married,' Lady Turner said, her eyes fixed on Sir Percy. 'That's it, Percy, never back down,' she called out, and then turned back to Sylvia. 'It is a wonderful sport.

You can get all that pent-up frustration out with a few slashes of the foil. If I am ever particularly annoyed with Sir Percy, I challenge him to a fencing match. I would wager it has saved us dozens of arguments.'

Sylvia regarded her companion, unsure if she was jesting.

'Dozens of arguments,' Rosa mimicked, fluttering down to sit on the arm of the bench.

'When you marry, I can recommend it.'

'I doubt all husbands are as forward-thinking as Sir Percy.'

Lady Turner snorted. 'I would agree, but I put it to you that it is on you to choose carefully enough that yours is.'

Sylvia pressed her lips together, not saying a word, and Lady Turner let her head drop back as she laughed.

'I know exactly what you are thinking, Miss Thompson, and you would be right.'

'What am I thinking?'

'You are thinking that not all women have the luxury of choice as I did.'

'How did you know?'

Lady Turner shrugged. 'We are not so different in spirit, you and I.' She fell silent for a moment and then regarded Sylvia intently. 'I take it you are the reason Lord Wilder is quite ferocious this morning.'

Lord Wilder *was* ferocious in his attack on Sir Percy, beating him back with no sign of mercy again and again.

'Perhaps. We had a lot to talk about yesterday. There were a lot of unexplored feelings, from both sides.'

'What was the conclusion?'

Sylvia inhaled slowly, feeling as if this were an important moment, this first time she said the words out loud.

'I told Lord Wilder we were not meant to be, that our time had been and gone, but there was nothing for us in the future.'

'Ah.'

'I also told him to settle things with Miss Willis one way or another.'

'Yes, *that* is important.'

Sir Percy threw down his foil and raised his hands in defeat, lifting the shield from his face to reveal a hot, sweaty countenance.

'Enough,' he said, a hint of laughter in his voice. 'I need a break. You have destroyed me.'

Hugh lifted his face shield as well and inclined his head, turning to where Sylvia and Lady Turner sat on the bench.

'Good morning, Miss Thompson,' he said, his voice light.

'Good morning, my lord.'

'Good Lord, she still calls you *my lord*?' Sir Percy said with a laugh. 'Do you hear that, Mary?'

'I do, Sir Percy.'

'Ha. My beloved wife stopped calling me Sir Percy three months before our marriage.'

'I still call you Sir Percy in public, my dear,' Lady Turner said.

'True. Although we're all friends here, aren't we? You are looking ravishing this morning, Miss Thompson.'

'Thank you, Sir Percy.'

'Did you see the beating he gave me, Mary? Thrashed

me before I could even pick my foil up. Terribly embarrassing, of course.' He looked anything but embarrassed.

'It is because you are a man of peace,' Lady Turner said, smiling at her husband and rising from the bench. 'You have peace in your heart.'

'What does that mean I have in mine?' Hugh asked.

Lady Turner cocked her head to the side and regarded him. 'Foolishness,' she said, softening the word with a smile. 'But we cherish you anyway. Come, Percy, I have a sudden hankering to stroll to the fishpond. Will you accompany me whilst you recover before your next bout?'

'Whatever you wish, my dear.'

Sylvia watched them go and was surprised to find Hugh making his way towards her and taking Lady Turner's place on the bench.

'It is a beautiful morning,' he said, his manner with her more relaxed than she had expected.

'It is. I could hear the birds singing from the window in my room, and I could not resist a trip outside.'

'Sir Percy and I sometimes used to sneak out of our rooms at school and go for an early morning excursion somewhere. We might take our horses from the stable or practice our fencing It felt like freedom when everything else was so constrictive.'

'I am impressed you risked the wrath of your teachers.'

Hugh's lips twitched into a smile of reminiscence. 'The other boys thought them strict, but after years of my father's draconian regime I thought their rules lenient and their punishments fair.'

'You were often caught?'

'Once or twice. There was another boy who liked to curry favour with the teachers. Sometimes he would see us depart and ensure the story of our illicit trip out reached someone who would punish us.' He shrugged. 'It didn't stop us, but we learned ways to get around it.'

He regarded her for a moment, his expression serious. 'Have you ever fenced?'

Sylvia let out a burst of laughter and then realised the question was a serious one.

'Never. When would I have had the opportunity to fence?'

'Pity. It is most rejuvenating.'

'Lady Turner was saying the same. I understand Sir Percy taught her.'

'Mary is fierce with a foil. She has a fiery focus and a determined glint in her eye. She may not have been fencing since childhood, but she isn't the sort to hold back.' He stood and held out a hand. 'Shall I show you?'

For a moment Sylvia didn't move, not thinking he was serious.

'You mean it?'

'Why not? It is a glorious morning, we are properly chaperoned, and there is nothing scandalous about an old friend teaching another to fence.'

Sylvia glanced over to where Sir Percy and Lady Turner strolled some distance away near the fishpond. They were careful to remain in view but with their eyes diverted so there was the appearance of a chaperon without any invasion of privacy.

'You wish to teach me?'

Suddenly his expression was serious. 'I thought a lot about what you said, Sylvia. You are right, of course. We have come too far along this path to ever go back to where we were. I was torturing myself and you, and I am sincerely sorry for it.' He shrugged, and she saw some of the familiar boyish enthusiasm in his eyes. 'I think we are both sensible enough to allow ourselves to be near one another, perhaps even enjoy a little of each other's company, whilst I find a path out of this mess I have created.'

It was what she had suggested, it was what she told herself she wanted, and Sylvia forced a smile onto her face and nodded with what she hoped was enthusiasm.

'We will not use the face shields,' he said. 'I will ensure my blade does not come near your face.'

'I may not be so lenient, or so controlled.'

'I will risk a blow to my visage,' he said, picking up the foils from where he and Sir Percy had dropped them. 'Hold out your hand flat, then curl you fingers like this.' He placed the foil in her hand, his fingers dancing over hers to help her adjust her grip. 'Good. Hold it firmly but do not clutch it. It needs to feel like an extension of your body, not a foreign object you are gripping on to for dear life.'

She tried to relax her grip a little, almost jumping in the air as she felt his hands on her shoulders. Her dress had a wide neckline, and momentarily his fingers brushed her bare skin, sending a shiver through her body. Exerting a very gentle pressure, he got her to drop her shoulders, and then stepped away with a satisfied nod.

'Move it around a little. Get a feel for the balance of the blade, how it moves through the air.'

It was surprisingly light, the metal flying through the air with the slightest flick of her wrist.

'The most important part of fencing, or indeed any sword fight, is stance and balance.'

'More important than the strength of your thrust?'

'Far more important. Turn your body sideways a little, and have one foot out in front. You will transfer your weight from back foot to front foot as you move forwards and backwards. If you are nimble and well-balanced, it will allow you to avoid your opponent's blows and then quickly lunge and place one of your own.'

He hesitated for a second before he came and stood directly behind her, his hands on her arms to guide the positioning of her body. For an instant, Sylvia forgot everything that had passed between them and could almost believe they were on the beach on the Isla Ana with Hugh ready to tumble her into the sand at any moment. She felt him pause behind her, his head bent and his breath warm on her neck. It took all her willpower to resist swaying backwards, to stop herself from tilting her head to present the smooth skin on her neck to receive his kisses.

With a cough, Hugh stepped away, not meeting her eye for a moment.

'I think you are ready,' he said with forced jollity. Taking his place beside her, he showed her how to slash her foil first in defensive moves and then to jab in the signature move to attack. The movements were fluid and easy to do without an opponent, but Sylvia suspected as soon as there was a blade flying in her direction, it would seem infinitely harder. 'Shall we fight?' he asked.

'I hope you do not think I will go easy on you, Lord Wilder,' Sylvia said, watching in astonishment as Hugh shrugged off his waistcoat and rolled up his sleeves. Whilst he had been fighting Sir Percy, he had shed his jacket, but she knew how much of an armour his formal clothes were for him. It was strange to see him with forearms bared and his shirt open at the neck.

'I would expect nothing less.'

He positioned himself a few steps away, and Sylvia mirrored his stance, holding up her foil as he did, tilting the tip forwards so it overlapped with his halfway between them.

'Why don't you start by attacking me?' he said.

Sylvia didn't move for a minute, conjuring up all the reasons it would feel good to land the tip of her foil on his chest. Then she attacked, her movement smooth but forceful. She revelled in the look of surprise in Hugh's eyes as she didn't hold back, and momentarily he was unbalanced. It spoke to what skill he possessed in fencing that he recovered so quickly, bringing his blade round to block hers with a clash of metal on metal.

She inched forwards, continuing the attack, but Hugh was firmly in control now, seeming to anticipate her every move and blocking it easily whilst still allowing her to get the feel of each thrust and swipe.

'Why doesn't it surprise me that you are a natural, Miss Thompson?' he called, grinning at her. It was the first real smile she had seen from him since they had spotted the ship approaching the Isla Ana over a year ago, and it pierced Sylvia's heart. She felt her balance wobble a little, and it took all her concentration to maintain her posture. There was even the familiar mischievous glint in his eye.

Sylvia felt a mixture of happiness that he was smiling again and grief that all it had taken to allow him to flourish was for her to set him free.

'I hope you are as skilled at defence,' he said, trying a few gentle thrusts in her direction. Sylvia experimented with how she raised her blade to block his, feeling the jarring of the impact even though the foils were light and her arm braced for it.

As he moved in her direction, there was a sudden flutter of wings and flash of red as Rosa swooped in, flying straight for Hugh's face. Instinctively he dropped his foil, raising his arms to protect his eyes as her talons swooped dangerously close.

'Get away, get away,' she screeched, flapping her wings even as Hugh backed away from her.

'Rosa,' Sylvia shouted, well aware of the damage the bird's claws could do.

At first she thought the parrot wasn't going to listen, but after a few moments and with a final flap of her wings, Rosa soared up into the air and then came to perch on Sylvia's shoulder.

Hugh straightened, his normally neat hair a mess, a superficial scratch down one cheek.

'Are you hurt?' Sylvia said, rushing towards him.

'Merely scratched.' He glanced up at Rosa on her shoulder. 'You are protective of Sylvia, aren't you.'

'*Stay away. Stay away.*'

Hugh held up his hands so he wouldn't seem a threat to Rosa.

'I am glad you have someone to protect you,' he murmured, his eyes coming up to meet Sylvia's. 'I often worried...' He trailed off.

Dropping her foil next to his, Sylvia leaned in, jumping as Rosa gave a squawk next to her ear and flew off to settle on the lawn a few feet away.

'You're bleeding.'

'I'm fine, Sylvia. It was a scratch, nothing more.'

She reached out, her fingers brushing his cheek, and for a moment, Hugh went completely still. His eyes came up to meet hers, and in that instant she knew they could say what they liked to one another, but words only took them so far. That deep longing, that desire for intimacy, wouldn't disappear overnight.

'It will heal,' he said gently, placing his hand over hers and then carefully removing it from his face. Sylvia swallowed hard and stepped back, aware she had overstepped again, unable to push away the torrent of emotion that was threatening to flood through her. 'And if it doesn't, I'll be left with an interesting scar. I could tell people all sorts of stories, but the one they would not believe is the truth.'

'That you were attacked by a bird thinking she was protecting me from a vile assailant.'

'Exactly.' He looked at her keenly and then glanced at Rosa where she was strutting about on the ground. 'She *hasn't* had to do that before, has she?'

'Protect me?'

He nodded. Sylvia smiled tightly, thinking of some of the less salubrious rooms she had rented over the past year. London was a difficult place to be young and single and without protection. Landlords were unscrupulous, and when people found out she was on her own, some thought of how best they could take advantage.

'I am settled somewhere safe now,' Sylvia said quietly.

'Now? What about before? Did something happen?'

In truth Sylvia knew she should gently reassure him she was fine and remind him it was none of his concern whether she lived in Mayfair or Whitechapel, but she had a sudden overwhelming desire to talk to someone about it all. This past year had been the most lonely of her life. Her world had shrunk to a basic, miserable existence since her brother had died. Her world had shrunk then, alone in the capital with no friends nearby and no family. It had been a time of rapid learning and more dangerous moments than she liked to admit.

'Sylvia,' Hugh said, waiting for her to look at him, and then his eyes searched hers.

'London is not a safe place for a woman alone,' she said quietly. 'I know that now. It is why I am so keen to make enough money I can get away.'

'What happened?'

It wasn't just one incident. It was a series of near misses and close calls that built up into a whole picture but were hard to explain individually.

'A neighbour forced himself into my rooms. I was accosted on the street when I stayed out too late one evening. I misjudged a stranger's seemingly friendly enquiry.' She shrugged. 'Nothing irreparable, but it has made me realise London is not where I wish to live if I have any sort of choice.'

Hugh looked serious, a deep furrow between his eyebrows.

'People are people wherever you settle,' he said quietly. 'Is there not someone you could seek protection from? A distant relative, even?'

'No.' Sylvia shook her head emphatically. 'Do you think I have not been through all this a thousand times, Hugh? I do not wish to be on my own—I never imagined this life for myself—but I have no living relatives, and I refuse to live on the charity of my friends.'

He opened his mouth to speak again, and she held up a hand to stop him.

'Whatever you are about to say, believe me when I tell you I have thought of it, considered it. I have been living with this reality for the past year, and it has not been anywhere near comfortable. If there was a solution, then I would grab on to it with both hands and never let go, but there isn't.'

He nodded slowly. 'I understand now,' he said, his voice low. 'This is why you think you need the book to succeed.'

'Yes. I am woefully unprepared for the real world. I have no experience of work, but my education is not robust enough to be hired as a governess. A few months ago, I got a position in a haberdasher's, serving customers and helping with the accounts. I was thrilled, but a month later the owner's debts became too much, and he lost the business.'

'I didn't know. I had no idea, Sylvia.'

She shrugged. 'Why would you?'

She let her eyes drift up to his, and a flicker of under-standing flowed between them. Sometimes she forgot how distanced from the world Hugh's life was. Clois-tered away in his vast estates, he barely saw the plight of the majority of the population.

'What will you tell everyone about the scratch?'

'The truth—that you commanded your avian guard to attack me, and she did so ferociously.'

'No one would believe that of poor Rosa.'

'I am impressed at how quick she was to your de-fence.'

'What on earth happened?' Lady Turner said as she and Sir Percy strolled back over.

'Don't tell her. I will never live it down.'

'Now my interest is piqued. Did you best him in a duel, Miss Thompson, and cut him with the foil?'

'That's jolly good going. Those things are capped at the end,' Sir Percy said, picking a blade up and testing the tip on the end of his finger.

'It wasn't the foil,' Hugh said, his eyes on Rosa strut-ting backwards and forwards across the grass.

'Rosa thought he was really attacking me,' Sylvia said, smiling at Sir Percy's and Lady Turner's shocked faces. 'So she swooped in to defend me.'

'I was caught in a whirl of feathers and claws,' Hugh muttered, frowning at his friends' expressions. 'It isn't funny. I could have lost an eye.'

'Pox on Hugh Wilder,' Rosa said, flapping up to Syl-via's shoulder as if sensing she was being talked about.

'Ha!' Lady Turner exclaimed, turning to Sylvia. 'You taught her to say that? Incredible.'

'I didn't teach her exactly,' Sylvia said quietly. 'She just picks things up.'

'I think this is my favourite weekend of the whole year,' Lady Turner said, linking her arm through Sylvia's. 'Have you had enough fencing? Shall we go inside and hunt down some breakfast?'

'That sounds wonderful.'

Guided away by Lady Turner, she risked a quick look back to see Hugh staring after her with a pensive expression on his face.

Chapter Fourteen

It was late one afternoon that Lord Wilder presented me with a gift, something he had fashioned with his own hands. Far from the trinkets or treasures two friends might normally share, Lord Wilder was excited to gift me a thin piece of rock, chipped and whittled to a sharp point and tied to a solid stick. He had made a spear for himself, too, and declared that afternoon we would catch our first fish.

'Oh, my!' Lady Montague exclaimed as Hugh wandered out of the house onto the terrace. 'Lord Wilder, what happened to your face?'

'A fencing accident,' he said, declining to elaborate any further. He had to suppress a smile at the memory of the morning spent teaching Sylvia the rudimentary basics of the sport. Perhaps this was what they had needed all along, a hard stop, an ultimatum to them both to realise that what they had once shared had changed.

For an entire year, he had tiptoed about this business, trying to use subtle means to satisfy everyone. He'd focussed his energy on persuading Captain Willis to release him from the promise he had made, concerned about breaking his word, but in doing so, he had lost sight of the reason he was doing it all along.

Sylvia.

The one and only reason. To protect her, to safeguard her reputation.

These past few days had reminded him what fire and passion he felt for Sylvia, how she made him feel whole when the rest of the time it was as if there was a part of him missing. Her ultimatum last night had made him realise what he risked. He wasn't sure protecting Sylvia's reputation was enough for him now. Now he wanted more.

He could acknowledge Sylvia was right. He needed to separate the issues he faced from one another. On the one side, there was the fact he still cared for Sylvia. On the other was the promise he had made Miss Willis. Merely *not* marrying Miss Willis wasn't going to miraculously bring Sylvia back to him. He could see that now. He needed to find a solution to satisfy everyone, where everyone got to keep their reputations and no one felt cheated.

This morning with Sylvia had felt good. There had been a hint of their old friendship, the feeling of ease and happiness that had made him fall in love with Sylvia in the first place. It was a reminder what it was exactly he was fighting for.

Realising Lady Montague was still talking, he turned to her with his most charming and attentive smile.

'...an unmatched success, that is what I heard one of the ladies say yesterday evening. I am sure you can imagine my pleasure at such words, especially as they were not meant for my ears.'

Guessing their hostess was talking about the success of her house party, Hugh nodded.

'It cannot come as a surprise,' he said lightly. 'Your parties have always had a reputation of being amongst some of the best of the season.'

Lady Montague tittered in pleasure as he refrained from rolling his eyes. Sometimes he wondered what the reaction would be if he came out and told the ladies and gentlemen he socialised with what he really thought. Of course, they were not all as bad as Lady Montague. There were some kind, generous, *interesting* people in the *ton*, just like in all echelons of society, but there were also some dullards.

Most of his lessons had come from his father, the late Lord Wilder having the much stronger personality and louder voice, but this skill he had learned from his mother. She had hated society events, hated balls and dinner parties, but every evening she would get dressed in her finest gowns and sparkle in her most expensive jewellery and head out to mix with those who would finally destroy her with their gossip. When Hugh saw her sadness, he would often ask her to stay, feigning a headache or sore tummy. She would kiss him and smile gently, and then tell him how important it was to put on a performance, to at least pretend you fitted in. The alternative was to be shunned or shamed. Sometimes Hugh thought being excluded might not be a terrible thing. Then he remembered how desperate his mother had been to get back the life she had once wished to reject.

'I do hope Miss Willis is enjoying herself.' Lady Montague said.

'I think she is, thank you.' It pained him to know he had neglected her again. When he was younger, he'd had this idealised view of himself, and he had vowed he would always be considerate, never dismiss another's feelings. However, as life had intervened, he had grown into a man sometimes he barely recognised. This weekend was the perfect time to talk to Miss Willis, to really understand what she felt about their arranged marriage, yet he still hadn't found the opportunity. He must do better.

'Good. I think the other ladies and gentlemen have been accepting of her, welcoming even.'

'Yes, they have.'

'I know how important that acceptance is,' Lady Montague said, her hands brushing an imaginary speck of dirt from her skirt.

Hugh looked up sharply, but at this moment there was no guile in the hostess's expression, and he thought she spoke without an alternative motive. It was always hard to tell with Lady Montague, but he supposed she was human underneath all her schemes and cunning.

She seemed to rally and gave him her normal bright smile as Lady French and Mr Otterby came out onto the terrace.

'I must gather the guests for a little game this morning. I am sad this is our last full day together, so we must make the most of it.'

Hugh inclined his head, wondering if he could slip away whilst this game was in progress. Perhaps he could use the distraction to take Miss Willis aside and talk to her as he should have long ago.

He resolved to go and find his future wife, to sit her down somewhere quiet and actually talk to her. He knew he had to ascertain what Miss Willis wanted, whether she truly wanted to marry him, to be his viscountess, or if it were something she was being pushed towards just as much as he. Only when he had that answer could he make his plans for the future, to try to find a way through that didn't ruin the life of a woman he suspected was merely caught up in the middle of this all.

He lingered for a few minutes before moving on, giving his hostess chance to walk on ahead of him, not wanting to be drawn into whatever game she was planning. As he rounded the side of the building, he saw Miss Willis in a group of guests gathered on the lawn. She was talking to a young gentleman, laughing at something he had to say. She looked young and carefree, and to an objective eye, he could see she was pretty even if he felt no stir of desire when he looked at her. She deserved the chance to choose her own future, not be encumbered with a man who did not care for her as a husband should.

'Are you coming over for the hunt?' Sylvia said as

she strolled up behind him, her hand brushing against his arm.

'A hunt?' he said, looking at the ladies and gentlemen in their morning attire, certainly not dressed for any sporting pursuits.

'A scavenger hunt,' she explained. 'Lady Montague is going to set us all some items to find, and the team who brings them back first will be the winners.' She smiled and gave a shrug, 'Most of this weekend I have participated in because it was expected I would be present and be seen, but this does actually sound fun. It is a glorious day, and I am eager to explore the gardens and estate a little more.'

Hugh nodded, thinking it would be a great opportunity to get Miss Willis alone to discuss their future.

'Ah, Miss Thompson, Lord Wilder, thank you for joining us,' Lady Montague said. 'Unfortunately, we have already formed teams, so I will have to pair you up together, although I am sure you do not mind.'

'Perhaps Miss Willis…' Hugh began, but Lady Montague interrupted.

'Ah, young love. Isn't it a wonderful thing, always wanting to be together. You will have a lifetime with your bride once you are married, Lord Wilder. Let someone else enjoy her company for a short time at least.' She turned away, and as Hugh went to speak again, Sylvia placed a hand on his arm, leaning in.

'Don't bother arguing with Lady Montague. Once she has finished explaining the rules, approach Miss Willis and her partner and just ask them directly. I will be paired with Mr Otterby quite happily.'

'Four items,' Lady Montague was saying, 'all from the house and the estate. Something to wear that is not your own, something to eat, something living, and something romantic. You have an hour. I will judge the best four items, and there is a prize for the winners. I cannot wait to see what you find.'

There was an excited chatter as the couples began to discuss what they might gather, and quickly everyone began moving away from the lawn.

Hugh was about to stride over to Miss Willis when he felt a hand on his arm.

'What did we miss?' Sir Percy said, arm-in-arm with his wife.

'A hunt for some items about the estate.'

Sir Percy raised an eyebrow and looked at his wife. 'What do you say, Mary? Do you wish to join in?'

'No,' she said with a laugh. 'Let's sneak off whilst everyone else is hunting.'

'You are a bad influence, Lady Turner,' Sir Percy said, and Hugh watched as they walked away.

'What is their secret?' Sylvia said as she stood beside him, looking after them as well.

'They are friends, great friends, before anything else. They actually enjoy one another's company. I suppose it is a good place to start with a marriage.'

'My parents were a little like that,' Sylvia said, a wistful note to her voice. 'They took every opportunity to be together. My father was a broken man when my mother died. He did his best, even tried to shield us from some of his grief, but you could see it in his eyes. Sometimes he would turn to the chair my mother used to sit in and begin to say something, only remembering a moment later that she was no longer with us.'

'Did they choose one another when they married?'

'In a way. My mother was the daughter of my father's business partner. I think it was always assumed one day they would marry, and they took their time getting to know one another first. It was no dramatic love story, but I could tell they did love one another fiercely by the time I was old enough to recognise it.'

Hugh thought of his own parents, the disdain in the looks his father would give his mother, the muted hatred in his mother's eyes for his father, hastily hidden. He'd often wondered what his life would have been like if his father had been different, if he hadn't pushed his mother to the edge of what she could tolerate and then watched her sink into the abyss of despair.

Quickly he pushed the thoughts away. Now was not the time to dwell on the grief he still felt. He had a job to do this morning, and he wasn't going to be distracted from it.

Looking around, he cursed quietly when he realised Miss Willis and her partner, Mr Otterby, had completely disappeared. He had no clue if they had headed inside the house or out into the wider estate.

'Did you see where Miss Willis and Mr Otterby went?' Hugh asked.

Sylvia spun around, her eyebrows furrowed as she looked for them. After a moment, she shook her head.

'No.'

'Damn.'

'You wanted to talk about your future with Miss Willis.'

'It is time,' he said, his voice gruff.

'Good. She will be pleased to have things settled.'

'I can hardly do it if I cannot find her.'

Sylvia shrugged. 'The game is one hour. At most you will have to wait a little over that. Then you will know exactly where she is going to be. You have waited a year, Hugh. One more hour is hardly going to make any difference.'

He grunted, knowing she was right.

'Come on. I have an idea where to find something living. Surely that has to be the hardest one.'

'I'm not trying to entice that bird of yours to perform.'

Sylvia laughed. 'I wouldn't dream of bringing you and Rosa together. She is traumatised enough, poor dear.'

'*She* is traumatised?'

'She thought you were attacking me.'

'She mauled me.'

'Hardly. A little light, friendly warning, that was all.'

'Hmm.'

'Come, accompany me. We will talk of nothing serious for the next hour, and then when we return, you can take Miss Willis somewhere quiet and discuss everything you need to. Otherwise you will brood on what has to be said.'

'You know me too well, Sylvia,' he murmured.

She smiled at him, her eyes twinkling with affection, and he felt a heaviness in his chest he could not explain.

'Where first?'

'To the fishpond. I saw tadpoles there the other day when I was exploring the estate, looking for you.'

'We will need something to collect them in,'

'You don't mean to carry them back in your hands?' she teased.

'Let us get a bucket from the stables, and then we can head over to the pond.'

They walked arm-in-arm to the stables, where one couple were arranging for a groom to ready a horse to be their *something alive*.

The fishpond was not too far from the house, tucked to one side behind the small walled garden. It was of good size, sunken into the ground so the surface of the water was below ground level. There were some lily pads floating on the top, their stems and roots just visible in the semi-murky water.

'Look there,' Sylvia said as they approached the pond. 'Do you see? Tadpoles.'

Sure enough, there were dozens of little tadpoles darting through the water.

'My brother and I would often spend spring days dipping for tadpoles in the local pond.' Sylvia smiled at the memory 'He was older, of course, and tried to boss me around as all good older brothers do, but he was always the one who ended up falling in.'

'What was the age difference between you?'

'Four years.' Sylvia pressed her lips together. 'We had a wonderful childhood. I feel blessed I got to spend it with him.'

'You must miss him.'

She nodded without saying anything at first, her eyes focussed on the writhing mass of tadpoles in the pond.

'Terribly,' she said eventually. 'He lit up the world. His smile, his energy. When he entered a room, everyone gravitated towards him. I often thought it was unfair he had such natural charisma when I was so shy, but he would tell me I was exactly as I was meant to be.'

'A wise man as well,' Hugh murmured.

'He was, and kind. He could tell through our letters how much I was grieving once our father died, and he insisted I come join him in Port Royal. I was so looking forward to seeing him when I was on the *Lady Catherine*, I could think of nothing else.' She shook her head. 'Then there was the shipwreck, and Captain Willis brought us back to England. Of course I thought we had some time. There was no indication, no reason to worry I would never see Robert again.'

Hugh realised for the first time the gaping hole the loss of Sylvia's brother had left in her life. He had been her only family, but more than that, he had loved her. She had gone from knowing there was someone who cared for her no matter what to being truly alone.

'I'm sorry you never got to see him again,' he said quietly.

'I am too. Do you know I still write to him? Foolish, isn't it? I still sit at my little table and tell him what has happened in my day or anything of note in the neighbourhood. I try to think of stories that would have made him laugh, I did love to hear his laugh.'

Hugh had the overwhelming urge to gather Sylvia in his arms and hold her close to him. She was exud-

ing a heartbreaking loneliness, and he realised he had
been so caught up in his own woes these last few days
he had barely noticed it, but it had been there all the
same. None of her connections were deep or meaningful now. She had no history with anyone still living, and
her circumstances meant she had not met anyone she
could trust and begin to build those new relationships.

That had been how he had felt when he boarded the
Lady Catherine a year and a half earlier. The voyage to
the Caribbean was poorly timed so soon after his father's
death. Hugh had known he should stay in England, es-
tablish himself as the new Viscount, make his mark on
the estates he held, and take up his position in Parlia-
ment. He hadn't mourned the loss of his father, but it
had thrown into focus how he had no living family, no
one who shared his name. Sir Percy had been there for
him, of course, and a small group of good friends, but
it was different to people who shared your blood. Then
he had received a letter from someone claiming to be
his half brother, sharing the same father. This man al-
leged the old Lord Wilder had taken his mother as a mistress on a trip to the Caribbean two decades earlier, a
trip Hugh remembered his father taking to look at some
land on St Lucia. Fuelled by this feeling of being alone,
Hugh had booked passage to the Caribbean without his
normal careful consideration of all the circumstances.

He shook his head ruefully at the memory. Of course
it had been a hoax, a rogue who had heard of the old
Lord Wilder's death and thought he might make a few
pounds from a supposed connection. After being rescued, Hugh had done what he should have all along and

sent an agent to investigate on his behalf, a sceptical man who had easily uncovered the scam. It had been a foolish decision to rush off to the Caribbean, one born of feeling suddenly alone in the world. He could understand a little how Sylvia was feeling now.

'Tell me of this cottage you hope to buy. Where are you planning to go?' He felt a pang as he said the words and wanted to grasp hold of her, to tell her she shouldn't be planning a future alone, but right now he had no right to ask anything of her.

Sylvia crouched down, eyeing up the pond and the tadpoles within. It would be quite a reach down, and they would have to be careful not to topple. The pond wasn't deep, but he didn't fancy traipsing back to the house sodden and covered in pondweed.

'There is this pretty little place on the south coast, a town called Rye. It is built by the sea on a hill, and the main street winds its way to a summit. We used to holiday there sometimes when we were children, there or a place nearby by the name of Winchelsea. I can imagine it can be bleak in winter—the area is surrounded by marshland— but I think it would be a lovely place to settle.'

'I can imagine you in a cottage by the seaside,' he said, wishing for a moment he could give up everything else and join her in her dream.

'I have this idea of perhaps a tiny cottage—it doesn't need to be much just for me—but also a little garden. I want to grow flowers and have somewhere I can sit in the sunshine.' She shrugged as if steeling herself against the possibility it might never happen. 'It depends on how well the book sells, of course. I am not expecting it to support me for the rest of my life, but if I could raise enough to pay the rent on a cottage for a year or maybe two, I am sure I could find a little employment to keep me going in the longer term. My publisher is hopeful for more than that, but even he admits it is hard to tell what will sell and what won't.'

Hugh suddenly had this image in his mind of Sylvia alone in her little cottage, struggling to put food on the table whilst he and Miss Willis grew fat off the profits off his estates. It left a horrible taste in his mouth, and his resolve hardened. He would set things right with Miss Willis, and then perhaps...

Letting the thought drift away, he smiled briefly. There would be time to reconcile with Sylvia, time to make her see their mistakes were not irreversible.

'How are we going to do this?' Sylvia said, moving closer to the edge of the pond.

'Careful. I'm not jumping in to fish you out if you fall in. You'll have to take up residence with the toads.'

'Why do you assume I will be the one to fall in?'

'You are leaning dangerously close to the edge whilst I am standing a foot further back. It is simple mathematics.'

'It won't be simple mathematics if I push you in,' Sylvia muttered.

'Let me see if I can reach,' Hugh said, kneeling down beside her. He took the bucket and reached down to the water below. The bucket skimmed the surface of the water, collecting a little, but it wasn't far enough under the surface to sweep up any tadpoles.

'Perhaps if I lie down,' Sylvia said, seeming not to

think of the white material of her dress as she lay down on her stomach on the grass. 'Here, give me the bucket.'

He rose and passed her the bucket, his eyes unable to stay away from the curve of her buttocks as her dress fell in waves of material over it.

'Do you remember washing day?' he said, the words out of his mouth before he could stop them.

Sylvia looked round sharply, her eyes wide with surprise. He could tell by the blush on her cheeks she did remember washing day.

'Do you mean…?'

'Sorry, I didn't mean to say that out loud.'

'Even thinking about it…'

'I cannot censor every single one of my thoughts, Sylvia.'

Her eyes bore into him, and then a hint of a smile appeared on her lips.

'I *do* remember washing day,' she said.

'I used to love washing day.'

'What made you think of that?'

He coughed, knowing he could not tell her it was the thought of her buttocks that had sparked the thought.

'The water, I suppose.'

She looked dubiously at the fishpond, a far cry from the bubbling pool they had bathed in on the island. They'd only had one single set of clothes with them, and they'd been battered and ripped by the shipwreck and the storm. There was some debris from the ship washed up on the island, and after a couple of months they had been forced to fashion some rudimentary garments to cover them as their clothes fell apart. Early on in their stay, before their clothes fell apart, they had agreed to have a dedicated time where one of them would use the natural pool in the middle of the island to bathe in without the other ever going near. Later on, once they had given up all pretence of resisting one another, they had still enjoyed washing day, where they scrubbed their clothes as well as their bodies, and lounged around naked from sunup to sundown.

'Can you reach?' he said, trying to distract her from the realisation that he still thought of her undressed and in his arms often.

'No.' It was hardly surprising. She was considerably shorter than he was. Even with her dangling over the edge perilously, the bucket was still only skimming the water.

He sighed and lay down on his front beside her. 'I hope no one happens upon us. I do not know how I could explain this away.'

She passed him the bucket, and this time he was more successful, scooping up half a bucket of water as he dipped it into the pond. They both peered in.

'No tadpoles,' Sylvia said. 'We need to get a little further out.'

He watched in amazement as she shuffled forwards, hanging out over the lip of the pond edge.

'Sylvia,' he said, a note of warning in his voice.

'Stop being so cautious and hold my legs.'

'I cannot hold your ankles.'

She scoffed, looking at him. 'I know you have touched dozens of women's ankles before. You've certainly touched mine.'

'Not in public.'

Sylvia glanced theatrically left and right. 'There is no one here. It is a hand on my ankle for a few seconds.'

'It is as though you are desperate to ruin yourself this weekend.'

This time she snorted, shaking her head. 'It is like nothing of the sort,' she said, wriggling forwards even more, hanging perilously low over the sunken pond.

'Good Lord, Sylvia, have a care. The pond is not all that deep. If you fall in and crack your head, that could be a nasty injury.'

She wriggled her ankles but didn't say anything, whooping ecstatically when she scooped a bucketful of water. As she pulled the bucket up he could see her balance teetering, and with visions of them both falling in the pond, he launched himself forwards and grabbed hold of her ankles. Sylvia stiffened at his touch, and he wondered if she had just suggested he hold her to unsettle him, thinking he would never really do it.

'It's heavy,' she said, hauling up the bucket, twisting as she did so and almost falling into the pond. Hugh lunged forwards and grabbed her by the waist, anchoring her as he reached down with his free hand to take the bucket from her and set it on the grass. Sylvia was now half-rolled onto her back, her skirts caught up around her knees, and Hugh's body was pressed close to hers, almost on top of her at the waist.

He knew how scandalous this would look if anyone came upon them and scrambled back quickly, knocking Sylvia off balance in the process and sending her rolling back towards the pond. Visions of Sylvia tipping over the edge filled his mind, and he reached forwards, grabbing the front of her dress and pulling as hard as he could. There was an almighty ripping sound that made both him and Sylvia call out in shock, and he felt the material give under his hand. Thankfully her roll backwards had been curtailed, but as he looked across at her he could see he had torn away the front section of her dress, revealing her stays and chemise underneath.

Sylvia looked down, aghast, scrambling to sit up.

As she raised her eyes to meet his, Miss Willis came into view round the corner of the walled garden, strolling alongside Mr Otterby.

'Miss Thompson, are you hurt?' Miss Willis said, rushing to Sylvia's side. Her eyes darted over the other young woman's dress, the huge tear apparent immediately.

'No, I am fine. Thank you for your concern.'

Miss Willis frowned, then looked at Hugh, her expression darkening.

'Did you do this?'

Hugh stood, brushing the dirt off himself, and went to offer Sylvia his hand, but miss Willis blocked his path to her, standing with her hands on her hips.

'Did you do this?' she enquired again, this time a note of hysteria in her voice.

'It was an accident Miss Willis, nothing more,' Sylvia said, and he could see she was doing her best to keep her voice light.

'You ripped her dress?'

'He didn't mean to,' Sylvia said.

Hugh stepped forward and saw Miss Willis flinch.

He couldn't believe she would think he was capable of whatever it was she was suspecting, although he knew the scene she had come upon was far from ideal with Sylvia splayed on the ground, dress ripped and him a few feet away as if she had shoved him off.

'We were catching tadpoles,' he said, keeping his voice calm despite the wave of horror rising inside him. *This* was how it all started, how lives were ruined and futures destroyed. One innocent thing misconstrued, one rumour started, and nothing was ever the same again. He got that horrible feeling, the one that built up from the bottom of his chest and threaten to suffocate him, as Miss Willis looked at him disbelievingly.

'Look,' Sylvia said, standing up, holding her ripped dress across her body. 'I got the tadpoles.'

'Damn tadpoles,' he muttered.

Sylvia thrust out the bucket and Miss Willis turned to peer inside.

'It was all an accident?' Mr Otterby said, a note of hope in his voice. He wouldn't want to get involved in an argument with a viscount, but his honour would demand he not stand by if a lady's safety were in question.

'Lord Wilder warned me not to lean too far,' Sylvia said. 'I didn't listen, and I almost toppled in. He lunged to grab hold of me, but all his fingers could grasp was the front of my dress. He managed to spin me round so I didn't fall in, but my dress ripped.' She looked down at the fabric. 'Nothing a little needle and cotton won't fix.

'Perhaps you could accompany me back to our room, Miss Willis,' Sylvia said, and he saw the young woman's expression soften a little. She nodded, and arm in arm he watched the two women quickly hurry away.

Hugh turned to Mr Otterby, who was grinning at him now Miss Willis's hard stare was not in the vicinity.

'A little rough and tumble gone wrong, eh?'

Hugh stepped up to the man, towering over him. He did not often use his height to his advantage, but he was glad of it now.

'She toppled. I caught her. That is all there is to it. I trust I can rely on your absolute discretion?'

Mr Otterby cleared his throat.

'Miss Willis will not say anything,' Hugh pointed out, 'so if I hear anyone else talking about it, I will know the rumour came from you.'

'I will not utter a word, my lord,' Mr Otterby said.

Hugh nodded quickly, leaned down to pick up the discarded bucket, and walked away.

'Damn tadpoles,' he muttered again.

Chapter Fifteen

Hundreds of fish darted this way and that in the shallows, and at first we expected it to be easy to aim and skewer a fine specimen for our dinner. Only once we had tried a few times did we realise the fish were too wary, too quick to swim away at the first hint of danger. Spear-fishing required infinite patience, the ability to stand completely still until the fish forgot you could be dangerous, forgot you were a living creature at all.

'You must tell me if he tried to force himself on you,' Miss Willis said, fire burning in her eyes as she stalked backwards and forwards across the floor in their bedroom.

She had been quiet on the walk from the lawn upstairs, and Sylvia realised this thought was what had been brewing the entire time.

Sylvia had shed the ripped dress and was now in the process of lifting her pink gown over her head. She wriggled it into place before answering.

'You can't think he is capable of that,' she said eventually

Miss Willis shrugged. 'I don't know the man. We've shared half a dozen stilted conversations. He has talked about his estates, a little about his family, but mostly about the weather or noteworthy events. I know nothing of his character, of what sort of morals he has.' She took a deep breath and then continued, glancing nervously at Sylvia. 'And I can see how he looks at you.'

'How does he look at me?'

'Like a man trapped in the desert who has just spotted an oasis.'

'No,' she said quietly. Perhaps once, but not now.

'I thought he may have been overtaken by his passion and forced himself on you.'

With her dress still undone, Sylvia took Miss Willis's hands in her own and led her over to the bed, pressing her to sit down.

'Lord Wilder is not like that,' she said emphatically. 'He is a good man. Stubborn and tenacious, and he always thinks he is right, but at his core, he is a good man. He would not tolerate bringing harm to someone, and he certainly would never force himself on anyone.' She made sure Miss Willis was looking her in the eye before she continued. 'You do not have to worry about his character. Of course he is flawed— there are things he gets wrong, and he is loath to admit them—but his heart is good, and he is a man of morals.'

'Do I have to worry about how he feels for you?'

Sylvia glanced away for a moment, not wanting to lie to Miss Willis but finding it hard to strike the right balance between the truth and the version they wanted everyone to know.

'Lord Wilder and I did once have great affection for one another. We were trapped on that island for a long time, and we became close, but the circumstances were exceptional. We both agree that our friendship would not flourish in the real world, and that is all there is.'

'Will you answer me one thing honestly, Miss Thompson?'

Sylvia nodded her head, knowing she might regret the promise.

'Do you love him?'

She felt the heat flood to her cheeks and her pulse soar as Miss Willis's eyes fixed on her own.

'In some ways, I think I do,' she said eventually, 'but not enough to overcome the hurdles that are placed before us.'

'Thank you for being honest,' Miss Willis said. 'And for reassuring me as to what sort of man he is. I have a lot to think about.'

'You do not regret coming here?'

'No. I felt trapped at home, walled in by my father's expectations and the implication that somehow it was my fault Lord Wilder and I were not already married. Something needed to change, and I wish to settle this matter once and for all.'

'Do you wish to marry Lord Wilder?'

'I would be a fool if I said no, wouldn't I?' She stared into the distance wistfully.

Sylvia took a moment before she spoke, trying to ensure none of her own wants and desires impacted the words she said to the young woman next to her.

'I am not foolish enough to say wealth and social status are not important when considering happiness. I have known a little of the worry that comes from not having an income, and it is terrible indeed. Nonetheless, I do not think it brings the happiness so many assume. You can be a viscountess and unhappy just as you can be the wife of a solicitor and very happy.' Sylvia smiled softly and thought of her parents. 'I think it is far more important to consider whether you can spend thirty or forty years tied in marriage to Lord Wilder. Is that something you want?'

'It would be easier to answer if I knew the man.' Miss Willis paused and then reached out and took Sylvia's hand. 'Can I confide in you, Miss Thompson? I feel as though you are the only person who might understand my torment.'

Sylvia hesitated for a second, but on seeing the pleading look in Miss Willis's eyes, she nodded.

'I do not think I ever told you anything of my life before the voyage on the *Chameleon*, the trip where we rescued you and Lord Wilder from the Isla Ana.'

'No, I don't think you have.' For a moment, Sylvia regretted keeping Miss Willis at such a distance. She could see now the young woman wasn't her enemy in all this, just another innocent caught up in the winds of fate.

'I didn't normally accompany my father on his voyages. In fact, it was my first time at sea. Normally he left me at home, in the care of my school mistresses in term time or a companion during the holidays.'

Realising quite how young Miss Willis must be, Sylvia felt a ripple of unease. Someone of sixteen or seventeen shouldn't be manipulated into a marriage when up until recently they had been sheltered from the harsh realities of life.

'I had got myself into a little trouble,' she said, looking down and biting her lip.

Sylvia let out a little involuntary gasp, and quickly Miss Willis shook her head. 'Not that sort of trouble, just I had developed a fondness of a young man I knew my father would deem unsuitable.'

'Where did you meet this young man?'

'On Saturdays we were allowed to walk into the local village from our school. I normally went with a group of friends, but one Saturday we argued, and I went in alone.' She smiled as she talked, remembering the fateful day. 'That's when I met him, Alexander. He's a farrier. He was an apprentice at the time, but now he's got his own workshop.'

Sylvia could tell by the dreamy, faraway look in Miss Willis's eyes that she still harboured feelings for the young man.

'Your father found out?'

'Foolishly, I told him. I thought he would be pleased. He was always going on about finding me a husband, a good, honest, hardworking man,' she scoffed. 'That wasn't what he meant at all. After making all his money, he wanted to use me to buy our way into the gentry.'

'He did not approve of Alexander.'

'He most certainly did not. He was due to leave for the Caribbean the next week, and he insisted I go with him so I would have no further contact with Alexander.'

'Then your father rescued Lord Wilder and me, and

it must have seemed like fate was handing him an opportunity he could not ignore.'

Miss Willis screwed up her face, coming to sit down beside Sylvia. 'I *do* see Lord Wilder is an attractive man, but he is so very old.'

Sylvia blinked and suppressed a smile, wondering what Hugh would think of being called *so very old*.

'What do you want now, Miss Willis?'

She remained silent for over a minute, contemplating the question. 'I am in love with Alexander,' she said eventually. 'I thought those feelings might fade, but they have not. I have seen him on only a handful of occasions since we returned, but each time I lay eyes on him, I feel as though my heart is going to burst through my chest.'

'Does he reciprocate these feelings?'

Miss Willis nodded. 'He does, but he knows I have much to consider.' She paused and bit her lip again. 'I know the sort of life I would have with Lord Wilder. It would be a life of comfort and luxury, one where I never had to worry about anything. What is more, I do not doubt he would be a kind if somewhat distant husband. I am also aware that if I break our engagement and choose a life with Alexander, I am choosing a harder life, but one with a man I care for.'

Sylvia squeezed Miss Willis's fingers, shocked by the revelation, and wishing she could take some of the angst and worry away for the young woman.

'I cannot tell you what to do, Honoria,' she said, using the young woman's given name as it felt too intimate a talk to be formal. 'I urge you to talk to Lord Wilder. He is far from the aloof man his outward façade sometimes projects. You may find you realise you do wish to marry him. He is a good man, a kind man. He would treat you well,' Sylvia paused and then decided to be open with the young woman as she had so openly confided in Sylvia. 'But I know all too well how difficult it is to ignore the pull of your heart.'

'I owe him an apology, for reacting as I did when I saw you lying there with your dress ripped. I believed...' She trailed off.

'It was a brave thing for you to do, standing there to confront him. Many would have merely averted their eyes.'

Miss Willis reached out and took her hand, squeezing it.

'I am glad I came here for another reason. Whatever happens with Lord Wilder, I hope we will remain friends.'

Sylvia swallowed, nodding, not able to bring herself to speak. She couldn't imagine the torture of having to see Miss Willis and Hugh married, growing happy in one another's company. Of course she wanted happiness for both of them, but it would be hard to witness Miss Willis having everything Sylvia had once thought would be hers. Yet it wasn't her place to push Miss Willis towards her young man, this Alexander. It had to be a decision she made of her own accord.

'Now, let's get you ready for lunch. It must be almost time,' Miss Willis said.

'I wonder if we have been missed at the culmination of the hunt,' Sylvia said.

'I am sure Lady Montague has noticed our absence. No doubt it will be a black mark against us.'

Chapter Sixteen

Our first row was over something as mundane as where to build our permanent shelter. We had tried a few rickety structures designed to protect us from the Caribbean storms that raged with surprising frequency, but as the weeks ticked by, we began to think of something sturdier...a place to call home. I wanted to stay as close to the beach as possible so we would not miss the chance to signal any passing ships, whilst Lord Wilder was adamant we chose a higher spot with better building terrain. We argued for three days before coming to a reluctant compromise of a spot with a view over the beach but on higher ground than I had suggested.

Hugh felt agitated. The whole day had been an unmitigated disaster, and now here he was, standing at the edge of the ballroom, scowling at anyone who came near, unsure if Miss Willis was going to announce to the room that he had taken advantage of Sylvia out by the fishpond that morning.

He had seen them briefly at lunch, seated far down at the other end of the table, but after the meal, the ladies had all been whisked off in carriages to the local village to shop for something or other. Sylvia had placed a reassuring hand on his arm as she had passed and murmured that everything was fine, but she was far from cautious most of the time, and he needed to know for certain what had passed between the two women.

As they had the previous evening, Sylvia and Miss Willis entered the ballroom arm-in-arm, heads bowed together in conversation. Hugh had to resist the urge to stride over, aware his every move would be watched and noted. Tonight was the night. Tonight he would talk to Miss Willis. He would find out her views on their engagement and then, depending on what she told him, see if there was a way out of this agreement.

Thankfully the two women greeted their hostess and then wandered in his direction.

'Miss Willis, Miss Thompson, I trust you had a good afternoon.'

'Yes, thank you,' Miss Willis said.

Hugh looked uneasily at Sylvia, but she just gave him a reassuring smile.

'Would you care to dance?'

'Are you asking me or Miss Thompson?'

He paused, Sylvia's name on his lips, biting it back.

'Both of you. Not together, of course, but the evening is early.'

'Thank you, yes, I would. Then I think we need to talk, Lord Wilder,' Miss Willis said.

As the first dance was announced, Hugh led Miss Willis to the centre of the ballroom, a feeling of anticipation washing over him. It was a heady sensation, knowing that finally he was going to be able to move forwards with his life. For a moment, he wondered what he would do if Miss Willis was set on the marriage. He had visions of Sylvia drifting further away as he desperately scrabbled for a way to appease everyone. He clutched at his cravat, trying to loosen it, but it had been expertly tied so sat snugly against his neck.

'It is very warm in here, isn't it?' he commented as he took Miss Willis by the hand. Suddenly he felt parched, as if he had been stumbling through the desert all afternoon, and wished he could abandon the dance to rush to find a drink.

With great effort, he took control of himself. All it would be was a little discussion, nothing more.

Out of the corner of his eye, he saw Sylvia take up a place with Mr Otterby. He frowned, wishing they were closer so he could hear what they were saying. It would have been a good opportunity to talk to Miss Willis. Hugh had attended hundreds of balls and dances in his time in society. He was an expert at enquiring after someone's health or reminiscing about mutual friends whilst stepping out a quadrille or twirling his partner in a waltz. Yet today, every time he reached for a topic of conversation, his mind wandered, and his eyes were drawn to the spot a few feet away where Sylvia was dancing. Miss Willis remained quiet too, and as he glanced down at her, he saw there was trepidation in her eyes.

'Is something amiss, Miss Willis?'

She cleared her throat and looked up at him.

'Let us talk in private, my lord.'

He nodded, that feeling of doom building even more and threatening to take his breath away completely.

After what seemed like an eternity, the dance finished, and he bowed, then escorted Miss Willis to the edge of the dance floor.

'Do you wish to find a private spot now to talk?'

'No, not yet. Everyone is far too observant at the moment. They will notice us slipping away. Let everyone relax into the evening a little more. Dance with Miss Thompson first.'

'Very well.'

They stood in awkward silence until Sylvia returned on the arm of Mr Otterby, who took one look at their solemn faces and excused himself.

'I believe this is your dance,' Miss Willis said, ushering them towards the dance floor.

Hugh offered Sylvia his arm, and he saw the flicker of a smile on her lips as she took it. Their dance was a quadrille, rapid and energetic. It meant he couldn't spin her in his arms one last time, or enquire as to what Miss Willis had said earlier in the afternoon, but he felt some of his earlier melancholy and anxiety begin to lift as they danced.

'I explained everything to Miss Willis,' Sylvia said as the music finished and they applauded the musicians. 'She understands it was an accident, nothing more.'

'She looked at me as if I was trying to force myself upon you.'

'She was very fierce, very protective. I like that about her.'

'She does have spirit.'

'That is a good thing if she is to be married to you.'

'I feel like I might take offence at your next words, but please explain.'

'You are very strong-willed, Hugh. You do not need a mouse for a wife. You need someone to challenge you, to keep you from getting bored.'

He laughed. 'Is that why I like you so much?'

Her eyes shot up to meet his, and for a moment, neither of them could move. Then Sylvia shrugged. 'I never pander to you,' she said, taking his arm as he led her off the dance floor. 'All your adult life, people have bowed and scraped because you are the all-important Viscount. Yet the people you truly like are those who do not stand on ceremony with you. Look at Sir Percy and Lady Turner. They treat you like a normal person, not someone elevated by his rank in society, and they are the people you enjoy the company of.'

'You have *never* pandered to me,' he murmured. 'I wonder why that is?'

'Because when we got to know one another, it didn't matter if you were a viscount or the lowliest beggar. Rank meant nothing on the Isla Ana. We were just two people stripped back to our cores, vulnerable with each other and able to be ourselves without the constraints of society getting in the way.'

It was the truth. For the first few days on the Isla

Ana, Hugh had been consumed by the practicalities, of finding fresh water and food, of building a shelter. He had worked alongside Sylvia, initially seeing her as a hindrance and then slowly realising she had strengths and skills of her own. They had spoken only when necessary at first, thrown together by this bizarre set of events, both shaken by the tragedy that was the sinking of the *Lady Catherine*.

Gradually, as it became apparent they might be able to survive on the tiny island, Hugh had felt something inside him relax a little, and he had seen the same in Sylvia. They had started to talk as they gathered fruit from the trees or collected water for drinking. It was a few words at first, but over the first few weeks of their entrapment on the island, it had grown until Hugh had realised he longed to hear Sylvia's voice first thing in the morning and last thing at night before they went to bed.

He had not realised how much he was falling for her until one calm night when they were sitting on the beach, looking up at the stars. They'd been talking of dancing, and Hugh had stood and held out his hand. Sylvia had hesitated, but only for a moment, and then she was in his arms. They'd danced a waltz by moonlight, and as he looked down into her dark eyes, he had realised he would give up everything for one kiss with this woman.

'Do you sometimes wish we were never rescued?' he asked.

The question made her stop where she was, and Hugh could see the difficulty she had answering it. Then she gave a too-bright smile.

'We shouldn't dwell on what-ifs, Hugh. We are here now. Our lives have been swept in a certain direction, and there is no turning back the tide.'

Miss Willis stepped forward and looked at them both. 'I wonder if it would be prudent to have Miss Thompson accompany us, as a chaperon,' she said, tilting her head to one side.

'I really don't think…' Sylvia began.

'Surely that is…' Hugh started.

'We are walking on a tightrope, my lord,' Miss Willis said pointedly. 'There is much speculation and gossip around the three of us. I do not wish to be caught somewhere alone with you, Lord Wilder, and fuel that gossip.'

'I agree a chaperon is a good idea,' he said, 'but perhaps we could ask someone else.'

'Lady Turner would not mind, I am sure,' Sylvia suggested.

'I do not know Lady Turner. You might trust her with this, but I need to satisfy myself that no one will speak a word of what passes between us. You do not mind, do you, Miss Thompson?'

He saw Sylvia hesitate and then shake her head.

'Good. Let us find somewhere quiet. We have a lot to talk about. Will you excuse me one second? I promised Mr Otterby a dance earlier. I should arrange to step out with him later.'

'This is going to be fun,' Sylvia said, closing her eyes for a moment once Miss Willis had darted across the room.

'I wish I could spare you from this,' he said. It was going to be a difficult half an hour, but perhaps in the end it would be for the best that Sylvia was there. It was her future as much as his or Miss Willis's they were discussing.

She shrugged, looking resigned to her fate. 'Miss Willis has been kind and understanding since she arrived. If she wishes me to be there, I owe her that. Many young women would have made much more of a fuss about everything than she has, and they wouldn't have looked to make me a friend.'

He inclined his head, knowing Sylvia was right. It was odd how Miss Willis had attached herself to Sylvia, but things could have been much worse. It would have been understandable if she had arrived with a set of demands and shouted them out until he had agreed to set a date and finalise their futures.

'All done,' Miss Willis said, returning with a smile. Now, shall we make use of the morning room? It will be quiet in there.'

They left the ballroom, Miss Willis and Sylvia first, Hugh waiting for a few minutes and then following behind. He found them in the cosy morning room, two candles lit to illuminate the darkness. Miss Willis was sitting on a comfortable chair in the middle of the room whilst Sylvia was perched uncomfortably on a hardback chair in the corner.

'Good,' Miss Willis said. 'Finally a chance to talk.'

'I must start with an apology. I know I have not been as attentive as a young woman might like from her fiancé.'

Miss Willis laughed. '*Inattentive* is letting yourself off lightly, my lord. You have been downright neglectful. I know you have visited my father on numerous occasions, but a few fleeting meetings hardly speak of a doting fiancé, do they?'

'It was never my intention to cause you any pain,' Hugh said, choosing his words carefully. It wasn't Miss Willis's fault he felt an overwhelming dread when he thought of this marriage, and he should have behaved better towards her. He should have asked her what views she held rather than focussing on her father. 'I have had a lot on my mind this year.'

'I understand, Lord Wilder, and I think I understand a little more of the bargain made between you and my father on the *Chameleon* now.'

Hugh glanced at Sylvia, but she was looking at her hands, her expression inscrutable.

'It feels a little underhanded, a little dirty, although I acknowledge marriages are frequently built on far less.' She cleared her throat and then looked directly at Hugh before continuing. 'I suppose what I need is clarity.'

'Clarity,' he murmured, wishing he had some.

'Clarity on your plans, your priorities, your wants for the future.' She took a deep breath, and he realised how much courage it must take for her to address him like this. She was a confident young woman, but she was at a disadvantage here. He could drag his feet forever if he so desired, and she would be able to do nothing about it.

'I have other…considerations…my lord. I want to know what it is you think you can offer me.'

'You are undecided?' He felt a flicker of hope.

'I am not my father, Lord Wilder. I have no desire to force you into something that would make you unhappy for the rest of your life, yet I get the impression you are not happy *now*. Of course I see the advantages of marrying you. I would be a viscountess with no need to worry about money or my position in society ever again, and Miss Thompson assures me you are a good man.'

Hugh glanced at Sylvia again, but her expression was inscrutable, her eyes downcast. The only movement was the gentle rise and fall of her shoulders.

'I have always prided myself as a man of my word, Miss Willis. I gave my word to your father I would marry you, in exchange for him keeping quiet about certain issues from my time on the Isla Ana. I do not wish to hurt your feelings. We do not know each other well, and much of that is my fault, but I will not deceive you.' He paused, glancing over at Sylvia, wishing he hadn't made such a mess of things this past year. 'I have been trying to find a way to break our engagement that will keep everyone's reputations intact and will keep your father happy.'

Miss Willis nodded thoughtfully.

'May I ask why, my lord?'

Unbidden, his eyes flicked across again to Sylvia, and Miss Willis held up her hand, nodding in acknowledgement.

'I see,' she said softly.

The young woman nodded and then stood, exhaling slowly. 'I think I need a minute, my lord. I am going to step outside for a breath of air.'

Before he could say anything to stop her, she was gone, closing the heavy wooden door quietly behind her. Hugh sank down into the chair Miss Willis had just vacated, resting his head on his hand. The words had not come as he had hoped. There had been no eloquent speech to persuade the young woman to release him from the promise he had made.

For a whole minute, neither he nor Sylvia spoke, both sitting there in complete silence, and then he stood up and let out a growl of frustration.

Sylvia stood too, and with a few steps had crossed the room, standing in front of him, her eyes still downcast.

'This is a disaster,' he murmured.

'A complete disaster,' she agreed.

He wanted to reach for her, to pull her close. Right now he needed nothing more than to have her body pressed against his. Every kiss they had shared flashed through his mind, and he knew exactly how her lips would taste if he lowered his mouth onto hers. He couldn't help himself. He raised a hand and ever so lightly brushed his fingers against her cheek, loving the sharp gasp she gave as his fingertips touched her skin.

'I wish we were never rescued,' he said, leaning forwards to whisper in her ear. 'I regret everything, every single thing, that has happened since.'

She pulled back, looking up at him, her eyes glistening with tears. 'I wish that too.'

He almost gave in to the urge to kiss her. She looked so beautiful with her cheeks flushed and her lips slightly parted. He knew she wanted to be kissed, and the thought of walking away from her hurt him physically, yet he knew his honour would not allow him to kiss her whilst Miss Willis was part of his life. It would be unfair to all of them.

They were standing close together, their bodies almost touching, and Hugh was so focussed on the woman in front of him that he didn't hear the door open behind them. The first he knew of someone else being in the room with them was the shocked gasp.

He spun, expecting to see Miss Willis, but instead there were four faces staring at them, a mixture of shock and glee. At the front of the group was Mr Otterby. He was accompanied by their hostess, Lady Montague, and behind them were Lady French and Mr Knox.

Feeling Sylvia's hand on his arm, her fingers digging into his skin, he turned back to her and saw the pure panic on her face.

'Lord Wilder,' Lady Montague exclaimed, 'I cannot believe what I am seeing. And with your fiancée not twenty feet away in the ballroom.'

'Not his fiancée.' Miss Willis's voice rang out loud and clear.

Hugh felt his whole world crumble and collapse around him. His whole purpose this past year had been to keep Sylvia safe, shielded from malicious gossip. It had been the reason he had agreed to the engagement to Miss Willis and the reason he had kept away from Sylvia, despite the often overwhelming desire to see her. Now here they were, caught together in a scene that was worse than any scandal they had been faced with so far. Even if he married Sylvia, the scandal would plague them their entire lives.

The image of his mother's face, drawn and thin, in the months before her death flashed into his mind. He could see history repeating itself and someone he loved hounded to an early grave by the horrible rumours that swirled around them.

'Honoria,' Sylvia whispered beside him, and he turned to see her looking guilty and stunned all at the same time.

'Lord Wilder and I broke off our engagement earlier today,' Miss Willis said, her voice with a hint of hardness in it as if challenging anyone to contradict her. 'We realised there were too many hurdles to overcome, and it left him free to pursue Miss Thompson.'

'I knew it,' Lady Montague murmured, a look of triumph on her face.

'Is this true, Lord Wilder?' Lady French asked, jostling her way further into the room.

He glanced at Miss Willis, who was smiling at him encouragingly. There was no malice in her eyes, no hurt or disappointment.

'It is true,' he managed to say as more people joined the back of the little group, drawn from the ballroom by the commotion.

Sylvia seemed to shrink beside him. All he wanted to do was to reach out and grab hold of her hand, to tell the onlookers to leave them alone, to stop taking pleasure in the affairs of others.

'I am delighted to announce Miss Thompson has agreed to be my wife,' he said, hoping no one would notice how his voice caught in his throat.

'What are you doing?' Sylvia whispered.

For a second he thought she might deny it, but even though her expression was severe, Sylvia nodded in confirmation.

'Hopefully this engagement will not be as long as your last, Lord Wilder,' Lady Montague said, drawing a titter of laughter from Lady French.

'I would wager there will be a wedding by the end of the year,' Miss Willis declared, then turned and made her way back through the crowd.

'Come, we will toast your good news,' Lady Montague announced, and slowly the little crowd that had gathered began to filter back through to the ballroom.

Hugh and Sylvia had no choice but to follow, and Hugh was relieved when Sir Percy and Lady Turner fell into step beside them, warding off the well wishes of strangers.

'I am ecstatic about this development,' Lady Turner said, leaning in so both he and Sylvia could hear her lowered voice. 'But do try to look a little happy. If I did not know the news at the moment, I would wager you were both going to Tyburn for hanging day tomorrow by the expressions on your faces.'

He tried to force a smile onto his face, drawing a harsh intake of breath from Sir Percy.

'Thank the Lord there are no children present. That is not a smile, Wilder.'

'I think I need some air,' Sylvia murmured, and he turned to see her face had drained of colour.

'Air later,' Lady Turner said gently. 'Right now you two need to look and act like the happy couple who have just got everything they have ever wanted. *This* is what people will be talking about for months. Do not give them any more fodder.'

Sylvia nodded, rallying a little, and Hugh wished

he could have a moment alone with her. He knew if he could just hold her hand, look into her eyes and tell her everything would work out, it would be good for the both of them.

Instead they were swept into the ballroom and handed champagne in crystal glasses.

'Tell us, Lord Wilder, about this extraordinary turn of events,' Lady Montague said, motioning for even the musicians to fall silent. 'A few hours ago the whole world thought you ready to marry Miss Willis, and now we hear you and Miss Thompson are destined to be together.'

Hugh wanted nothing more than to stride out of there, taking Sylvia with him, but he knew now was the time to step up.

'Spin them a yarn,' Sir Percy said into his ear as he stepped forwards. 'You can make anyone believe anything when you want to.'

Hugh looked down at his glass for a few seconds, composing himself, and then lifted his eyes to meet the crowd, a smile filled with warmth and delight on his face.

'I do not wish to bore you,' he said, taking Percy's advice and imagining he was stepping up to a mock political debate as they had done at school. It was all about charm and dazzling your audience so they never realised you hadn't said much at all. 'But it is a tale I could tell again and again, so perhaps for a few minutes, you will indulge me.' He reached back and took Sylvia's hand in his own. 'The start of our relationship was unconventional, to say the least. At first we were merely two people with no common interests trapped on an island together. Then, as time passed, we realised we actually liked one another. Now, I know there are many reasons we marry. Money, perhaps, isn't that right, Lady French?' The older woman smiled at the jest, 'Or to align two great families, like Lord and Lady Montague. But the marriage I am most in awe of is that of my dear friends Sir Percy Turner and his wife, Lady Turner. I have long admired their dedication to one another, and I have wanted to base my marriage on the same foundation of friendship as they did theirs.'

Lady Turner pressed her lips together as if trying not to cry.

'That is why, when Miss Thompson and I renewed our acquaintance and realised we cared for one another in the same manner, I knew I had to ask her to marry me.' He cleared his throat, his eyes searching for Miss Willis but not able to find her anywhere. He didn't blame her for sneaking out. He would have done the same if he were able.

'So I give you the future Lady Wilder, my beautiful future wife.'

He raised his glass in a toast, and the whole room mirrored his gesture. For the next few minutes, they were surrounded by the other guests wishing them well.

'Good speech,' Lady Turner said as she leaned in and gripped his hand once the furor had died down. 'Suitably romantic. Hopefully most people will just remember the love story, not the circumstances in which you were found.'

'I am delighted, old boy,' Sir Percy said, clapping

Hugh on the back. 'Absolutely ridiculous how long it's taken you to get to this moment, but I am so happy you're here now.'

'You haven't said a word,' Hugh said to Sylvia. Since confirming she had accepted his proposal, the proposal he had never actually made, Sylvia had been silent by his side. The well-wishers gabbled on, and Sylvia had managed to summon a smile, but it was forced and un-natural. 'I know it is a lot to take in.'

'I need to get out of here,' Sylvia murmured.

'I will accompany you.'

'No,' she said sharply. 'I need to be alone.'

Without another word, she slipped away, looking wraith-like as she dodged between the groups of guests. Hugh followed her progress with his eyes until she was out of the ballroom and disappeared from sight.

Running a hand through his hair, he turned back to his companion, unable to think of anything but the de-spair on Sylvia's face as she had left.

Chapter Seventeen

We soon lost track of the days. It was difficult to keep count when each day was identical to the last. Nevertheless, we tried, carving a groove on a tree trunk for each day we spent on the island, and soon five turned into ten and then twenty. By this time, rescue seemed increasingly unlikely, and we turned our thoughts to how we would live more permanently on the island.

Sylvia felt a mess. She had flopped down on the bed the night before without even bothering to undress or unpin her hair. For hours she had lain there, thinking again and again of the look of agitation, then bewilderment, then resignation on Hugh's face as he realised there was no option but to propose to her.

She knew he desired her still, that part of him still wanted her. As he had said just before they had been discovered the evening before, if only they had never been rescued. Yet it was far from enough. He didn't want to marry her. If he had, there had been ample opportunity over the last year to break things off with Miss Willis and seek Sylvia out. Instead she was now just another burden for him to carry, a responsibility he hadn't asked for but would do the right thing by.

Sitting up, she slowly took the pins out of her hair, setting them on the bed beside her before crossing to the little table and picking up her hairbrush. It was only then that she noticed the piece of paper folded neatly. Last night she hadn't looked at anything but the canopy above her bed.

Carefully she picked it up and unfolded it, her eyes dancing over the neat, unfamiliar handwriting as she read.

Dear Miss Thompson,
I am sorry for leaving without saying goodbye, but I thought it for the best if I was no longer here to complicate matters. I wanted to write to thank you for your friendship over the last few days and wish you the very best for your future. I also think I should perhaps explain why I did what I did and beg your forgiveness.

I did come here to Somersham Hall to speak to Lord Wilder and decide on my future. It has been a long year of uncertainty, but I think deep in my heart I knew something wasn't right.

When I learned of what my father did, I was appalled, although not altogether unsurprised. He is a doting father with slightly dubious morals, but I am sorry you were ever caught up in one of his

schemes. I truly had no idea he had blackmailed
Lord Wilder into proposing to me.

I looked for comfort in the familiar and spent
some time with Alexander before I came to Somersham Hall, reminding myself of what we shared
and what my life would be like if I chose him.

When I arrived at Somersham Hall, I could see
from the very first moment there was something
between you and the Viscount. The shared glances,
the spark as one of you enters the room and the
other can't help but look. I know many young ladies would be jealous, but I don't think I ever regarded Lord Wilder as mine to be jealous of.

I watched you earlier this morning from the
window as he showed you how to fence, and I
could imagine you two happily married with a
brood of children.

I knew I could not stand between you. I want
what you have, but I do not think I would ever get
that from Lord Wilder.

I realised I already have a man who looks at
me the way Lord Wilder looks at you. He may not
be wealthy, but he is kind and hardworking, and
I do not need anything more than that.

This is the part where I must ask your forgiveness. This evening I arranged the little meeting
between the three of us, insisting you come as
a chaperon. I know Lord Wilder wanted to talk
to me about cutting off our engagement, but I
thought it the opportunity for a little more. I had
always planned to step outside, and after a min-

*ute or two, I arranged for Mr Otterby to burst
in on you with some of the other guests. He was
happy to oblige, thrilled to be included in the little subterfuge.*

*Please do not hate me. I know there are a hun-
dred reasons why you feel you and Lord Wilder
should not be together, but I can only see the way
you both light up when the other is near. That is
special.*

*Perhaps one day you will visit me in Ports-
mouth, and we will both be happily married.*
With warmest wishes,
Honoria

Sylvia staggered back across to the bed, unable to
take it all in on the first read-through. Honoria had set
everything up the night before, not out of malice, but
because she thought she was doing the right thing, the
kind thing.

Closing her eyes, she let the paper drop onto the bed.
Clearly Honoria did not understand Lord Wilder. Sylvia
knew she didn't either, not fully, but she was starting to.

Now she would become one more obligation for him
to feel stressed about. If she was completely honest with
herself, she did want to marry him, but not like this. She
wanted him to realise how in love with her he was, to
declare he could not live without her, not be forced into
marriage by a series of unfortunate events.

'I deserve more than that,' she said quietly.

With a sigh, she set the letter aside and continued
getting ready. She needed to be away from this house,

away from the nosiness of their hostess and the rest of the guests, and most importantly away from Hugh.

Of course she would marry him. It would be foolish of her not to. Whatever he had said last night in his clever speech it wasn't enough to stem the gossip entirely. By tomorrow, half of London would know they had been found almost embracing in a room alone together, without a suitable chaperon. The scandal Hugh had been so desperate to avoid would find them. It meant Sylvia had no other options. She would have to accept his proposal, once one actually came.

Downstairs Hugh was pacing backwards and forwards in the hallway like a wounded tiger, agitated and ready to snap. She had seen pictures of the great beasts in her father's books and was fascinated by the brightly coloured but ferocious animal. His expression didn't brighten when he saw her, and she had the urge to sail past him with not a single word, but she knew she couldn't afford to be so petty.

'You disappeared last night,' he said with no preamble.

'I told you I needed some time alone.'

'I thought you would come back. Lady Turner even went and knocked on your door.'

Sylvia had heard the gentle knock half an hour after she had fled the ballroom but hadn't been able to bring herself to move to answer the door. She'd wanted the whole world to disappear and leave her alone in her misery.

'We have a lot to talk about,' Sylvia said.

She let herself be led out onto the terrace behind

the house and then down the few steps onto the lawn. There was a stone bench twenty feet into the garden, positioned to allow the people resting there a good view over the parterre. They sat, and Sylvia's leg brushed against Hugh's, sending a shiver through her. She hated that even when she was angry, he could still make her want him.

'I do not think there is any way around it,' Hugh said after a moment. 'We shall have to be married. Too many people saw us in the morning room together, and Lady Turner assures me it looked as though we were embracing from her position near the back of the crowd. There will be gossip and scandal whatever we do, but society in general will forgive a young couple who are a little indiscreet before their wedding day but go on to marry quickly.'

'Is that what we are?'

Hugh paused and looked at her, but didn't answer, instead pushing on with the speech he had prepared.

'We will do things right, get the banns read and aim to be married within two months at the most. There will be speculation, of course, but there is still time before the season starts for some other scandal to come along and take the focus away from us.' He nodded in satisfaction. 'In a year, perhaps two, people won't have forgotten this weekend, but it will be a more distant memory. We will be able to breathe a little easier, go about our lives without it hanging over us.'

'Two years?' Sylvia asked, incredulous.

'The gossips have long memories.'

She stood, shaking her head. 'It sounds like you have

everything worked out, Hugh. I will leave you my address. Please notify me as to what date you want me to be available.'

He was too shocked to reply, and Sylvia got a little spark of satisfaction by the confusion on his face. If he was going to treat it all as a huge disaster to be managed by treading a path to satisfy society, then she could be distant and cold too.

'Sylvia,' he called, and she heard footsteps behind her. 'What are you doing?'

'You do not need me. At least not yet. On the day of the wedding, I am sure it will look better if I am there, but for the rest of it, you are capable of organising everything on your own.'

'Why are you being like this? I know it is a shock, the scandal an inconvenience.'

'An inconvenience,' she exploded. 'That is exactly what you are treating me like, Hugh. The biggest inconvenience you have ever faced.'

'You can't stand there and pretend you are pleased with how events have turned out.'

'Once I would have been thrilled to be marrying you. Once it was all I ever dreamed of. Foolish me thought it would be something joyful, not an ordeal to try to manage with no happiness whatsoever.'

'Happiness,' he said, as if it were a foreign concept.

'Yes, Hugh, happiness.' She sighed loudly. 'I do not feel the need to know all the details of the arrangement. I need some time and space to take in everything that has happened.'

Before he could say any more, she strode away, torn

between desperately wanting him to chase after her and tell her he *did* love her, he'd just been distracted by everything that had occurred and just needing to be alone.

Without stopping, she dashed back inside and up to her room, wishing she had her own carriage, a horse even, anything that meant she did not have to rely on the whims of Lady Montague to arrange her onward travel.

Three hours she sat in her room, changing position every now and then but otherwise completely bored to her core. She had long ago finished the one book she had brought with her. She had made the bed to her satisfaction, despite knowing the maids would strip the sheets as soon as she left. Now she was staring out the window.

There was a soft knock on the door, and Sylvia went to answer it, hoping it might be a message from Lady Montague. A timid maid stood outside, shifting from foot to foot.

'Lady Montague asked me to give you a message, miss. She's given her carriage to the Knoxes to get them home. When it returns, the driver will take you into town.'

'Thank you. Do you know how far away the Knoxes live?'

'I heard the groom say it was at least an hour away, miss. I don't know where exactly.'

Sylvia looked at the clock anxiously. There was one coach on Tuesdays from Sevenoaks to London, leaving at one o'clock and getting to the capital late afternoon or early evening depending on the road conditions.

If she missed that, she would be trapped in the town for another night, having to spend some of her closely guarded, dwindling funds on a room for the night.

She glanced down at the trunk at the end of her bed and out at the glorious day.

'How long does it take to walk into town?'

'A little under an hour, miss.'

'Is it easy to find the way?'

'Oh, yes, you follow the road downhill until you come to the end of it and then turn left. It climbs quite a hill, but that road takes you into the High Street eventually.'

'Thank you.'

The maid hurried away, and Sylvia picked up her trunk. It was a little awkward to carry, but she managed to tuck it under her arm, adjusting it so it was well-balanced, before she left the room.

'Come on, Rosa,' she said, and the bird fluttered from the bedpost and perched on her shoulder.

'You can't mean to walk, Miss Thompson,' Lady Montague said, rushing out of the drawing room as Sylvia descended the stairs. 'The day is warm, and it is quite a distance into town.'

'I do not mind, Lady Montague, I enjoy walking.'

'I am sure one of the other guests can take you. Lord Wilder, perhaps. He has not departed yet.'

'No,' Sylvia said sharply, and then smiled to soften her response. 'I am eager to walk, Lady Montague. I must thank you for a wonderful weekend and for giving me the opportunity to do my reading to your guests.'

Lady Montague waved a dismissive hand. 'Always a pleasure, my dear. I think we both got something out of you being here. You truly are going to walk into Sevenoaks?'

'Yes.'

'Well, then, I wish you all the best, Miss Thompson, and I hope our paths cross again soon.'

Sylvia hurried out before anyone else could stop her, head bent and walking faster than was ideal in the heat of the morning. She felt beads of perspiration form at the back of her neck as she marched the length of the long drive, only slowing down once she was out of sight of the house and on the road.

She took a moment to rest in the shade, adjusting her bonnet so it would shield her from the worst of the sun. It was a glorious day, beautiful for the time of year, and she resolved to slow down and try to enjoy it. There was still plenty of time to make the journey on foot to Sevenoaks before the coach left for London.

Starting out again, she allowed herself to breathe deeply and slowly let go of the tight restraint she'd kept on her emotions and thoughts this morning. Everything had changed, her plans, her hopes for the future. All dashed in a few seconds of indiscretion.

'It isn't all bad,' she murmured to herself. If she had been told a year earlier, before they had left the Isla Ana, that she was going to be married to Hugh, to be his wife and spend the rest of her life by his side, she would have been ecstatic. It was all she had wanted, all she had dreamed of. Perhaps one day she would be able to recapture that excitement.

For a moment, she let herself be taken back to the island in her thoughts, almost feeling the warm Caribbean breeze on her skin. The little flashes of memory were intoxicating, and she thought of the time they lay on the sandy beach under the shade of the palm trees, her head resting on his chest, his hand tracing lazy circles on the bare skin of her arm. Most of the time on the island they did not talk of the future. For weeks after they had first washed up on the island, Sylvia had thought of little else but rescue, but as time had ticked on and she and Hugh had built a life for themselves, they hadn't often spoken of what might happen if they were rescued. The possibility seemed so distant, so unlikely. That afternoon, though, Hugh had turned to her, his eyes heavy and his lips soft as he kissed her, and he'd told her he wanted to spend the rest of his life with her in his arms. Sylvia had felt happy then, happier than any other time in her life.

Coming back to the present, she knew of course she could refuse him, but that would be foolish. He wasn't wrong to worry about scandal and gossip. It was a malign force that pervaded everything and everywhere. The notoriety might help her sell a few more books, but her plans for a quiet existence in Rye would have to be vastly readjusted. Gossip was not limited to London, and she knew small communities could be even more judgemental and unaccepting, especially of a stranger.

No, the only sensible option was to marry him.

Feeling her heart squeeze in her chest, she tried to focus on the little things around her. The blossoms on the trees and the wildflowers in the hedgerows. But it was no use. All she kept seeing was Hugh's shocked face when he realised he would have to marry her.

She understood, or at least partially. He was pathologically scared of scandal, yet this past year had been nothing but speculation and gossip directed at him. She knew that the tragic death of his mother and the way she had been hounded out of society still had a huge impact on how he responded to things, yet it hurt that he could not see beyond that and find some positives in the situation.

Sylvia adjusted the case under her arm and wondered if things might be different once they were married. Maybe he would relax a little, realise that she was not like his mother and would not be traumatised by the gossip.

She felt the tears prick her eyes, knowing it would not be the case. She didn't fit into his world, his expectations. Just as he hadn't wanted to marry Miss Willis because she wouldn't make the perfect Viscountess, he would be thinking the same about her. It had been the reason he had started to pull away from her when they were rescued, and it was why he looked so glum now they were destined to be married. It hurt to know she had been forced upon someone.

The clattering of hooves and rumble of carriage wheels approached from behind, no doubt one of the guests leaving Somersham Hall. For a moment she wondered what it would be like to have her own carriage, ready to transport her around the country on a whim.

With a groan she saw a carriage painted shiny black with a gold crest on the side. It rolled to a stop beside her. Before the wheels had even stopped moving, Hugh jumped down.

'What do you think you are doing?' he demanded.

'Walking.'

'Where to? With your trunk under your arm? You are aware how far away the town is?'

'To town to catch the coach. Yes, with my trunk, and yes, I know how far it is.'

'You're being ridiculous.'

'How am I being ridiculous? I need to be on the coach to London at one o'clock. If I waited for Lady Montague's carriage to return, it would be far too late. We do not all have our own carriage and set of horses available at the snap of our fingers.'

'Get in,' he said, his voice brooking no argument.

'Thank you for your kind and gracious offer, Lord Wilder, but I prefer to walk.'

'Get in.'

She ignored him and began to stalk away, wishing she didn't look so unbalanced by carrying the weighty trunk.

She heard an exasperated sigh, and then he strode after her.

'If this is what our marriage is going to be like, you will drive me to a premature grave.'

'Don't give me ideas,' she muttered. 'Being a wealthy widow is looking like a great option right now.'

'Sylvia, stop.'

She paused and turned to face him.

'Stop being so stubborn and let me take you into Sevenoaks. We can sit on the opposite sides of the carriage and not say a word to one another if you would prefer.'

She eyed the carriage. The trunk was getting very heavy.

'Fine.' It would be fifteen minutes by carriage at the most to the town. Surely they could manage being civil for that long.

He reached out for her trunk, gripping hold of it and walking back to the carriage, and passing it up with ease to the groom who sat behind the horses. Rosa fluttered from her shoulder and took up a perch on the top of the carriage, looking like a majestic watchman.

'My lady,' he said with an exaggerated bow, holding out a hand to help her up.

Ignoring the proffered hand, she climbed up, taking a place on the plush seat and sinking into the cushions.

Outside she heard Hugh murmur something quietly to the driver, and then he got in himself, closing the door.

True to his word, he sat in silence as the carriage made its way through the narrow country lanes. It was hilly in this part of Kent, beautiful green rolling countryside with oak trees in every field and sheep grazing on the land. The sunlight was dappled on the road, but every so often, they would come out from the cover of the trees into the golden light. Apart from the fateful trip to the Caribbean, Sylvia hadn't travelled much in her life. Her childhood was spent in the upmarket town of Tunbridge Wells, and she had been to visit friends and family across Sussex and Kent, as well as spending some time in London, but she hadn't ever been anywhere else either in the country or the world. She yearned see a little more of the different cultures she had glimpsed on her travels to meet her brother in Port Royal, but there was something magical about this part of England, something that made her realise no matter where she went, she would always end up here.

Hugh cleared his throat but still didn't speak, his eyes on her, studying her carefully.

Turning her attention back to the window, she contented herself with observing the countryside.

Half an hour later, she leaned even further out the window, trying to catch a glimpse of the town they were heading for.

'Are we going in the right direction?'

Hugh didn't answer, and Sylvia looked over at him, frowning.

'The sun has been on our left the whole time, which means we're heading north, not south. I thought Somersham Hall was a little north of Sevenoaks.'

'We're not heading to Sevenoaks.'

'What? That is where the coach leaves from.'

'I know. You're not getting the coach.'

'What do you mean?'

'We need to talk, and we can hardly do that if you run off back to London without even saying farewell.'

'You've kidnapped me?'

'Don't be ridiculous.'

'Ridiculous? I am in your carriage going to some unknown destination when you said you would take me to Sevenoaks.'

'*Kidnapping* is rather dramatic a word.'

'What would you call it?'

'Taking you home in the comfort of my carriage.'

'I don't want you to take me home.'

He waved a hand. 'I will drop you wherever you wish.'

'Here. I wish to be dropped here.'

He shook his head, a frown on his face. 'Wherever you wish within reason,' he corrected himself.

'Stop the carriage.'

'No.'

'Hugh, I am being serious. Stop the carriage.'

'We're in the middle of nowhere, Sylvia. I'm not stopping the carriage.'

She reached up and banged hard on the roof of the carriage.

'It won't do any good.'

'Why not?'

'I've instructed the driver not to stop unless I give the command.'

Sylvia leaned out of the window, drawing in a great breath of air.

'Stop,' she shouted, loud enough to make the driver look round. She saw his face was set in a stony expression, and before she could make eye contact he turned back to face forwards.

'I told you he won't stop.'

'You really have abducted me.'

'I hardly think a magistrate would see it that way. "Yes, your honour, my fiancée got into my carriage of her own free will, and I transported her back to her lodgings in London."'

'That is not what is happening here.'

He shrugged and settled back in his seat.

'We have three to four hours together, depending on the congestion when we enter London. May I suggest you inform me when you are calm enough to enter a rational discussion?'

Sylvia gripped the handle on the door and, with a

deep breath, flung it open. She wasn't thinking clearly, her mind clouded by a fog of rage. All she wanted was some time away from Hugh, some time to resign herself to the fact she was marrying a man who saw her as a burden.

'Hell and the devil, Sylvia. Are you trying to get yourself trampled by the horses?' Hugh shouted as he pulled her back onto her seat, slamming the carriage door closed.

With her heart pounding in her chest, Sylvia sat back in her seat and closed her eyes. For a long time she didn't speak, didn't move, didn't do anything but breathe in and out, aware how foolish her last action had been but unable to settle the fierce emotions that were raging inside her.

They travelled for almost an hour in complete silence. She was aware of Hugh's eyes on her, watching her cautiously like you might do to an unpredictable injured animal, but she merely sat there, seething, every slight, every hurt bubbling up to the surface.

Chapter Eighteen

Later, after we were rescued, we learned the locals called our island the Isla Ana. In the Taino dialect, Ana is the word for flower, and all over the interior of the island were the most beautiful tropical blooms. On the day we thought might be my birthday, I was awakened to the smell of fresh fish cooking over a fire and the largest and brightest bouquet of flowers I have ever seen placed outside the entrance to the shelter. Lord Wilder reminded me that although we were far from home, some things are still worth celebrating.

For over an hour, the only movement from Sylvia was the rise and fall of her chest and the blinking of her eyelids. She sat like a statue, rigid and proud, her face fixed into a scowl.

This was not his finest moment, far from it, but he had panicked when Lady Montague had told him Sylvia had left already, opting to walk the four miles into

Sevenoaks rather than spend twenty minutes in the carriage with him. When he'd seen her struggling along, the trunk under her arm, he knew he had to get her into the carriage so they could properly talk.

Outside he heard a faint shout, and then the carriage began to slow. Quickly he looked out the window, trying to ascertain what the problem was, aware that if they stopped, Sylvia was likely to jump out and run. She could be unpredictable like that, ruled by her emotions. Even if they were miles from anywhere, she would make a dash away from him just to make the point she didn't want to be there.

Hugh sighed, knowing he was handling this badly. He had honestly thought that if he'd got Sylvia inside the carriage, she would relax a little and agree to his plan of taking her back to London. He needed to talk to her, to make her see that whilst he was preoccupied with ensuring they were not hounded by the gossip surrounding their engagement, he was genuinely thrilled with how things were working out. In the space of a few days, he had reconciled with Sylvia and broken free of his unwanted engagement. Now he was engaged to the woman he should have married all along.

'I can see a cart ahead,' he said as he sat back in his seat, looking at Sylvia. 'I don't know if it is blocking the road.'

Their carriage stopped, and a moment later, Hopkins, the driver, popped up by the window.

'Looks like an accident, my lord. I'll go and check, see if there is a way past.'

'Is anyone hurt?'

Hopkins shrugged, and Hugh glanced at Sylvia. Knowing he had to go and help, he gave her a firm look.

'Stay here.'

She didn't respond. Didn't even acknowledge his words.

Quickly he hopped down and took in the scene. An old cart was lying at an angle, one wheel missing from the back right. The wheel itself had rolled away some distance and was splintered and broken in the road. There was a horse, a docile-looking sturdy workhorse, standing still attached to the cart. At first Hugh couldn't see anyone with the cart, which seemed strange. At the very least, the owner should have uncoupled the horse from the splintered cart before going for help.

'Hello,' Hopkins called, looking around in puzzlement.

Hugh walked around to the far side of the cart, hoping he wasn't going to find some poor farmer half-squashed underneath.

There was no one there.

'That's odd,' Hugh murmured. He glanced over to where Hopkins had hold of the horse's bridle, murmuring calming words.

Before he could say anything more, two men stepped out of the trees, pistols raised and aimed at Hugh and Hopkins.

'Don't move,' one said with a thick country accent.

Hugh glanced at the carriage, wondering if Sylvia had worked out what was happening. He hoped she stayed hidden inside. There was no need for the bandits to even know she was there.

'It looks like we've landed a right rich one here,' the second man said, stepping forwards and holding his pistol up against Hugh's chest. It wasn't the first time Hugh had been robbed, and he knew the danger came from the nervousness of the highwaymen. They were skittish like horses. One twitch over the trigger of the pistol and it could be the end of someone. 'Your money, *my lord.*'

'And your valuables,' the first man said. 'Quickly.'

With smooth, calm movements, Hugh removed his coin purse and gently threw it at the feet of one of the men. It made a satisfying clink.

'I have no jewellery,' he said, holding up his hands to show they were not adorned with rings as was the fashion amongst the wealthy.

'Is this all you carry?' one of the bandits sneered. 'Search him.'

The second man approached cautiously, patting Hugh down whilst keeping his eyes fixed on Hugh's for any hint of rebellion. They were well-practised at this routine, and Hugh thought they must have been at it a while. They were not foolish youths, either, instead men of around his own age, although it was apparent they'd had harder lives than him. One had a long scar down his cheek that continued onto his neck, a nasty-looking wound that had healed poorly. The other was missing several teeth. Despite their coarse appearances, they were well-built, muscular and strong, and Hugh wondered if they had spent time in the army. There was something about their demeanours, about the seamless way they worked together, that made him think they'd had some sort of training.

'Tie them up,' the leader of the two said, passing the rope to his companion.

Now was the time to act if he was going to do something. He weighed up the options carefully. The bandits hadn't shot them on sight, which they would have been easily able to do from their positions in the trees, and now they were tying them up. It hinted that they weren't proposing to kill Hugh and Hopkins, merely leave their two victims bound whilst they made their escape. If he tackled them, there was a good chance someone would get hurt.

His only reservation was Sylvia. No doubt she was quivering in the carriage, hoping the two men didn't approach. If he was tied, incapacitated, and the bandits did look inside the carriage, Hugh wouldn't be able to protect her.

'Don't think about it,' the man with a rope said in a low growl. 'I can see the rebellion in your eyes. I will shoot you without a second thought.' He called back over his shoulder. 'This one is looking at me funny.'

'Tie them up and be done with it.'

Roughly the bandit prodded them over to a tree with his pistol, making them stand with their backs to the trunk on opposite sides, which he wrapped the rope round. He pulled it tight, digging the rope into Hugh's middle and trapping his hands by his sides.

'Let's see what you've got in these fancy boxes, shall we?' the leader said once he was happy Hugh and Hopkins could not escape. Hugh felt a stab of panic as the man approached the carriage, pulling himself up to the top to throw down the trunks that were secured on top. He jumped back down, then went to peer inside the carriage. Hugh swallowed hard, bracing himself for Sylvia's scream.

Panting from exertion, Sylvia tried to make her breathing as quiet as possible. She had jumped out of the carriage the moment Hugh's back was turned, fuming at him holding her hostage as he had. She meant to walk along the road until she came to a village where hopefully she could ask a friendly farmer for a ride on his cart to Sevenoaks or at least directions to the town.

Something had made her pause as she slipped round the back of the carriage. Perhaps it was an innate sense of danger. Perhaps it was a need to see that no one was truly injured, crushed under the cart with the broken wheel. She turned back, meaning to reassure herself all was well before she continued on with her plan.

All had not been well. As she had watched, the two bandits had come out of the trees, pistols raised and pointed at Hugh and his carriage driver. The men were tall and muscular, difficult to overpower even without their guns.

She'd waited for them to spin and turn their pistols on her, but it had never happened. Whilst they were distracted, she had made a dash into the trees, trying not to make a sound. That was where she was hiding, behind a fat tree trunk, wishing her skirt was a little more practical for running through woodland. Somewhere above her she heard the flutter of wings, and with relief she saw Rosa come to rest on a tree branch nearby. At least that was one less thing to worry about.

Carefully she peered out, watching as one man climbed on the roof of the carriage and threw down the trunks. The other man's attention was still on Hugh and Hopkins, even though they were tied to a tree.

Glancing over her shoulder, she tried to work out her options. She couldn't just leave the two men there, but it would be dangerous to try something, especially as the bandits were armed as well as much stronger than her.

She had heard stories of highwaymen, of carriages being stopped in the dead of night on dangerous strips of road, but never had she thought she would bear witness to such an event, in the middle of the day as well.

Both men were next to the trunks now, leaning over the first, scrabbling through the contents. It was Hugh's trunk, and they seemed pleased with a couple of items, pocketing them as they rifled through. With a flare of panic, Sylvia realised they would move on to her trunk next, and then they would realise a woman had been in the carriage. No doubt they would come looking for her, incensed she had tried to get away. Either she needed to run now, to make a dash through the trees before they realised she had been there, or she had to make a move to confront them.

Her gaze rested on a hefty fallen tree branch about as long and thick as a man's arm. Silently she bent down and picked it up, weighing it in her hand. It was heavy, but not too heavy to manoeuvre. With her eyes fixed on the two bandits, she picked her way through the trees to the edge of the road, taking her time and getting as close as possible without being seen.

The two men were just turning to her case, their backs to her, bending over the buckle that secured it. Sylvia took a quiet step forward and then another. She glanced over to where Hugh was tied to a tree, his eyes wide as he saw her emerge from the shadows of the woods. She could tell he was willing her to go back, to not do anything foolish, so she bent her head, ignored him and focussed on the task ahead.

Silently she crept forwards, getting within touching distance of the two men as they managed to open the case. She raised the branch as high as she could.

'It's women's clothes,' one of the bandits said in puzzlement.

Sylvia struck, bringing the branch down hard on the first man's head. He toppled sideways, his body sprawled out in the dirt. His companion was quick, and before Sylvia had a chance to raise the branch again, he was halfway up on his feet, spinning round to face her.

She did the only thing she could think of. She rushed at him, arms spread wide, using the momentum to crash into him and push him to the ground. Sylvia knew he had a pistol and was aware of the hard metal between them as her body landed on top of his. He'd gone down with a thud, and she knew he would be winded for a moment. Her only chance was to be quick. His strength far outmatched hers, and if he had the chance to grapple with her, all would be lost.

Before he could recover, Sylvia drove her knee as hard as she could into his groin. He let out a low, wounded groan of pain and instinctively curled up into a ball. Sylvia grabbed hold of his pistol, taking it easily from his hands as he rolled around in agony. She scrambled backwards, grabbing the other man's pistol as well.

'Don't move,' she said, aiming a pistol at the injured man.

'You wouldn't shoot,' he rasped, half sitting up.

'Move one more inch and we will find out,' Sylvia said, sounding much calmer than she felt.

The bandit regarded her for a moment and then sank back onto his elbows.

Sylvia stepped away, keeping her eyes locked on the two men, aware the one she'd hit over the head with a branch could come round any moment. With two of them conscious, they might try to rush at her and overpower her.

'That was the most foolish thing I have ever seen,' Hugh said, his voice low with suppressed agitation.

'You're welcome.' Sylvia had known he would be disapproving, reprimanding her for putting herself in danger. She stepped towards the tree, holding the pistol steady in her hand, and crouched down, her eyes only momentarily flicking towards the rope that bound Hugh and Hopkins. Using one hand to unpick the knot would take a while, but she was aware she couldn't lower the pistol for a second. 'Keep still,' she murmured as Hugh began to strain against the ropes.

He stilled and she started to pull at the knot, wriggling her fingers into the gaps between the overlapping strands of rope until she felt it loosen. Something caught and she looked down, trying to work out if it were loose enough for the men to slip out. At that moment, she heard a scrabbling, and her head whipped round to see the conscious bandit on his feet and barrelling towards her.

Beside her there was a blur of movement as Hugh slipped out from the loosened rope, but Sylvia could see it would take him a few seconds to overpower the man, seconds they did not have. As Hugh darted past her she raised the pistol, aimed, closed her eyes and then squeezed the trigger.

The sound of the gunshot echoed around the surrounding woods, causing birds to take flight from the trees and small animals to flee in a frantic rustle of leaves. Sylvia swallowed and then opened her eyes, wondering if she had just killed a man.

Hugh and the bandit were on the floor, tussling. There was blood, but at this moment it was impossible to know where it had come from. Hopkins dashed past her, having escaped from his bonds too, but by the time he had reached his master and the bandit, Hugh had the other man pinned to the ground.

'Sylvia, the rope,' Hugh shouted.

With her hands still shaking, she untangled the rope from around the tree and brought it over to him. Only when the bandit's hands and feet were bound did Hugh stand up and come over to her.

'Are you hurt?' There was deep concern in his eyes as he checked her eyes, hands roaming from her shoulders down her arms and then up over her head.

'No,' she said, still shaking.

'That was a very brave and very foolish thing to

do,' he said quietly. 'You could have been captured or killed, and then…' He trailed off, breaking eye contact and shaking his head.

'What should we do with these two, my lord?' Hopkins asked.

'Take them to the local town. Perhaps they will have a magistrate to deal with them.'

'Yes, my lord.'

'Get them into the carriage, Hopkins. I will sit inside with them with the pistol. Sylvia can sit up top with you until we unload these two criminals.'

He groaned slightly and held onto his arm, and Sylvia looked down in consternation.

'You're bleeding.'

He smiled ruefully. 'Someone shot me.'

'I hit you?'

He shrugged off his jacket to reveal a bloodied shirt-sleeve, and Sylvia gasped. After tearing the hole in the material, he prodded at the wound for a moment, then gave a satisfied nod.

'A graze, nothing more. The bullet clipped me, but it is not embedded.'

Sylvia forced herself to look at the wound even though she sometimes felt a little light-headed at the sight of blood. It was not deep, but blood trickled from it in a constant narrow stream.

'We need to bind it.'

He nodded, watching as she searched the open trunks still lying discarded on the ground to find something of the right size and shape to wrap round the wound. She tied it tightly, making Hugh flex and relax his arm to ensure it would put pressure on the wound whatever he was doing with his arm.

'The second man was starting to come round, my lord, so I've tied him up too,' Hopkins said, crouching down to close the two trunks, fasten them and carry them back to the carriage.

'Are you harmed in any way, Hopkins?'

'No, my lord, just annoyed I let them get the better of me.'

Hugh turned back to Sylvia, his brow creased into a furrow.

'What were you doing in the woods? Before the bandits revealed themselves.'

She cleared her throat, all thoughts of running away long gone. All she wanted was to bury herself against Hugh's chest, to feel his warmth, the reassurance of his beating heart.

'It doesn't matter,' she said quietly.

'Miss Sylvia Thompson, you are one of the most reckless women I know. When you came out of the trees holding that branch, I nearly died of a heart seizure.'

She suppressed a smile. 'The bandit I hit did go down nicely, didn't he?'

'That is not the point. You could have misjudged the distance and whacked him with that big stick only to anger him.'

'I didn't, though.'

'You didn't.'

After a moment's hesitation, he reached out and wrapped her in his arms, holding her tight. Sylvia felt as though a great weight was being lifted off her shoulders and buried her head in his chest, inhaling his scent and revelling in the warmth and security she felt there. Later she would remember why she was so incensed with him, later she could go back to being angry, but right now she was just glad they were both alive.

Chapter Nineteen

When we caught sight of the Chameleon for the first time, I thought it a mirage. For weeks we had not talked of rescue, thinking we must be so far off the trade routes only a ship blown wildly off course would ever be passing. Instead we had thrown ourselves into making the island our home. Now, with the ship on the horizon, neither of us could quite believe what we were seeing.

Manhandling the two bandits out of the carriage, Hugh handed them over to the waiting magistrate, who directed some men to escort them into the local gaol.

'You have my sincere thanks, Lord Wilder. These men have been terrorising travellers on this road for months. We've sent out patrols but never caught sight of them.'

'Are they locals?'

The magistrate shook his head. 'I don't think so. I have never set eyes on them before. They've never come up before me in court.' He cleared his throat. 'I have a comfortable house and a good cook if you and Miss Thompson would like to stay before continuing your journey. We have a local doctor, too, who could have a look at that wound.'

He glanced at Sylvia, and she gave a minute shake of her head.

'Thank you for the kind offer, but we are eager to be on our way home.'

The magistrate shook his hand and then bid them a safe journey, turning to follow the two bandits across the square towards the tiny gaol.

'We can still make it home before nightfall,' Hopkins said, looking at the position of the sun in the sky. 'At least we will make the outskirts of London, if you want to try.'

'I think that is for the best, Hopkins. Thank you.'

They returned to the carriage, Hugh helping Sylvia up and waiting until she was comfortable on the seat before he sat down himself and closed the door. In a matter of minutes they were back on the country lanes, travelling at a moderate pace.

Opposite him, Sylvia sat with her eyes closed. He could see she was shaken by their ordeal, more so now she'd had time to consider the consequences had anything gone wrong.

'Do you want to talk about it?' he said softly.

She opened her eyes and looked over to him, and he had to resist the urge to bundle her onto his lap. He had this fierce protective instinct when it came to Sylvia. All he wanted, all he ever wanted, was to keep her safe from the horrors of the world.

'I keep feeling that panic I did when the bandit grabbed hold of me as we tumbled to the ground. I knew then I'd done something I might not get out of.'

'It was a very brave thing to do, Sylvia,' Hugh said. At the time he had been furious she would put her life in danger like that, but there was no need to reprimand her again. Now she needed reassurance that the world was still the same around her, that she was safe and nothing more bad would happen to her.

'I was petrified,' she said quietly. 'I watched them tie you up, and I knew if they spotted me, if they caught me, they would be able to overpower me so easily. Then I would be completely at their mercy.' He saw her eyes glaze over a little and quickly leaned forward to take her hands in his own. There was so much to discuss, so much to unpack between them, but right now he could see what she needed was gentle physical contact. Something to remind her she was still alive.

Her eyes flicked up to meet his, and Hugh felt a throb of desire and something deeper pass between them. He realised with a flush of pleasure that she was his to comfort, his to care for. It might not have come about in the best way possible, but it would mean they would wake up side by side every morning and fall asleep in one another's arms. *If* she ever forgave him.

The weight of responsibility began to press on his shoulders as he felt the burden of keeping Sylvia safe manifest itself. Their marriage would be blighted by scandal from the very first, and he would have to battle to keep it from permeating every aspect of their lives.

'Will you hold me?' She spoke the words so quietly he had to strain to hear them.

Moving carefully to sit beside her, he wrapped one arm around her shoulder and pulled her gently to rest against his chest.

For a few minutes they sat like that, bodies pressed together as if the past year had not driven a wedge between them. Hugh realised that despite everything, despite the way his hand had been forced, the potential for a life-ruining scandal and the perilous ordeal with the bandits, he felt happy for the first time in a very long time.

'You're smiling,' Sylvia said as she looked up at him. There was a look of bemused puzzlement on her face.

'Yes,' he said.

'We've just been attacked by highwaymen.'

'Yes.'

'We could have very nearly lost our lives.'

'Yes.'

'I shot you.'

'Yes.'

She shook her head, a smile tugging at the corner of her lips too. Hugh had the overwhelming urge to kiss her and, tired of fighting the desire that surged within him, he leaned over and brushed his lips against hers.

The kiss set off a reaction inside him. It felt like he was coming alive again after months of hibernation. Suddenly he forgot everything that had seemed such a big issue only a few hours ago and lost himself in the feel of Sylvia's lips and the heady scent that always intoxicated him.

He growled with satisfaction as she gripped his head, pulling him closer to her. Then, before he knew quite how they had got there, he'd spun her round and pulled her onto his lap.

They kissed as though they had been separated for a decade, desperate for one another's touch. Hugh felt the conflict rage inside him, torn between wanting to take his time, to savour every moment and driven by a need to quickly take in every part of Sylvia in case this was the last time.

'I've missed you,' he murmured, pulling away a little and nibbling on her earlobe. She shuddered as she always did, and Hugh wondered how he could have ever let her go. Surely nothing could have been as important as the woman in his arms. Quickly he pushed at the material of her dress, wanting to see as much of her as possible, hearing her gasp as the cold air hit the delicate skin of her breasts.

'I've missed you too,' Sylvia whispered in his ear, and Hugh felt hope and love surge up inside him. Somehow they would find a way through this, and once they had, their reward would be to experience this pleasure every single day.

'I am going to make love to you at least six times a day when you are my wife.'

'You will barely have time for anything else if you do that.'

'What is more important?'

'I know you have other demands on your time.'

'Everyone else will have to wait.'

He ran his hands over her body, feeling the warmth

of her skin through her chemise. Her dress was bunched at her waist, and he cursed the ridiculous number of layers women were expected to wear.

Quickly he pulled at the laces that held her stays in place, throwing the stiff garment on the floor with a surge of triumph.

'When we are married, you will not wear so many ridiculous layers,' he murmured as he lowered his head, kissing the base of her neck and then trailing down lower. He loved the taste of her, the feel of her, and he wanted to lose himself in her arms forever.

'Shall I walk around naked for the whole world to see?'

'No.' He growled possessively. 'Do not tease, Sylvia. This is a serious matter.'

'Then perhaps I will walk around naked only in our bedchamber.'

He felt a swell of victory at her words. It was the first time she had acknowledged their future together.

'Yes, better,' he said as he kissed her breast through her chemise. He loved the way she responded to him, the instinctive rocking of her hips towards him, the way she thrust her chest forward, eager for his touch. Ever since that first night they had spent in one another's arms on the Isla Ana, it had felt as though they were made for one another. Their bodies fit perfectly together and seemed to move in harmony.

Sylvia leaned down and kissed him again, her breath coming a little faster now. Her cheeks were flushed, and he thought she looked more beautiful than she had ever done before.

He groaned as he felt her hand reaching for him, pressed between their bodies. He lifted his hips, and she smiled as she succeeded in loosening his waistband, her hand slipping inside. Her fingers were warm and soft as she gripped him, and he pulled her closer so he could kiss her deeply.

Lifting her hips, he helped her to shift and then felt the exquisite tightness as he entered her, loving the sigh of pleasure that escaped her lips. She moved slowly at first, rocking backwards and forwards, letting her head drop back, loose strands of hair tumbling over her shoulders.

'I have dreamed of this every single night since we last lay in each other's arms,' he murmured in her ear.

'Me too,' she said softly.

Overcome by desire at her words, he gripped her hips and began thrusting up into her harder and faster, over and over until he felt her clench and climax, and he followed, waves of pleasure rippling through him.

For a long moment they didn't move, her chest pressed against his as the movement of the carriage gently rocked them. It felt good to hold her, as if finally he was exactly where he needed to be.

After a few minutes, Sylvia slipped from his lap, straightening out her chemise and picking up the battered fabric of her stays from the floor of the carriage. She didn't attempt to put it back on, instead adjusting the neckline of her dress so it preserved her modesty.

'Sylvia,' he said, his voice low. He knew they needed to talk, needed to repair this great rift that was between them.

She shook her head. 'Not yet, Hugh. I'm not ready yet.'

He nodded silently, wondering what she was trying to puzzle out.

'Will you sit with me, then?'

For a minute he thought she might refuse. Then, without a word, she slipped onto the seat beside him, her body nestled against his.

Chapter Twenty

*We signalled with fire, building up a great bon-
fire on the beach to catch the crew's attention on
the Chameleon, then waited for what seemed like
an eternity to see if the merchant ship would turn
towards us. At first it seemed like it would sail on
past, but at the last moment, it changed course,
and we knew we were saved.*

It was dark when Sylvia woke. The movement of the
carriage had lulled her, soothing away all the fears and
worries until she had lost the fight to keep her eyes
open. She'd slept long and peacefully, not plagued by
dreams as she sometimes was, but that meant it took a
few seconds for her to work out where she was.

'We're almost home,' Hugh said as she shifted against
him.

Sylvia stretched and then looked out herself, recog-
nising the narrow cobbled streets of the area she had
called home these last few months.

'How do you know where I live?' She had mentioned

Whitechapel, but they were fast approaching the street Sylvia rented a room on, and she certainly hadn't told him where that was situated.

He coughed, as if embarrassed, and looked out of the window.

'Good Lord, it is a hellhole.'

Sylvia shrugged, unable to think of anything to say. She wasn't about to reassure him it was actually a decent area. It wasn't. She never went out after dark and always walked quickly through the streets even in the middle of the day. There were parts of Whitechapel you never went to, dark alleys and dangerous corners that everyone knew to avoid, but most of the people who lived there were just normal people, down on their luck or born into poverty. People who did desperate things to ward off desperate times.

Right now she was more interested in how he knew where she lived.

'Hugh, how do you know where I live?' She repeated, her tone firmer this time.

He cleared his throat again and then gave a world-weary sigh. 'I was hardly going to let you disappear off into London without checking on your welfare, was I?'

'You followed me?'

'No, at least not most of the time. I paid a man to check on your well-being every few weeks. He informed me when you moved to your current lodgings.'

Sylvia thought back to the times when she had felt a sensation of being observed, and turned and thumped Hugh on the arm.

'You could have simply knocked on my door and enquired about how I was. Would that be too simple?'

'You told me in no uncertain terms you never wanted to see me again, to stay away.'

Sylvia let out an exasperated sigh and turned back to look out the window.

The carriage navigated the final couple of twists and turns and rolled to a stop in front of the tall, narrow building where Sylvia had her room. Outside he heard Hopkins jump down and hurry round to the door, letting in a gentle breeze as he opened the door.

'No,' Hugh said, gripping hold of her wrist as she went to get out.

'No?'

'I can't let you stay here.'

'This is my home, Hugh,' Sylvia said, suppressing a laugh. He looked so serious, so adamant. 'Anyway, if you knew where I lived the last seven months, why didn't you protest then?'

'I knew the address. My agent did not convey *quite* how insalubrious the area was.'

'Insalubrious.' She laughed.

'It's unsafe. It's unsanitary. It's unsavoury.'

'*This* is how the majority of the population live.'

'You are not the majority of the population. You are the future Viscountess Wilder.'

Sylvia rolled her eyes. 'What do you propose? I come and live with you before our wedding?'

He blanched at the thought as Sylvia knew he would.

'Exactly. There is no choice. I live here. It hasn't done me any harm the past seven months.'

* * *

Hugh eyed the building and shook his head. Trying to push away her frustration, Sylvia remembered the sinking feeling she'd experienced the first time she had viewed the poky room and the dank building it was situated in.

'I am weary, Hugh. It has been a long and eventful day. I know we have a lot to discuss, but right now I want my bed.'

She slipped her hand from his grasp and stepped out of the carriage, smiling despite everything as Rosa fluttered down and landed on her shoulder, leaning her feathery head into Sylvia's.

'Shall I bring your trunk inside, miss?' Hopkins asked, making to follow her.

'I'll take it,' Hugh growled before Sylvia could answer.

'I will take it,' Sylvia said, reaching out for the case. 'My landlady does not allow men in the building.'

'That is something at least.'

'Goodnight, Hugh,' Sylvia said. She needed to get away from him and the maelstrom of emotions she felt whenever she looked at him. In the carriage, for half a wonderful hour, it was as if the past year had melted away, all the feelings of hurt and regret nothing more than a horrible dream. It had been wonderful to be back in his arms, to feel that surge of desire and pleasure and let herself succumb to it. Part of her wanted to block out everything else, to pretend all the pain she was feeling didn't exist and just focus on the fact that soon she would be married to Hugh. Then she would be able to fall asleep in his arms with no one to reproach her.

Even though it would make things simpler, Sylvia knew she couldn't just forget everything that had passed between them. She couldn't forget Hugh's reaction to the idea they would be forced to marry, his focus on minimising the scandal rather than feeling any real happiness they would be together again.

She tucked the trunk under her arm and stepped away from the carriage, irritated when Hugh followed her a few steps.

'Mrs Tenyson will not allow you inside,' she said, a weariness coming over her. She didn't want to fight with him, but for once she wished he would listen.

'I will walk you to your door, then.'

She looked at the twenty feet between the carriage and the front door of her building and decided arguing about it was too much effort. Instead she walked briskly to the door and fumbled for her key.

One of the reasons she had eventually chosen this room to rent was the security. Unlike many other places she had looked at when searching for somewhere to live Mrs Tenyson kept a locked front door, only allowing residents past. The older woman lived in a small set of rooms on the ground floor and could often be seen poking her head out to check her tenants weren't sneaking anyone they shouldn't inside.

For Sylvia it was ideal. She had no friends in London, no one she might want to entertain in her room, so she had embraced the extra security, knowing it would be difficult for a thief or intruder to get past Mrs Tenyson's watchful eye and feeling safer because of it.

'I wondered if you were ever coming back,' Mrs Tenyson said as she shuffled out from her room, opening the door before Sylvia could turn the key. 'Your rent is due tomorrow.' The older woman paused and squinted up at Hugh, her face taking on a pinched expression.

'Thank you for walking me to the door,' Sylvia said, turning to Hugh. 'As you can see, I am safe now.'

'No men allowed,' Mrs Tenyson barked, although Sylvia could tell she was thrown by the cut of Hugh's clothes. He was far better groomed and turned out than most of the men in Whitechapel.

'It is a pleasure to meet you,' Hugh said, reaching out and taking the older woman's hand, bowing low over it. 'I am Lord Wilder, a friend of Miss Thompson's.'

'Lord,' Mrs Tenyson squeaked, and Sylvia rolled her eyes.

Hugh knew how to manipulate people, and although he did not use his charm and status often, when he did, the results were stunning. Mrs Tenyson, normally a dragon when it came to protecting the reputation of her lodging house, beamed up at him.

'Yes. I wanted to thank you personally for taking care of Miss Thompson these past few months. She tells me she does not have to worry for her safety when she is in her room here, for yours is the most secure lodging house in all of Whitechapel.'

'I try my best, my lord. We tolerate no visitors here.'

Sylvia fixed him with an exasperated look, but he simply ignored her.

'Now, Miss Thompson and I have had a difficult day. We travelled from Kent and were accosted by highwaymen on the road. Thankfully the rogues are now in the custody of the local magistrate, but given our ordeal, I thought it prudent to check Miss Thompson's safety before I left her.' He bestowed his most charming smile on the older woman. 'I do not wish to push against your rules, but perhaps, if you accompany us, you would permit me to see Miss Thompson back to her room and watch her turn the key in her lock.'

Mrs Tenyson hesitated, and Sylvia could not believe her normally draconian landlady would even consider the suggestion she let a man into the lodging house.

'It will be for a minute, perhaps two, and I would be in your debt.'

Mrs Tenyson nodded, and Sylvia couldn't help but shake her head in disbelief. The older woman stepped to the side and let them pass, locking the door behind them.

'I will be here to let you out the front door in two minutes, my lord,' she said, regaining the slight edge to her voice Sylvia knew well, but she didn't push to follow them upstairs.

Sylvia's room was on the second floor, one of four on this level with an identical pattern repeated for another two stories. It meant there were fifteen women living in the lodging house alongside Mrs Tenyson, and often the landings and stairs were busy with people coming and going, but tonight it was quiet. She knew a couple of the young women worked late into the evening, both serving maids in a tavern a couple of streets away. The rest, it would seem, either had not yet returned or were safely locked into their rooms.

They ascended the stairs, Hugh so close behind her he would have bumped against her if she stopped suddenly.

'I am hardly going to get attacked here,' she muttered.

'You can't stay here, Sylvia.'

She scoffed. 'I've been living here the past seven months.'

'I told you I was not aware of the extent of your circumstances.'

'So if you had been informed you would have swooped to my rescue, would you? Perhaps you would have sped through the streets of Whitechapel on your noble steed and swept me away from this world.'

'There is no need for sarcasm.'

'There is every need for sarcasm, Hugh. *This* is my life, and the only reason you are even here objecting about it is because someone has forced you to ask me to marry you.'

He remained silent, brows furrowed.

'Gather your things. You can stay at my house until we are married.'

'I thought the whole point of this all was to avoid scandal. It will look like you're moving your mistress in if I stay before we are married.'

'I'll move out. Stay with a friend. Sir Percy has a big old house I am sure he won't mind me rattling around in for a while.'

Sylvia sighed. 'No, Hugh. This is something you cannot arrange to your satisfaction.' She slipped her key into the lock on her door and turned it, pushing open the door. The look on Hugh's face was pure shock at the simplicity of the room, and Sylvia tried to see it through his eyes. There was a narrow bed pushed up against the wall, a wooden chair and table for eating or writing with a candle set upon it, and a wooden trunk where she kept all of her personal possessions. The only other piece of furniture in the room was a washstand, a raised wooden frame where Mrs Tenyson would place a tepid bowl of water every morning.

Sylvia's favourite part of the room was the huge window that took up nearly one wall. It had a narrow window ledge below it that she could just about perch on, feet up, and watch the world go by on the street below.

Despite the simplicity of the room, it was clean, and had a few homely touches like the quilt on the bed she had saved from her parents' home or the small miniature of her brother she kept on the little table.

'It is safe and it is clean and it is warm,' Sylvia said, turning and placing a hand on Hugh's chest, some of the irritation she had felt with him draining away. 'You know where to find me now, and perhaps in a day or two, we can arrange to meet to discuss this whole messy situation.'

'Tomorrow,' he said eventually. 'Tomorrow I will send the carriage for you.'

'Fine.'

He nodded and took one final look around the room. 'Lock the door before I go.'

Stepping back, he watched her as she closed the door. Sylvia heard his footsteps receding when she had turned the key in the lock, and only then let out an exhausted sigh. Despite sleeping for a couple of hours in the carriage, she felt as though she could fall straight into bed, her body was so weary.

Crossing to the window, she looked out, seeing Hugh

leave through the front door of the lodging house and then pause, turning to look up at her. He gave her a nod of acknowledgement, a serious expression on his face.

Sylvia pulled the curtains closed and undressed quickly, collapsing onto the bed in her nightgown.

'What do I do?' she murmured. For a moment, she allowed the pleasure of the memory of their intimacy in the carriage wash over her. It had been wonderful to feel that closeness again, and she wondered if perhaps that would be what marriage to Hugh might be like. Once he had pushed past the worries about a scandal, his concerns that she would not be the Viscountess he had imagined for the role, that her bloodline was not as impeccable as his father had insisted he look for in a wife, perhaps they could settle down into something resembling happiness.

Sylvia closed her eyes. Maybe that could happen if she could get past this overwhelming feeling of being unwanted, being forced upon Hugh. Once marriage and a life with Hugh by her side had been everything she had wanted, but in her dreams he had wanted the same too.

'Enough,' she murmured, blowing out the candle that flickered by her bed. It was still early, but she would try to sleep. It was better than lying awake and torturing herself over everything that had happened.

Chapter Twenty-One

Our first contact in months with another human was with Captain William Willis, owner of the Chameleon and the man who swept to our rescue, commanding his sailors to lower the rowboat into the water to come and meet us on the Isla Ana. I was so shocked I could barely speak, and it was with wobbling legs that I boarded the ship that would take us back to civilisation.

Hugh didn't care it was far too early to call in polite society. Sylvia's living situation had shocked him. Vaguely he had realised she must be getting short on funds, although the man he had set to watch over her assured him every month she was doing fine. Her father had been a solicitor, but Sylvia had told him whilst they were on the Isla Ana he had died in debt. That debt had swallowed the modest house Sylvia had grown up in and most of their possessions. The little bit of money she had been able to scrimp and save had paid for the ticket to join her brother in Port Royal.

She'd always hinted her brother was more worldly-wise than her father, and he assumed the money she had been living off these last months was the small inheritance she had received after his premature death. Without an income, the money would go fast. Hugh knew all this, but seeing the reality of her situation made him feel terrible.

No wonder she had been so keen for her book to succeed. It was the only way she saw out of the life of poverty she was living now.

The carriage rolled through the streets of Whitechapel, bustling despite the early hour, and then rolled to a stop in front of Sylvia's lodging house.

'I will not be long,' he told Hopkins as he jumped down, heading straight for the solid wooden door.

Mrs Tenyson shuffled out to greet him, smoothing down her hair.

'I shall let Miss Thompson know you are here, my lord,' Mrs Tenyson said, giving him a smile that revealed a mouth without many teeth left.

'Thank you. Might I have a moment of your time first, Mrs Tenyson?'

'Of course,' she said, looking taken aback. He was led through to a clean but dingy set of rooms just to the left of the front door and bidden to sit in one of the sagging chairs.

'It is a delicate matter, but I hope we might come to some arrangement.'

'I can't let you visit her, my lord,' Mrs Tenyson said, straightening her back. 'Whatever your title, I cannot make exceptions. That is how a lodging house gets a name for itself, and before long it becomes no better than a bawdy house.'

Hugh shook his head. 'It is not what I am asking. Miss Thompson and I are engaged to be married. I have arranged for her to come and live with a friend of mine until the wedding. Now, I know her rent is due today, and it will be an inconvenience finding someone at short notice. I thought it only right you get compensated for the next month and a little more for your trouble.' He took out his coin purse and handed over four shiny coins. 'I trust this is enough.'

Mrs Tenyson looked at the coins as though they might be magical and disappear in a puff of smoke any minute. Quickly she tucked them into a pocket and stood.

'I'll see if Miss Thompson needs any help with her things.'

Hugh stood too, happy to get out of the dark room and back into the sunshine.

'I don't understand. You're evicting me?' he heard Sylvia say as Mrs Tenyson hustled her downstairs a few minutes later.

'You're getting married, Miss Thompson. The outstanding rent has been paid for the room. It will be difficult to find someone else to take it, but I hope I can fill it eventually.'

Mrs Tenyson opened the door and handed Sylvia's case out to Hugh.

'There is a wooden trunk upstairs if your man wants to fetch it.'

'Hopkins,' Hugh said, motioning with his head for the man to follow Mrs Tenyson.

'What have you done?' Sylvia demanded as she hurried outside. 'You've made me homeless.'

'Luckily I know of a place you can stay.'

'Tell me you jest, that this is all some perverse joke.'

'Do not fear. I am not inviting more scandal. Sir Percy and Lady Turner have invited you to stay with them until our wedding. They have a large house and are more than happy to set aside a number of rooms for your convenience. Lady Turner is a suitable chaperon and above reproach.'

'I had a home. I don't need to stay with your friends.'

'You do not like Lady Turner and Sir Percy?'

'That is beside the point. They seem like very pleasant people, but I do not know them.'

'I am confident you will get to know them quickly.'

'Hugh, stop,' Sylvia said, reaching out and placing a hand on his chest. The touch sent a wave of protectiveness through him, and he strengthened his resolve. She would not live here any longer. 'I know my living situation has shocked you, I can acknowledge that, but it does not give you the right to come in here and upend my entire world. I need to have a say in what happens to me. I have been living completely independently for the past year, and I do not intend to hand over all my autonomy to you.'

Hugh glanced at the building behind her, where Hopkins was hauling the heavy wooden chest down the last of the stairs. He had thought of nothing but removing Sylvia from a dangerous situation. Hugh was aware this single-track focus was something he struggled with sometimes, looking at only one goal and never considering the consequences.

'I'm sorry,' he said quietly. 'I couldn't sleep with worry. I thought of you here…' He held up his hands to ward off the outburst he knew was coming. 'I know you've lived here safely these last seven months, but I didn't want you at risk a moment longer than you had to be.'

She looked slightly mollified by his explanation.

'I know I should have asked you instead of orchestrating things like this.'

'You should. I would have said no, but you should have asked.'

'Please come live with Sir Percy and Lady Turner. Or if that doesn't suit, let me rent you some rooms somewhere a little more salubrious, perhaps with a maid or a companion to keep you company.'

She looked at him long and hard and then gave a miniscule nod of her head.

Hopkins hauled her trunk up onto the roof of the carriage, and Hugh reached out to help her up.

'I will get Hopkins to take your things to Sir Percy's house, but I wonder if you might indulge me with a little diversion first?'

'Where to?'

'Somewhere quiet, peaceful, where we can talk.'

'I think that sounds like a very good idea, Hugh.'

He nodded, wondering how they would end the morning. In his sleepless state of worry the night before, he had done a lot of thinking, and he realised it wasn't enough to marry Sylvia. He wanted so much more than a stilted relationship with his wife.

Hugh was desperate not to repeat his parents' mistakes, but in striving to keep Sylvia sheltered from the same sort of scandal his mother had endured, he knew he had pushed her away. Somehow he needed to fix things.

They rode in silence, Sylvia looking thoughtful as she stared out the window. Only when they reached their destination did she stir from her position.

'Where are we?'

'The Old White House, my favourite pleasure garden in London.'

They descended from the carriage, and Hugh felt a ball of anxiety sitting like a stone in his stomach. There was a sense that the next hour or so would determine both their futures, and the sort of marriage they would share.

Chapter Twenty-Two

Every morning when I woke in my small cabin on the Chameleon, I forgot where I was for a moment. I felt confused to be looking up at wooden planks rather than rough branches with patches of brilliant blue sky visible through them. It was difficult to adjust to the sheer number of people on the ship as well, a vast difference from the company of just Lord Wilder and Mrs White.

Once Hugh had paid the price of their admission tickets they walked quietly side by side down the winding paths through the gardens. In the distance there was a large round pond with stone benches set around the edge, but for now she was content to wander through the bright blooms of the flowerbeds.

Hugh cleared his throat, and Sylvia could see he was nervous. In a way she was glad. It meant he finally realised what was at stake here. She felt a surge of hope.

'I wonder,' Hugh said, looking at her, 'whether we can have an emotional amnesty?'

'What do you mean?'

'Don't you feel hurt, betrayed, devastated by what has happened between us?'

She nodded. 'Completely.'

'I was thinking about this last night. We are both still holding on to grievances of the past. If we speak them, without any argument or effort at justification from the other person, with them just listening, then perhaps we might be able to put it to one side.'

Sylvia nodded. It would be difficult, but Hugh might be right. She was still seething about things that happened a year ago. The hurt and betrayal clouded every conversation they had.

'I know things have been far from ideal, Sylvia. Last night I was sitting there, and when I stopped and thought about how things were between us, I couldn't believe it. We went from sharing everything to this cold animosity.' He paused, using his free hand to rub at his brow. 'I know much of this is my fault, Sylvia, but it has felt like everything is out of my control.'

'I know what you mean. I feel the same way.'

'Then yesterday, when you tackled that bandit to the ground, I had this awful ominous feeling that he would get the better of you. I would lose you, and it felt as though my heart was ripping in two.' He took a deep breath. 'I don't want to lose you, Sylvia. To bandits, highwaymen, or because I am pigheaded enough to ruin everything good in my life.'

They walked through an arch to a fragrant rose garden, filled with dozens of varieties of pink and white roses. Bees buzzed amongst the blooms, and Sylvia felt a little glimmer of positivity.

'Come, I know somewhere private and out of the sun where we can talk.'

He gripped her hand, and Sylvia felt the familiar spark of excitement pass between them as she always did when Hugh touched her, but she didn't pull away her fingers. They walked briskly, dashing along the winding paths, until a small summer house came into view. It was wooden, painted white, and had climbing roses woven through the open slats, giving it a magical, fairy-tale look.

'In here,' Hugh said, leading her inside.

It was cooler in the summer house away from the direct sunlight, but the front was completely open, so it was not gloomy like some of these places. There was a wide bench around the wall providing a comfortable place to sit.

Hugh exhaled as he sat, and Sylvia realised how nervous he was. It was out of character, but perhaps it showed how eager he was to get this right. She never wanted to repeat their experience with the bandits again, but it wasn't all completely bad if it led to them finally finding a way through this.

'You go first,' he said with a smile. 'I will keep silent, no trying to justify my behaviour, no arguments. Tell me everything you've wanted to scream and shout at me about this last year.'

Sylvia took a few moments, knowing it was important to be completely honest but also aware that she didn't want to destroy Hugh completely. She would tell

him everything that had irked her, but there were ways
to go about doing that.

'I think much of my discontent stemmed from how
happy I was on the Isla Ana,' she began slowly. 'I never
questioned why we worked so well together, why our
relationship was seemingly perfect. Then that ship appeared, and it was as if a carpet had been ripped out
from underneath me. You changed in an instant. Up
until then I hadn't once doubted we would marry if we
ever got rescued, but I could see all the uncertainty in
your face. You were worried what a relationship with
me would look like in the real world. That hurt, Hugh,
more than anything I have ever been through. I realised
I didn't mean as much to you as I thought.'

She saw him open his mouth to protest and then
promptly close it again as he remembered the rules.

'Then, when you announced seemingly out of nowhere
that you were planning on marrying Miss Willis, it felt
like you had reached into my chest and pulled out my
heart when it was still beating.' She closed her eyes for
a minute. 'Even knowing why you did it, knowing you
overheard me express my doubts of the hardiness of our
relationship to Captain Willis, I cannot understand why
you did not come to me. So much hurt could have been
prevented if only you had spoken to me, instead of deciding unilaterally that you were going to make some
foolish and noble sacrifice to keep my reputation safe.'
Shaking her head, she pressed on. 'When I saw you walk
away from me along the docks, it was like my whole
world had come tumbling down. Then there was nothing from you, from a man who only weeks earlier had

professed his undying love for me. It felt as though you had decided to move forwards with your life, and you wanted to cleanse yourself of all memories of me. It was a terrible time. I was thrust into society with no one to guide me, no one to protect me. Then news reached me of my brother's death, and I realised I was truly alone.'

Sylvia paused for a moment to catch her breath. As she spoke, she could see the impact her words were having on Hugh, but for once she wasn't holding on to the anger or the self-pity. One by one the words floated away, leaving her feeling lighter, unburdened.

'I longed for you this whole past year. I longed for you to reappear and tell me what a terrible mistake you'd made. I longed for you to save me, but you didn't.' Sylvia bit her lip, knowing she was going to have to open much fresher wounds before she got to the end. 'And then, when Miss Willis arranged for us to be found together, the dismay and panic on your face were so difficult to see. There was no happiness, no pleasure at the thought of marrying me, and that hurts more than anything else.'

She fell silent, watching Hugh's face as he nodded and took everything in. Gently he reached out for her hand.

'Sylvia, I am so sorry,' he said softly. 'I am sorry for hurting you and sorry for not seeing what I was doing to you, but most of all, I am sorry for not celebrating the fact that finally we can be together.'

'It is your turn now,' she said softly, knowing his words would be hard to hear and wanting this part done and over with so they could think about the future.

'Are you sure?'

'Yes. I will try to stay silent.'

'I acknowledge I have this little voice inside that drives me onwards. I think it is my father's voice, his cruel tones always telling me I had to be better or what a disappointment I would turn out to be. If I am honest, Sylvia, I hated the man, but I cannot silence his opinions. When we were about to be rescued, I did, for a few minutes, panic about what the future would look like. I'd planned everything out. For years I had known at what age I would marry and where I would look for my bride. I had a list of attributes she would possess and connections she would bring to the marriage, and then there we were, and all those plans were being dashed to pieces.' He shook his head ruefully. 'I couldn't see that I had the chance of something much better, something real, something strong.'

Sylvia nodded, pushing aside the anger she always felt reliving that moment on the beach when he had begun to withdraw, and finally trying to understand what had made him act that way. His explanation didn't excuse his behaviour, but it did make her realise that some reactions are out of our control.

'Then, on the ship, when I heard you say you didn't think we would be together in England, I was devastated. Even though it went against everything I had ever planned, I knew I loved you.' He closed his eyes for a moment. 'I wish more than anything else I had not reacted as I did, that I did not panic. I wish I had spoken to you then. Instead I was too easily influenced by Captain Willis's words, too quick to believe the scandal he was threatening would blight our lives as soon as we landed if I did not do as he said.'

'Because of your mother.'

'Probably.' He gave her a quick smile, 'My family are not good advocates for married life, are they?'

'No. All families have difficulties, but from what you say, your parents' marriage was not one I would like to emulate.'

'My father was a scoundrel, yet I cannot get him out of my head.'

Sylvia squeezed his hand, wondering what Hugh would bring up next, hoping it was nothing they wouldn't be able to overcome.

'I became obsessed with protecting you from scandal,' he said quietly. 'I can see that it was perhaps not a healthy reaction, but I thought if I could not protect you physically, this was the next best thing. I kept my distance because of it, even though this whole year I have thought of little but you. I set a man to keep watch over you, to report back how you were doing, and I lived for those scraps of information.'

Sylvia felt her heart begin to beat faster in response to his words.

'I know how I reacted when it became clear we would have to marry. I apologise, Sylvia. It was not well-done, and I can see how much it has hurt you. Again, my focus was on the scandal that could ensue, not the wonderful fact that we will be married. In truth, I am ecstatic, for even if you still cannot forgive me, I have years and years to make it up to you. It is just I have been so focussed on protecting you, it has taken a while to see what a blessing this is.'

'You mean it?'

'How can I not?' He smiled at her, a hint of sadness in his expression. 'I love you, Sylvia. I have loved you ever since you poked me with a stick on that beach on the Isla Ana. I think once you loved me too. I just hope one day you will find your way back to loving me once more.'

'This last year has been so very difficult,' Sylvia said slowly, 'But do not ever think I stopped loving you. That was why it was so heartbreaking to be apart from you. Hugh, all I have ever wanted is for you to see we can live a happy life no matter where in the world we are. If you wish me to act like I was born into the life of a viscountess, I will. If you would rather we lock ourselves away from the world and live as recluses with only one another for company, that suits me fine too. I do not care as long as I am with you.'

He closed his eyes and pressed his forehead against hers.

'I will try my hardest to leave my worries about scandal behind us.'

'No need to go out and do anything dramatically scandalous,' Sylvia said.

'But perhaps I can take a few more risks,' he murmured, leaning forwards to kiss her.

'Hugh, anyone could walk past and see us.'

'Let them. I am kissing the woman I am going to marry in a few short weeks. What on earth can be wrong with that?'

Sylvia surrendered to the kiss, feeling the same ecstatic feeling she always did when his lips met hers. There was much work to do between them, much still to repair, but already she felt brighter, more positive. Hugh was right. They had their whole lives to make up for the lost time. Hopefully in a few years, the time they had spent apart, and the mistakes they had made, would seem like nothing more than a distant memory.

Chapter Twenty-Three

As the weather turned cooler and we neared England, my thoughts turned to the future. Much had changed in the months we had been away, and I too was coming back a different person to the one who had departed. I needed to find my place in this new world.

'You have nothing to be nervous about,' Lady Turner said, resting her hand on Sylvia's. 'I have known dear Hugh for a long time, and I can see you two are well-matched. You have overcome such obstacles already. Nothing will stand in the way of your happiness now.'

'Do you know what Hugh told me on my wedding day, my dear?' Sir Percy said from the other side of the carriage.

Sylvia shook her head.

'He told me he thought I was the wisest man he knew for marrying a woman not because of her fortune or her family name, not even because of her beauty, although of course Mary is stunningly beautiful. He knew I was marrying Mary for love and for the friendship we shared. *That* is the firmest base for a marriage. You have that with Hugh. I am not saying there won't be trials and tribulations, but your love will mean you can overcome anything this life throws at you.'

These past five weeks, she had grown close to both Lady Turner and Sir Percy, who had welcomed her into their home, urging her to treat it as her own. Early the day before, she had asked if Sir Percy might walk down the aisle of the church with her to the altar, in the position her father or brother might have taken had they still been alive. He'd been visibly touched by her request and agreed readily.

The carriage slowed to a stop outside the little church. Hugh and Sylvia had debated whether to organise a grand wedding, an affair that would not be forgotten and hopefully would ward off any scandal that was attached to their names for their hasty engagement. In the end they had decided it wasn't worth the sacrifice of having people they didn't like at their nuptials, instead opting for a quiet affair in the chapel in Fenstanton near to Hugh's country estate. Their only guests were to be their witnesses, Lady Turner and Sir Percy, and Honoria and her new husband, Alexander Tarrant.

Honoria had not returned home to her father after her stay at Somersham Hall, instead embracing her future with the man she loved and staying with friends until the banns were read and she and Alexander could marry. Sylvia had found Honoria to be a dedicated letter writer and felt she knew every aspect of the young woman's life. When Hugh suggested they find a place for the

newlywed couple on their estate, far from the anger of
Captain Willis, Sylvia had quickly agreed, knowing she
would appreciate having a friend so close by. Honoria
and her husband had moved to a pretty little cottage
close to Elmwood Hall three weeks ago and had been
delighted to be asked to be Sylvia and Hugh's witnesses
for the wedding. Hugh was helping Alexander find suitable premises for him to set up his farrier's workshop,
something the local area sorely needed since their last
farrier had moved away a few years earlier.

Captain Willis had been furious not only with Honoria's marriage to Alexander, but also that Hugh had
broken his promise. He had almost gone through on
his threat to expose the fact that Hugh and Sylvia had
been alone, unchaperoned on the Isla Ana until Hugh
had pointed out it would matter much less when he and
Sylvia were married. Instead Hugh had paid Captain
Willis a princely sum and suggested the man settle it
on his daughter. It was still to be seen if Honoria's father would mellow towards her and pass on the gift.

'Let me go and check everything is ready for you,'
Sir Percy said, hopping down from the carriage.

Sylvia peeked out at the church. They had visited
on a handful of occasions in the last week when they'd
made the decision to move from London to the countryside. Lady Turner and Sir Percy had magnanimously
agreed to accompany them so Lady Turner could continue in her role as chaperon, but the rules were easier
to bend in the country. It was a pretty little church with
a square tower and heavy wooden doors that took up
almost one entire end of the building. Inside were rows

of pews and beautiful stained-glass windows that ran down both sides of the church.

She had expected to be almost overwhelmed by nerves, but instead, a calmness overtook her now they were here. There was nothing to be nervous about. She was marrying the man she loved. This would allow them to start their lives together properly, officially. It wouldn't matter if they were caught kissing in the gardens or if they danced a little too close together at balls. From today she was free to love Hugh without having to hold anything back.

'Everything is ready,' Sir Percy said as he returned along the path to the carriage. He reached up and helped first his wife and then Sylvia down.

'You look beautiful, my dear,' Lady Turner said, leaning in and giving her a kiss on the cheek. 'Hugh is a very lucky man.'

Sylvia watched as Lady Turner hurried away to take her seat inside the church, taking a moment to smooth down her skirt and check her hair was in place.

'Shall we?' Sir Percy said, offering her his arm,

Hugh turned from his position by the altar as the door opened for a second time and couldn't help but smile as he saw Sylvia walk in. At first she was a silhouette, the details of her blunted by the glorious sunlight behind her, but then the church door closed, and he saw her in all her beauty. She was wearing a simple white gown, gathered underneath her bust before the material cascaded to the ground. Her hair was pinned, but only loosely. Hugh smiled, realising she had chosen nothing ostentatious, taking inspiration from their time on the Isla Ana, favouring a simple dress that allowed her beauty to shine through.

It felt like it took an eternity for her to walk down the aisle, but when she paused by his side, he reached out for her hand immediately, eager to say the words that would bind them together forever. Sometimes, if he was feeling a little maudlin, he mused about the future he could have had, separated from Sylvia, pining for her but never confessing it to himself. He couldn't believe how close he had come to that future, and every day he was grateful for the way things had worked out eventually.

'Are you ready?' he asked, leaning in close and catching a hint of her delicious scent.

'Yes,' she replied, her eyes flicking to his lips.

Together they turned to the vicar, Hugh feeling a swell of happiness as the ceremony to bind them together began.

'Welcome to our bedroom,' Hugh said, sweeping Sylvia inside.

Sylvia giggled. She had sneaked into the bedroom on more occasions than she could count this last week, but it felt good to step inside with no creeping around for appearances' sake.

'Fair warning. I plan to keep you closeted in here for at least a month, perhaps two.'

The room was huge, dominated by a comfortable four-poster bed and with a large bay window looking out over the gardens of Elmwood Hall. Sunlight streamed through the windows and alighted on a little writing desk that Hugh had brought in specially in case she wanted to write some more.

'I have something to show you,' Hugh said, almost jumping up and down in excitement. He handed her a printed piece of paper and pointed to a paragraph. Sylvia's eyes flitted over the writing. It was one of the London gossip sheets, a few days old and folded in the middle as if it had been tucked into an envelope. About halfway down the front page, someone had marked a star in ink.

She began to read at the marked place.

This week saw the much anticipated The Rescue, by Sylvia Thompson, available for sale at bookshops in London. There was an unprecedented crowd waiting for the establishments to open, and I am told the shops sold out within a matter of minutes.

The contents of the book I cannot comment on, as people have been guarding their copies closely, but I am told it is a fascinating read of endurance and bravery.

In the knowledge that Lord Wilder and Miss Thompson are due to be married later this week, perhaps it contains a few hints of romance too.

That was it. The next paragraph went on to talk about an upcoming wedding between the Duke of Wiltshire and the daughter of the Earl of Essex. Even though the description of her book was short, Sylvia felt the smile on her lips and flung her arms around Hugh's neck.

'It sold out within minutes,' she squealed.

'My clever wife.'

'I am a woman of independent means now, my lord.'

'I shall have to be careful not to upset you. Luckily I am your faithful servant in every way, dedicated to satisfying your every whim,' he said, wrapping his arms around her and picking her up. Sylvia loved how easily he could lift her and felt a spark of anticipation as he set her down on the bed, then stood in front of her. 'Now, I am not one to complain,' he said, loosening his cravat and then whipping it off. 'And these past few weeks, I have enjoyed the subterfuge of creeping around and indulging in a little intimacy wherever we could snatch the opportunity. But now you are officially my wife, I think we should spend at least a day, perhaps more, getting to know every inch of one another again.'

His meaning was made clear as he lifted his shirt over his head, revealing the toned torso below. He was less tanned than when they were on the Isla Ana together, but he had maintained the chiselled form he had built by hauling tree branches and climbing rock faces.

Pulling Sylvia up to her feet, he made short work of the fastenings of her dress, and soon she was left standing in only her chemise and petticoats.

Hugh slowed down, running his hands over her arms, making the skin pucker and the little hairs stand on end. She wanted to press herself against him, but before she could, he had lifted the chemise over her head and disposed of her petticoats.

'Do you know what I thought when I opened my eyes

on the Isla Ana and saw you looking down at me?' he murmured in her ear, pulling her close.

'That I was an angel?'

'Guess again.'

'That I was the most beautiful woman you'd ever seen.'

'You are not wrong, but it wasn't my first thought.'

He was kissing her now, brushing his lips against her skin in a way that made her moan with desire.

'That I was a native and going to spear you and eat your brains for dinner.'

'No, nowhere near.'

'Tell me.'

He paused, breaking away from kissing her a second, and looked at her with a smile filled with love.

'I thought, "I am going to make this woman mine."'

'That's a very primitive way of thinking.'

'Primitive?' He shrugged. 'It worked, though, didn't it? Now you are mine, and I am yours.'

'You belong to me?'

'Forever. Every part of me.'

Sylvia smiled, wrapped her arms around his neck, and pulled him in for a long kiss.

Epilogue

'No peeking,' Hugh chided her.

Sylvia smiled, lifting her face to feel the warmth of the sun. The boat rocked a little, dipping in the waves, and a moment later she tasted the salty sea spray on her lips. She felt the reassuring weight of Rosa on her shoulder, the bird's claws tickling through the fabric of her dress.

'Can I look yet?'

'Not yet. Two more minutes.'

She had a very good inkling of what she would see and felt a swell of excitement at the prospect. They had been married a little over a year, and their wedding in England felt a long time ago. For the past seven months they had been travelling, first across Europe and more recently around the Caribbean. They had been to visit her brother's grave in Port Royal and met some of the men he had worked with. It gave Sylvia a sense of who her brother had been in the last few years of his life, seeing where he had lived and worked.

Now Hugh had arranged a mysterious trip for them,

a couple of days' sail from Port Royal on a small but sturdy boat. The first night had been stormy, and Sylvia had sat wrapped in Hugh's arms as the boat rocked, but the rest of the journey was without any surprises.

'You can open your eyes,' he said from his position at the rail beside her.

Sylvia opened her eyes to see the familiar beach of the Isla Ana. It looked as beautiful as ever, the sun glinting off the sand and making it appear golden.

'Hugh,' Sylvia said as she noticed the rowboat that was being lowered down with a large hamper already in it. 'What have you planned?'

'I thought we couldn't come to the other side of the world and miss the opportunity to visit the island where it all began.'

'We're going to row over?'

'The boat can't get any closer.'

She leaned in and whispered in his ear. 'Can we tell them to go away and leave us?'

He kissed her, and Sylvia felt the same happiness swell inside her as she always did when his lips brushed against her own.

'I already have,' he murmured.

Sylvia's eyes widened in surprise.

'Do not fear, only for a day. They will come back tomorrow lunchtime to pick us up.'

'Hugh,' Sylvia said slowly, 'what if something happens to the boat? What if it sinks or a storm rolls in?'

She eyed the island. Often they spoke of their time there, reminiscing about the very start of their love, and they'd both at various points dreamed about going back.

'Nothing is going to happen, my love,' Hugh said, wrapping his arms around her. 'If we are not back in Port Royal in four days, I have hired a whole host of captains with their boats to come looking for us.'

Sylvia felt some of the tension ebb away. Normally she wouldn't be so worried about such a thing, but she was keeping a secret from Hugh that made her a little more cautious. She thought she was a few months pregnant, three, possibly four. Although she shared every part of her life with Hugh, she wanted to wait a little longer to be sure. Soon after their wedding, she had realised she was pregnant, but they had lost that baby very early on. They'd both been devastated, and it had been the prompt to push them to start this journey across the globe. Sylvia wasn't quite ready to go home yet, so soon she would tell Hugh, but for now she didn't want him to worry.

Hugh helped her down into the rowboat and then dropped down himself, taking up the oars and pulling the boat swiftly across the water. He had removed his shoes, so as soon as they got close enough to the shore, he jumped out and pulled the boat up onto the sand.

Sylvia slipped off her shoes and stockings and stepped out, taking a moment to feel the peace of the Isla Ana descend over her. It was as though they had been transported into another world. She leaned down and skimmed her fingers over the surface of the water, sighing as her toes sank into the sand.

'Shall we walk around the island first, and then perhaps we can have lunch?'

'That sounds perfect, my love.'

The beach went all the way round the edge of the island, narrow in places and wide in others, but always made of the same beautiful white-gold sand. They stopped to paddle their toes in the sparkling water and marvel at a group of turtles swimming in the shallows. Rosa fluttered up into a nearby tree, watching them from her perch in the greenery.

'This was the best idea ever,' Sylvia said, feeling her heart swell with love for her husband.

'Once I used to think this was where I was happiest,' Hugh said quietly. 'But it isn't true. I have realised now I am happiest wherever you are.'

'The sunshine and scenery don't hurt, though.'

'No,' Hugh murmured. 'They don't hurt.'

* * * * *

If you enjoyed this story, make sure you pick up
Laura Martin's Matchmade Marriages miniseries

The Marquess Meets His Match
A Pretend Match for the Viscount
A Match to Fool Society

And why not check out one of her other great reads?

The Captain's Impossible Match
One Snowy Night with Lord Hauxton
Her Best Friend, the Duke
The Brooding Earl's Proposition

Get 3 FREE REWARDS!

We'll send you 2 FREE Books plus a FREE Mystery Gift.

PRESENTS
His Innocent for One Spanish Night
CAROL MARINELLI

PRESENTS
Bound by the Italian's "I Do"
MICHELLE SMART

FREE
Value Over
$20

Both the **Harlequin® Desire** and **Harlequin Presents®** series feature compelling novels filled with passion, sensuality and intriguing scandals.

YES! Please send me 2 FREE novels from the Harlequin Desire or Harlequin Presents series and my FREE gift (gift is worth about $10 retail). After receiving them, if I don't wish to receive any more books, I can return the shipping statement marked "cancel." If I don't cancel, I will receive 6 brand-new Harlequin Presents Larger-Print books every month and be billed just $6.30 each in the U.S. or $6.49 each in Canada, a savings of at least 10% off the cover price, or 3 Harlequin Desire books (2-in-1 story editions) every month and be billed just $7.83 each in the U.S. or $8.43 each in Canada, a savings of at least 12% off the cover price. It's quite a bargain! Shipping and handling is just 50¢ per book in the U.S. and $1.25 per book in Canada.* I understand that accepting the 2 free books and gift places me under no obligation to buy anything. I can always return a shipment and cancel at any time by calling the number below. The free books and gift are mine to keep no matter what I decide.

Choose one: ☐ **Harlequin Desire**
(225/326 BPA GRNA)

☐ **Harlequin Presents Larger-Print**
(176/376 BPA GRNA)

☐ **Or Try Both!**
(225/326 & 176/376 BPA GRQP)

Name (please print)

Address — Apt. #

City — State/Province — Zip/Postal Code

Email: Please check this box ☐ if you would like to receive newsletters and promotional emails from Harlequin Enterprises ULC and its affiliates. You can unsubscribe anytime.

> **Mail to the Harlequin Reader Service:**
> **IN U.S.A.:** P.O. Box 1341, Buffalo, NY 14240-8531
> **IN CANADA:** P.O. Box 603, Fort Erie, Ontario L2A 5X3

Want to try 2 free books from another series? Call 1-800-873-8635 or visit www.ReaderService.com.

*Terms and prices subject to change without notice. Prices do not include sales taxes, which will be charged (if applicable) based on your state or country of residence. Canadian residents will be charged applicable taxes. Offer not valid in Quebec. This offer is limited to one order per household. Books received may not be as shown. Not valid for current subscribers to the Harlequin Presents or Harlequin Desire series. All orders subject to approval. Credit or debit balances in a customer's account(s) may be offset by any other outstanding balance owed by or to the customer. Please allow 4 to 6 weeks for delivery. Offer available while quantities last.

Your Privacy—Your information is being collected by Harlequin Enterprises ULC, operating as Harlequin Reader Service. For a complete summary of the information we collect, how we use this information and to whom it is disclosed, please visit our privacy notice located at corporate.harlequin.com/privacy-notice. From time to time we may also exchange your personal information with reputable third parties. If you wish to opt out of this sharing of your personal information, please visit readerservice.com/consumerschoice or call 1-800-873-8635. **Notice to California Residents**—Under California law, you have specific rights to control and access your data. For more information on these rights and how to exercise them, visit corporate.harlequin.com/california-privacy.

HDHP23

Get 3 FREE REWARDS!

We'll send you 2 FREE Books plus a FREE Mystery Gift.

FREE
Value Over
$20

Both the **Romance** and **Suspense** collections feature compelling novels written by many of today's bestselling authors.

HARLEQUIN
PLUS

Try the best multimedia
subscription service for romance
readers like you!

Read, Watch and Play.

Experience the easiest way to get
the romance content you crave.

Start your **FREE TRIAL** at
<u>www.harlequinplus.com/freetrial</u>.